RHAPSODY CREEK

Recent Titles by Freda Lightfoot

LAKELAND LILY
LARKRIGG FELL
LUCKPENNY LAND
WISHING WATER

LOVE ALTERS NOT *
WINE AND ROSES *

* *available from Severn House*

RHAPSODY CREEK

Freda Lightfoot

This title first published in Great Britain 1999 by
SEVERN HOUSE PUBLISHERS LTD of
9–15 High Street, Sutton, Surrey SM1 1DF.
Originally published 1992 in paperback format only under
the pseudonym of *Marion Carr* and title *Hester.*
This title first published in the U.S.A. 1999 by
SEVERN HOUSE PUBLISHERS INC of
595 Madison Avenue, New York, N.Y. 10022.

British Library Cataloguing in Publication Data

Lightfoot,   Freda
        Rhapsody creek
        1.   United States - History - Revolution, 1775-1783 - Fiction
        2.   Love stories
        I.   Title
        823.9'14 [F]

        ISBN 0-7278-5405-4

Printed and bound in Great Britain by
MPG Books Ltd, Bodmin, Cornwall..

CHAPTER ONE

'You cannot be serious. No one in our family has ever done such a thing, and ours is one of the oldest and most respected families in the whole of Charleston.' Kristina Drayton stared at her niece in open dismay.

'Then it will be a new experience for us,' said Hester with determined brightness. 'Dear Aunt Kizzy, don't fret so. We must look upon it as an adventure.'

'I well know your taste for adventure. Haven't I suffered getting stuck up more sodden creeks than I care to mention because of it?'

'That was before the war, Aunt,' said Hester regretfully. 'When life was all picnics and fun, and I was young.'

'Tch! You are young still at not yet twenty. Why will you not settle for a quiet life, Hester? And think of the risk, with the dreadful British all over town. I'm sure I cannot look upon turning my beautiful old house into— into——' Words apparently failed Aunt Kizzy for she dived into her crochet bag and pulled out a small bottle of pink pills. 'Oh, my. My poor heart will not stand for it. The very idea makes me quake.'

Hester looked up from the large book, balanced precariously on her lap, which she had been studying for some time and sighed. 'Nonsense. There is nothing at all the matter with your heart. And you know that you like people. All Southern women enjoy having guests to call. What is the difference, except that this time they will be paying for the privilege of eating your pecan pie? Do you know there is a wonderful receipt here for hot pepper sauce? I must write it in my home book.'

Kizzy looked shocked. 'You are surely not planning to do the cooking yourself, even if the ingredients could be found?'

Hester's brown eyes twinkled, yet she pushed back the thick strands of golden-brown hair which had fallen forward with a tired gesture. It had been a long day. A long week, in fact. A week in which her entire life had changed. On Monday she had still had a brother, albeit unheard of for two years.

She had written countless letters to his commander during that time, asking for word. George had joined the war in 1778, much to poor Kizzy's dismay, after the American victory at Saratoga. If Hester were less charitable, she would conclude that her brother had thought the war to be almost over at that stage. But by the following spring all news from him had ceased. Had the British taken him captive during the long Revolution? Had he died in some lonely corner of a field where he still lay unmourned and unburied? If only they knew. While there had been silence they had still hoped, but over the months that hope had gradually seeped away. Now the news they had dreaded had been given to them. According to his commander, poor George had indeed died, but not fighting for his country as he would have wished. Like his parents before him he had succumbed to the yellow fever and, at just nineteen, Hester Mackay had found herself without a relative in the world, save for Aunt Kizzy.

'You do not truly imagine that Susy could cope with running a lodging house all by herself? I do not, and I see no shame in earning an honest living. At least this way we can conduct our business discreetly, in our own home.' Hester straightened her slender shoulders with characteristic determination. She was not in the habit of bemoaning her lot or looking longingly backwards on to an easier, more affluent lifestyle. Her parents had died when she and George were quite small and dear Aunt Kizzy had been like a mother to the two orphans. But the money they had once taken for granted had gradually been used up over the years and now, with prices sky high, and George gone, their security was even more shaky.

'If George had lived he would have gone into the bank with old Mr Shelton. But things are different now and we must accept that.' Hester reached out to grasp her aunt's small mittened hand and give it a little squeeze. 'But you don't have to worry. It is my turn to take care of you.'

'But we have no man to protect us,' wailed Aunt Kizzy, clasping her niece's hands as if she would never let go. 'How shall we go on without even an uncle or cousin to care for us? Oh, if only I had married that Wilber Marshall.'

Hester burst out laughing and, setting down the book on the hearthrug, went to sit beside her tiny aunt and hug her close. 'Oh, my sweet darling. You know you have always disliked him intensely. And we can manage perfectly well without a man to protect us. Goodness, I have two hands, haven't I? Eyes, ears and a brain between them, or so I've been led to believe. You must not worry for another second.'

Aunt Kizzy slanted her shrewd grey-eyed gaze sideways at her beloved niece. 'And what does Carter Lois say about all of this? Will he permit it?'

Hester bridled. 'I need no one's permission to earn an honest living, not even Carter's,' she flatly stated, while guiltily remembering the unpleasant scene which had taken place that afternoon when she had asked him if she might place her advertisement for rooms to let upon his door, along with the others listing horses or buggies for sale. He had been quite frankly appalled.

'You cannot mean to subject genteel Miss Kizzy to the comings and goings of perfect strangers in her own home?' he had said.

'You can be assured she will not even notice we have guests. They shall use the main drawing-room and we shall be cosy in the upstairs parlour of an evening as we like to be. Nothing will change, except that we will not be constantly concerned over how to manage our bills.'

Then he'd talked of 'having patience' and 'biding her time', of not being impulsive as she so often tended to be. 'The war cannot last forever,' he said. 'By next fall it will be all over, my general store will be singing along and we can marry at last as I so long to do.'

'And in the meantime?' Hester stiffly asked. 'A person can get pretty hungry in eighteen months.' Then she had seen the bleak despair in his eyes and her tender heart had been touched. Instinctively she put out a hand and patted the lapel of his silk waistcoat. 'Oh, Carter, we cannot go on any longer in this fashion. Aunt Kizzy's funds are limited. While we still had hopes of George returning we were prepared to struggle. Now. . .' She swallowed the fresh threat of tears. 'We cannot live on hope any more, we must needs have something more substantial.' She looked him straight in the eye. 'You do see that, don't you? And it will all be conducted with perfect propriety, I assure you.'

'But what will people think?' Carter said.

'*Sensible* people will think that young Miss Hester has got her head screwed on right and knows how to look after that old aunt of hers. Others will say I've taken leave of my senses,' Hester said with a smile, placing the small square of white card firmly in his hand.

Glancing down, he read the few simple lines. 'Rooms to let in home of two ladies. Only respectable ladies or gentlemen need apply.' The address followed but Carter's frown had deepened and, watching his reaction, Hester gave a tired sigh.

'Is there something else wrong?'

'I do think you should confine the accommodation to ladies only. It would not be at all proper for two ladies to entertain a gentleman.'

'But we have Jonas in the house,' said Hester, thinking of the old black retainer who had served Miss Kizzy for as long as she could remember. 'He guards us like a hawk. You need have no fears on that score and gentlemen are so much less finicky. Besides, how many ladies do you know who would be likely to need a room, whereas gentlemen move about on matters of business, do they not?'

She gazed up at him, brown eyes so softly velvet and entrancingly trusting that he wanted to melt right into them. Drat this loan he'd taken out to expand his store. But the British armies had to have supplies and they were running up a fair-sized bill which he looked forward to collecting when hostilities ceased. He did not class himself as either a Loyalist or a Rebel, but he was certainly a realist and if there was money to be made out of this war he would make it. But he couldn't begin to consider taking a wife until every cent had been paid and all his plans were complete. Besides, for all her present poverty, Hester Mackay was not the kind of woman who could live in a dime store. The Mackay family had had money when her father had been alive and married into one of the most respected families on the river front. What was more, somewhere out west there was an old plantation house that Carter would dearly love to get his hands on, in addition to the over-sized frame house in which Hester lived with Aunt Kizzy. For the moment his hands were tied, but it would not do to disagree too strongly with Hester. She was a woman with decided opinions, which he'd often discovered to his cost. He must keep her sweet if he was to win her.

'Very well, Hester, my dear. But you will allow me

to vet anyone who calls and insist they leave if I think them unsuitable?'

Hester felt the familiar surge of rebellion whenever Carter put on his officious, paternal air, but she desperately needed that card on view in his window, so she smiled and even managed to flutter her lashes, which was not at all her usual way of doing business, and the matter was settled. But now Aunt Kizzy herself was proving to be a problem.

'I think you are simply tired, dear Aunt. Funeral services are most depressing, and it was so hot today. You will feel quite differently after a good night's sleep.'

Two large tears trickled down the thin old cheeks. 'But it seems so *wrong* to have a funeral service for Georgy, though I was glad enough to pray for his poor soul. How can he be dead? Why, we didn't even have a casket to bury.' Fresh tears spurted and Hester hugged the old woman tighter, swallowing her own with a quiet desperation so as not to worsen the flood of emotion that racked them both.

'George is gone. Even though they never found his body, we know that he is dead. Didn't Colonel Bouvier tell us that the fever raged throughout that camp?'

'But those poor boys were all left behind when the rest of the company moved on. How could the colonel allow such a thing?'

Panic gripped Hester. How could she cope? Her confidence at her own ability to see them through the difficult, lonely days ahead was as fragile as a butterfly's wing. And if she did not put an end to this soul-destroying grief it would be crushed to dust. 'The colonel had to leave them, darling Kizzy. He could not risk the lives of all the men who were still healthy when there were battles to be fought, a war to be won. And we will win. The British will be defeated and justice will prevail, make no mistake. And George would not have you pine for him. Now off to bed and I'll bring you a cup of chocolate to help you sleep.'

There were protests and kisses and smiles but quietly, and with unusual obedience, Aunt Kizzy for once did as she was bidden.

As soon as the room was empty, Hester's defences crumbled and, covering her face with her hands, she wept silent, heartbreaking tears. When she was done she dried her eyes and sat in the quiet drawing-room for some long time, her eyes fixed upon the fire screen that stood before the empty grate and then moving over the marble fireplace itself and up to the matching portraits of her parents above. The beloved face of her mother, smiling, serene, with a merry twinkle very like Hester's own lurking in the corners of those fine hazel eyes.

And her father. Handsome, bearded, soberly watching everything she did. Hester could remember neither of her parents since she had been only four at the time of their death. George, at three years older, declared he had a memory but Hester doubted it. Their parents had been busy, hardworking people with less time for their children than they would have liked, or so Kizzy told her. John Mackay had come to America from Scotland as a boy of sixteen. After several failed business ventures he had married Margaret Drayton, much to the disapproval of her family. But by the time he was forty-three he'd been well on his way to making a fortune as a cotton planter when he and his beautiful young wife were struck down with the all too common yellow fever. Now the plantation house on Rhapsody Creek stood empty. Young pine saplings had reclaimed the land and the Spanish moss that hung on the live oaks gave it a ghostlike quality. Hester had not visited for over six years, not since that momentous year of 1775 when America had declared its intention of breaking free from its colonial status. She had no inclination to return now that George was gone.

Her brother had once had dreams of returning, of working the land. With the price cotton was fetching these days it might well have been worth it. Everyone was predicting a boom period when the war was finally over. But Hester had no inclination to return to Rhapsody Creek, nor to plant cotton.

She shivered as if a goose had stalked over her grave.

But George would not now have to choose between going into a bank or reworking his parents' old plantation. George was gone, for all his death was unofficial, and Hester must learn to cope without him. It wasn't that they had been particularly close as brother and sister, for he had always been an introspective kind of person, keeping his secret, private thoughts very much to himself. But they had rubbed along well enough and she would miss his quiet presence. She would sell Rhapsody Creek, of course, as soon as she could. It was worth little now but every dollar counted and it was of no use to her out in the back of beyond. Living in this pretty pine and cedar house in Charleston with Aunt Kizzy was much pleasanter. Hester could not imagine anything which would take her back to life in the rural wilds of Georgia. And if Carter Lois succeeded in making even a modest fortune in his general store Hester guessed she would have to make up her mind to marry him, or spend the rest of her life here as an old maid, just like Aunt Kizzy.

The only response to the placing of the advertisement in Carter's window was the sharp clicking of disapproving tongues as the Mackays' fortunes were picked over and reworked at sewing bees all around town. Hester, resolutely closing her ears to the tittle-tattle, set about cleaning the old house with vigour, though June was not the ideal month for such an activity. Before the war there would have been no question of the family staying on the coast for the entire summer. They would have headed out west to Rhapsody Creek where there was less danger from mosquitoes and fever.

But Susy washed the bed linen happily enough, while Hester swept out all the rooms and polished the mahogany furniture till her own face was reflected in its shine. Jonas went so far as to agree to trim the box hedges and paint the shutters in addition to his normal tasks of looking after Miss Kizzy's horse and buggy and generally fetching and carrying for her. But, for all he was a slave, Hester never asked him to work in the large kitchen gardens, for that would have been beneath his dignity. She merely chivvied ten-year-old Joe, whose job it was to provide the house with fruit and vegetables, to plant much more this spring and work harder at keeping the strawberry beds weeded.

Three weeks had gone by and the house and yard were as spick and span as Hester could make them and still no one had come. It was bitterly disappointing. After all, the town was bustling with merchants, cotton factors and ship owners besides the despised redcoats. They all had to stay somewhere, for goodness' sake, why not here? Yet there hadn't been one single enquiry from the placing of her card in Carter's store and a terrible suspicion dawned upon Hester. The next instant she was striding through the house calling for Jonas to fetch the buggy round.

'Yes, ma'am,' said Jonas, hastily dropping the papers he'd been using to clean the silver. Always ready to take out the buggy, he knew too well that when Miss Hester spoke in that particular tone there was no point in arguing.

'If you're going to the store to see Mr Carter,' called Susy with uncanny perception, 'yo could bring back a slab of bacon. And a wedge of cheese wouldn't go amiss. There ain't a bite of food in this whole larder.

How'm I supposed to feed us all? Aw, and let me check my flour.'

Hester jittered with impatience while Susy reeled off her list of needs, knowing all the while there was no way of paying for them. It would have to go on Carter's 'slate' yet again and she so hated to be in debt. Jonas tacked up Captain, Aunt Kizzy's old grey and brought the small carriage to the door but then Aunt Kizzy delayed matters still further by insisting Hester go upstairs and fetch her parasol since it was midday and the sun was strong.

'Southern women take care of their skin,' said Aunt Kizzy scoldingly. 'What a worry you are to me, Hester.' Privately Hester thought that if all she had to worry about was the whiteness of her skin, life would indeed be sweet. As it was, their debts were fast overtaking their income and if she didn't find a solution to their troubles soon she'd have to marry Carter Lois simply to settle them.

By the time the carriage started on its lumbersome path down East Bay towards Queen Street, Hester was in a veritable ferment of youthful impatience. She did not even take time to enjoy the glint of sun on the river as she so loved to do, or admire the magnolias that bloomed beneath the palmettos in the gardens of the fine white mansions that lined the wide street. She barely had time to nod a good morning to the carpenters and builders busy repairing and rebuilding where cannon fire had done its worst. Charleston was suffering but refusing to be beaten. It would rise again as it always did after turbulence, whether made by man or nature. But this morning there was not even time for the pride she usually felt for her own beloved city.

'Oh, do hurry, Jonas. Mr Carter may well be closing for lunch soon and the whole morning will have been wasted.'

'I reckon we're going fast enough, Miss Hester.'

'Jonas!'

The old man twitched his eyebrows and reluctantly clicked the horse to go faster. 'Yo shore is in a fine lather this morning, Miss Hester. Mebbe yo should leave it till this afternoon to see Mr Carter. Whut he done to vex you so?'

Hester chose not to answer. The less Jonas knew, the less he would fuss. 'Faster, Jonas, it's almost one o'clock already.' But Jonas kept the horse to a steady pace barely above a walk till, unable to restrain herself any longer as the words she must say to Carter Lois buzzed in her head, Hester wrenched the reins from the old man's grasp. 'Oh, give them to me. Gittup, Captain. Go on, boy.' The horse was startled from its dozing amble in the sun into a brisk trot and still Hester urged it onward. The carriage rattled round the corner into Queen Street at such a pelting rate, Hester did not see one tall gentleman strolling idly across the road until she had almost run him down.

She heaved on the reins, managing at the last moment to drag the carriage off its collision course though it rocked dangerously and for one heart-stopping moment she felt certain it would overturn. A loud oath rent the air as the dark-haired man flung out his arms to fend off the huge animal bearing down upon him.

'Lawd sakes, Miss Hester, that was a close one. See what I telled you. Don't do no good to drive like a tearing buzz-fly.' Deliberately, Jonas reached over to tug on the ribbons and slow the horse to a walk. Equally irritated, Hester looked back over her shoulder to frown her displeasure at the offending pedestrian who had so stubbornly got in her way. He was standing in the centre of the street, his face a picture of fury as he dusted the sand that the wheels had spurted at him from the sleeves of his fine coat. Obviously some foolish seaman unused to traffic. Well, he'd take more care in future. Stubbornly she paid no heed to the fast frightened beating of her own heart. The only creature not to be perturbed by the incident was Captain, who returned to his usual amble in a self-righteous huff.

Jonas drew the carriage to a halt outside Carter's General Trading Company and, stepping down, asked Hester for the shopping list. 'Now yo stay cosy here, Miss Hester, and ah'll slip in and get yo purchases and tell Mr Carter yo want a word with him.'

But Hester was tugging at her mittens and snapping down her parasol. 'I think not, Jonas. I shall deal with the matter myself.' At which declaration she began to climb down from the carriage, much to Jonas's despair. He'd tried all his life to turn Miss Hester into a lady and all his efforts had been a miserable failure. She still insisted on doing everything herself. He was greatly relieved to find the store almost empty, most sensible folks having gone home for a bite of luncheon and a quiet nap in the heat of the day. Miss Hester however, judging by the way she strode past the young clerk who bobbed his head to her from behind the long counter, was bristling with pent-up fury. And Jonas guessed that Carter Lois would not particularly enjoy this visit, for all he quickly set aside the coffee beans he was grinding to come eagerly towards her, hands outstretched and a smile planted from ear to ear.

'Hester, what a surprise, and how charming you look. I always said that blue was your colour.'

'Where is it?'

Carter came to an abrupt halt, one hand half reaching for Hester's frozen in mid-air at her tone. 'W-where is what, Hester, my dear?' He rubbed the hand instead over the pale fronds of his hair, which stuck out, Hester thought, rather like sprouting corn.

'I am not your dear, and you know well enough what I am talking of. Where is my card?'

'Card?'

Hester was almost fizzing with fury and very close to tears. All her plans could go to nothing because of this silly man and his old-fashioned prejudice. Hadn't they all had enough of suffering with almost two years of British occupation? With valiant self-control she kept her calm. 'My advertisement.' The steel in her voice should have warned him. 'The one you promised to display in your window. I do not see any sign of it.' But Carter Lois was as stubborn as he was mild and he merely gazed blankly back at her for a second before finally allowing a quiet smile of benign patience to creep over his pale features.

'Ah, the advertisement for letting your aunt's rooms. Well, now, Hester, I didn't reckon it was a good idea to go rushing into anything, so I took it out again.'

'*You* didn't think. . .'

'I reckoned as how you needed time to consider.' Wiping his hands on his long white apron, Carter took Hester carefully by the elbow and led her over to the pot-bellied stove, stiflingly hot on this June afternoon, but where a pot of coffee bubbled, filling the room with its aromatic fragrance. Beside it two old men played a quiet game of checkers. They didn't even glance up from the contemplation of their next move as Carter offered Hester a chair and she ignored it.

'Here's Miss Hester called to see us,' said Carter with a cheerfulness beginning to show signs of strain.

'How ar'ya, Hester?' said one, eyes still fixed on the checker pieces.

'Very well, thank you, Mr Elliot,' replied Hester as politely as she could before turning back to her argument. 'Now Carter, really, you had no——'

'How's Miss Kizzy?'

'Went to young Georgy's funeral,' said the other. 'Fine gathering but mighty queer without a coffin.'

Hester was forced to give her full attention to answering the queries of the two old gentlemen, accept their condolences, though by no means for the first time, discuss the weather, the state of the economy, and the possible end to the war now that the French had thrown in their lot. And not once did they lift their attention from the game. Then she had to put Jonas to ordering the supplies from Carter's young clerk if he wasn't to stand gawping and listening to every word she said. At last she was able to return to Carter, who had drifted away to get on with weighing out an order of herb tea for Mrs Winborough. 'Do you think we might discuss this very private matter in your office?' she asked.

'Why certainly, Hester, my dear, such as it is.'

The 'office' was no more than a small area of the shop partitioned off by shelves and barrels of flour, crackers and corn meal and such, but it gave a modicum of privacy behind which accounts were written out and trading deals struck.

'I do understand, Carter,' Hester began in a conciliatory fashion, 'just how you feel. But you have to see my point of view. Aunt Kizzy has little enough money to live on, certainly not enough to feed us all. I've depended on George these last years and now that he is gone I must needs shift for myself.' She smiled appealingly up at him, her temper quite gone, for really Carter Lois wasn't worth the trouble of it. She wondered she had ever considered him as a possible husband, for he had little to recommend him and certainly nothing you could call spunk. Not once had he disagreed with a word she'd ever said to him. Until now. And even this was in a peevish, underhand sort of way. She as good as told him so. 'You might have at least discussed it with me, rather than simply do nothing about it,' she said, rather tartly.

'But Hester, my dear,' he purred, 'you know I have only your best interests at heart. If you are in need of funds you only have to say. Admittedly cash is a little tight just now, but I reckon I'll soon have enough and to spare. In the meantime you're more'n welcome to run up an account.'

Hester clicked her tongue in dismay. 'I can't do that indefinitely. However would I settle it with no income? Carter Lois, you don't listen to a word I say. Are you a complete fool?'

She could feel her impatience starting to grow again. Many was the time Aunt Kizzy had told her she should have been descended from the Irish rather than the milder-mannered Scots with such a temper. And while she struggled to control her scorn of her would-be-betrothed, and yet persuade him to fall in with her wishes, Hester did not notice the door of the store open and a stranger walk in, his fine grey coat somewhat tarnished with dust, and with one sleeve torn.

'My only concern is for your happiness,' Carter was saying. 'There'd be no question of your paying me back, not in cash anyway.'

Hester went very still and her brown eyes darkened to almost black beneath frowning brows. 'What are you suggesting?'

Carter had the grace to flush with embarrassment. 'Oh—only that soon enough you'll be my wife and so all your debts will be mine in any case.'

'All my debts. . .?' Hester gasped. 'Wife? I never. . .' Carter could not have chosen a worse line of argument.

The interested stranger drew nearer.

'It's been understood between us for some time,' said Carter in his flat reasonable voice. 'You know that is true, Hester, dear. Why, ain't I building a fine house for us out on Meeting Street?'

Hester was appalled. She hadn't known any such thing. In fact she'd paid little heed to Carter's patient courtship these last years. Her entire concentration had been on survival through the difficult days of war, and

on discovering the whereabouts of her lost brother.
But it seemed that had been a mistake.

'I never asked you to build a house, Carter Lois.'

'Well, as a newly wed couple we have to live somewhere.'

Hester squirmed with a mixture of embarrassment and rebellion. 'Seems to me you take too much upon yourself. You should have checked with me first.'

Carter puffed out his chest self-righteously. 'It's a man's duty to provide, Hester. And you know you want to marry me really, so don't be coy. Anyway, reckon there won't be a whole lot of choice left. For every soldier who comes back from the war, there'll be half a dozen belles clamouring for him. You'd best put aside all that nonsense of letting rooms and taking in lodgers and be grateful for my offer, Hester Mackay. Husbands are going to be hard to come by, you mark my words, particularly one as well set up as I intend to be.' He reached for her. 'So come on, honey. Let's stop spatting and seal our bargain with a kiss, else you'll turn into a dry old maid like your aunt.'

'Sounds reasonable enough to me.' The stranger had reached the small office unnoticed and was leaning against a cracker barrel, his tanned face creased in amusement. It was the most fascinating argument he'd had the pleasure to eavesdrop in a long while, and what an odd-assorted pair. He found himself laying bets on which one would win. The rather plod-hopping shopkeeper, or the deliciously provocative young girl in the pale blue dress and bonnet. He glanced interestedly across at Carter to find him almost smirking in a most superior manner which would surely not endear himself to any young lady with her dander up.

Hester whirled to face him, the perpetrator of this unlooked for intrusion, in startled surprise. Clutching his side in an evident agony of delight, blue eyes twinkling outrageously, was the tall dark man her carriage had almost run down a few moments earlier. It was Carter who had made her angry. Carter who had insulted her, and yet there was something in the arrogant tilt of this stranger's handsome head, and in his unfortunate facility for getting under her feet that set her blood to boiling-point. 'How dare you, sir?' she cried. The loud crack of her hand across his cheek startled him far more than the pain it brought. But in its wake came laughter, not a matching anger.

'What a delight she is,' the stranger said with evident glee. 'What a harridan, an absolute termagant of fire and brimstone, hellbent on decapitating me twice in one short morning's work. Ma'am, if you cook as energetically as you drive and make love, I'd be more than pleased to take one of those rooms you have on offer.'

CHAPTER TWO

THERE was complete stillness in the room. Hester and Carter ceased their petty quarrelling. The clerk behind the counter stopped cutting crystallised ginger for Miss Kizzy's order and Jonas stopped his toing and froing with parcels to the waiting carriage. Even the two old men stopped playing checkers and lifted their grizzled heads to examine the tall dark stranger, and listen.

And in the silence Hester too found herself examining him with frank, startled hostility. Deep-set, gentian eyes met her gaze with a wry, almost questioning amusement and the wide lips quirked with matching laughter. He bore the tanned complexion of one who had evidently been at sea for some long time, but his clothes labelled him a gentleman. Such an appearance was not unusual in Charleston, though he was taller and more powerfully built than most. But Hester's reaction to him was. Only to look at him set her heart scudding into tiny rapid beats of excitement. A reaction which horrified her. For not only did this stranger appear arrogant, overly self-assured and decidedly inquisitive, but he was, without question, English.

Mr Elliot and his companion got up from the checker board and, without a word of farewell, walked from the store, abandoning their game unfinished.

Hester felt a compelling urge to follow them and escape the suddenly stifling atmosphere of the general store. Few Charlestonians maintained any respect for the British since they had occupied the town for almost two years now, not always in a gentlemanly manner. Notable citizens had been held captive at St Augustine downriver. Even humble prisoners had often never been heard of again. Once this uncomfortable war was over, wounds would heal eventually, no doubt. Brother would again speak to brother. But not yet. Not yet. And certainly not with such a man as this with his uppish manner and supercilious laughter.

But what on earth had possessed her to do such a madcap thing as to strike him? He did not look at all the sort of man accustomed to such treatment. She could feel damp tendrils of hair drooping on to her forehead and down her neck, escaping the tidy confines of her bonnet. And her cheeks positively burned. She saw the stranger open his mouth, revealing a flash of strong white teeth, as if he was about to say something more. But pivoting adroitly upon her heel, Hester cut him by presenting her back to his all too disturbing gaze. With frigid control she spoke to Carter.

'It must be the heat which has got to me this morning, Carter. I feel quite faint. I shall return home at once and you can send the rest of my packages on later, if you will.'

Carter was at once all concern. 'But of course, Hester, my dear. You do look—well—feverish.' He stepped back a trifle in alarm. 'I should go to bed if I were you. You look positively unwell. We don't want you going down with anything d-dreadful.'

Hester bit back fresh irritation at his words for she knew that it was his own health he was chiefly concerned with and not hers at all. Everyone in the South feared the least sign of fever. Without a glance at the stranger, and lifting the skirt of her narrow dress well away from any danger of brushing against his highly polished boots, she swept out of the store, head held high and slender back stiff with national pride. It said all too clearly that no one would find her conversing with an Englishman.

But Benjamin Blake's long strides took him to the door before her none the less, and as he held it politely open, he watched her go with a small smile. He even, much to Hester's further annoyance, held up Jonas by exchanging pleasantries, would you believe, so that she was forced to tap her foot most indignantly upon the pavement before Jonas bethought himself to hand her into the carriage.

They drove home in silence and at a more sedate pace than their outward journey, with Jonas in the driving seat. On arrival home she did not join Aunt Kizzy in the rocking-chairs on the piazza, the long porch which ran the full length of the house, but fled to her room, where it took most of the afternoon before she felt quite herself again. What a very disagreeable man he must be to deliberately jay-walk in front of her carriage and then to eavesdrop upon a perfectly private conversation, which for some reason afforded him immense amusement. Why, she sincerely hoped she never clapped eyes on him again, for all he was a fine handsome figure of a man.

But her wish, even had it been sincere, was not to be granted. The very next morning Hester was out in the yard, a chicken she was plucking held between her knees and the skirt of her dimity cotton dress rucked up, showing bare brown legs and feet in anything but a ladylike fashion. Her mind was busily engaged upon how to pay for the restocked larder without compromising herself further with Carter Lois when she was startled by a polite but very masculine cough.

'Forgive me for intruding but no one heard me ring the front doorbell. Perhaps you would be so good as to tell your mistress that a Mr Benjamin Blake begs leave to pay his respects and make enquiries about a room.'

Hester jerked her head up in stunned dismay. She could hardly believe her eyes. Her first thought was, Oh, why had she not thought to tidy herself this morning, just in case someone called? To her shame she knew herself for a dusty frump. Jonas was right to scold her continuously for her rebellious, tomboyish behaviour, for to be caught thus by this insufferable man was galling in the extreme. Really, it was too much to bear. The slow pulse which started to thrum deep inside her stomach gave the lie to her displeasure and she had to work very hard not to show the intrigue and delight she felt at sight of him.

Drat the man, was he following her? She was about to ask him when she became aware how his gaze slid insolently over her, missing nothing of shapely calves, trim ankles, nor the mass of golden-brown hair that tumbled unrestrained over shapely shoulders. She gazed helplessly up at him, his tall, lean body seeming to stretch endlessly upwards. Wide powerful shoulders slouched slightly forwards as he examined her with undisguised interest from mischievous eyes, half closed against the sun.

'Why, I do believe. . . Can it be. . .?' Frank brown eyes met enigmatic blue and Hester knew them to be insincere. The Englishman had known well enough whose house this was. But how on earth had he persuaded Carter to part with her address? And then she remembered his brief exchange with Jonas and knew the traitor, if that was the correct term, to be closer to home.

Hester found that she had dropped the chicken and in one single movement, as unflustered and dignified as she could make it, she picked the carcass up with trembling hands while drawing down her skirt hem and getting to her feet without the least sign of haste. They stood gazing at each other for some long moments while Hester unconsciously traced the planes of his tanned cheekbones down to the squared jaw. She noted the patrician line of his nose beneath the lowering black brows, and the sensual droop to his lower lip.

Her mind devoid of any sensible words, she stood dumb, rooted to the spot.

'Benjamin Blake, ma'am, at your service,' he gently reminded her in case she had forgotten in the long silence, and, sketching a deep bow, smiled. It was a lop-sided sort of smile, rippling with sensual awareness, and left Hester feeling suddenly decidedly weak. There was a certain knowing quality to it, as if he understood her perfectly well and challenged her to deny it.

'Lawd sakes, Miss Hester, what yo doing with dat chicken? He won't be fit to eat the way yo carrying on. And just look at dat dress. What yo thinking of, getting it all soiled? Have you found yourself a wardrobe full of dimity dresses dat this one don't matter none?' The screen door had banged open to reveal Susy at her most disapproving, hands on hips, face a pucker of displeasure.

'I'm—I'm sorry, Susy.' Hester brushed ineffectually at the stains down the front of her dress.

'Yo could least have worn an apron, chile. Ain't you got no sense?'

One large masculine hand reached down and gently picked a feather from Hester's hair. She felt herself flush to the very roots. Taking the chicken from her limp grasp, Benjamin presented it to the negress with his most winning smile.

'I believe the fault was mine. I startled your mistress so that she dropped the chicken upon her skirts.'

It was absolute nonsense of course, and both ladies were aware of it. There was a small stunned silence and then Susy burst into peals of merry laughter. 'Lawd sakes, if we ain't got a gennelman here, Miss Hester. Tongue as smooth as a bob-cat's fur.'

Hester ground her teeth in a fresh spurt of anger. Were he truly a gentleman he would have done her the courtesy of not recognising her when he found her thus employed, and tactfully returned to the front door, which he should never have left. The man's inquisitiveness was rife, and clearly showed that the British had no manners. But she must guard her temper if she were not to look a complete fool. This man was no Carter Lois and she was still half prepared for a reprisal in return for her being so misguided yesterday as to strike him. Drawing herself to her full if moderate height of five feet three, Hester addressed the stranger with apparent composure.

'I very much doubt we can have anything to say to each other so I will bid you good day.' She moved towards the kitchen door.

'One moment, ma'am.' Benjamin Blake put out a hand to grasp her arm and Hester looked down upon it as if it were a insect. After a long moment he gave a sardonic laugh and removed the hand, succeeding in leaving the impression that it was at his own behest and not hers. 'If you recall, I was interested in a room?'

It took all her will-power not to actually gape at him. Did this *Englishman* imagine that she, a proud Southern woman, would take him into her home? 'You must be mad,' she said, and flushed with surprise that she had actually spoken the words out loud.

'Must I?' Benjamin Blake frowned, and then the lop-sided smile was back and Hester's heart gave a betraying leap at sight of it. It held a certain charm, she had to confess. 'What have you to fear? Now that de Grasse is in the West Indies it will only be a matter of time before he brings his men into action. And, with the French actively on your side, that will give a whole new perspective to the American cause. In the meantime, the British remain in Charleston, and they must be housed. I assure you we will do our best not to inconvenience you more than is absolutely necessary.'

Hester stared at him, aghast. 'Are you saying that you wish to house *redcoats* here?'

He gave a little chuckle. 'Would that be so very

dreadful? They are simply frightened young men who need to be fed and have a clean bed to sleep in, like any other. I could commandeer the rooms, but I would rather treat you fairly.'

Hester's lips almost curled with disbelief. 'When did the British ever treat us fairly?'

Benjamin Blake pretended not to understand her. 'I guessed you were of Scots extraction with a name like Mackay and of course with your passionate personality. While I have to admit the Scots and the English have had a tempestuous relationship in the past, I sincerely hope that will not prejudice you against me in the future.' The wide lips tilted teasingly and Hester felt her own give an answering twitch before she managed to control them.

'I am an American, Mr Blake, and proud of it, though my ancestors were indeed Scottish. Nevertheless, whatever I may think, I cannot offer you rooms for I have my aunt to consider.'

'Is that someone at the door, Hester?' called Aunt Kizzy exactly on cue and Hester looked at her visitor with velvet appeal in her brown eyes.

'If Aunt Kizzy thought for one moment that I might let Englishmen into her beautiful home, she would withdraw her permission to let the rooms at all. And that would spell disaster for us. Please go.'

'To where? Do you thnk anyone else will be more charitable?' Benjamin asked, a weariness showing at last in his tone and taking the edge off his bewitchingly confident smile. 'Do you think I have not tried? It is not for redcoats that I seek accommodation in point of fact, but half a dozen of my own men, from my own ship. We did not expect the red carpet treatment, but have business to transact here in Charleston and must needs stay somewhere.'

'Hester?' The voice from the piazza had grown more

insistent. 'I can hear voices. Who is it? Bring them here and let me see.'

'One moment, Aunt.' Hester was in despair. Despite herself she did feel a certain sympathy for the stranger but not for a moment would she let him see it. 'Will you please leave, at once? You'll spoil everything.'

'Pardon me for intruding, Miss Hester,' said Susy. 'But if dis 'ere gennelman can pay his board, it shore don't bother me none that he ain't American. And dem groceries ain't getting no cheaper, dat's for shore.'

Hester had forgotten about Susy still standing there and drinking it all in. And now the truth of her statement was so obviously indisputable that Hester could think of nothing to say in reply. The whole situation was decidedly confusing.

'I assure you that unlike the soldiers I can pay a fair price, and in advance, naturally.' So saying, Benjamin Blake began to peel bank notes from a roll he took from his inner pocket, making Susy's eyes pop. And when he mentioned the sum he was prepared to pay for the privilege of lodging with the Mackays Hester's very nearly did the same.

'*Hester*,' called Miss Kizzy with not a trace of patience left in the stentorian voice.

Hester met his frank gaze with sad resignation and, taking a step backwards, allowed him to enter the stairhall. 'Coming, Aunt. You'd best follow me. We'll have to let Aunt Kizzy decide after all,' she said stiffly.

'Presumably it is her house.'

Hester's head jerked back at his impertinence. 'Yes, but we share it now that my brother is. . .is.'

'I see.' She was surprised to see something like kindness in those narrowed eyes, which even now, inside the shady house, regarded her through half-closed lids in a shrewd, almost calculating way which at once disturbed and excited her. 'It is decidedly galling to live on charity. I know that well enough from my own experience. You have my heartfelt sympathy, Miss Mackay.' The bitter note in his tone astonished her and she blinked rapidly as, searching his face for any sign of insincerity, she found none.

She led him briskly from the garden door in the side of the house, through the stairhall to the front of the house, which was set at right angles to the street. This way the piazza faced south-west to catch the breeze. It was a favourite place to entertain when, as today, the inside of the house was stifling.

Miss Kizzy was seated in one of the rockers set on the piazza, but, instead of rocking and enjoying the light breeze that motion created, she was sitting bolt upright, hands clasped tight upon her bony lap and her small mouth drawn into a tight rosy bud. Hester saw at once that this would not be a pleasant interview. Miss Kizzy could be the sweetest and dearest of aunts when she had a mind to it, but she also held the power of a strict disciplinarian. By no means had she quaked in her duty at bringing up two robust youngsters and as she now regarded the young man Hester had brought Miss Kizzy began to see that that discipline must be further exercised. She had given in to George's sudden desire to join up and look what a mistake that had been. She wasn't about to make another. Good heavens, on no account did she want a man in one of her best bedrooms. He would get boot polish on the four-poster and leave his shaving soap all over the furniture. She eyed the young man with open disfavour.

Hester, recognising the familiar expression, swallowed nervously and performed the necessary introductions.

'Delighted to make your acquaintance, ma'am,' said Benjamin Blake, bowing dutifully over the older woman's proffered hand. He felt it freeze even as his fingers touched it.

'English?'

He inclined his head slightly in agreement. 'I cannot deny it.'

Miss Kizzy drew in an endless breath and as Hester waited for the explosion that would surely come she found herself holding her own.

Then suddenly the old lady grinned. 'We'll lick you, you know,' she said.

'I dare say you might, ma'am,' Benjamin said with a warm smile. 'But it isn't over yet and the British do not take kindly to defeat.'

Lids snapped over pale grey eyes. 'Nor do we Americans.'

'Quite so,' said Benjamin, mildly enough, but Hester broke in upon the argument as she considered her aunt to be taking the presence of this Englishman too light-heartedly.

'The British must go,' she said, very decidedly. 'They interfere too much in our lives and try to manipulate everything to suit themselves. It was that foolish tax on tea which precipitated the war in the first place. The Declaration of Independence was signed over five years ago, yet still they fight on. What right have they to impose their laws upon us? When will the British ever accept that they can no longer control us?' she finished, rather breathless in her fervour.

'The motherland has no wish to lose the colony,' Benjamin explained, 'and dislikes the idea that her favourite child rebels.'

Hester bridled. 'America is not Britain's child. She is the equal of any country, whether it be France, Spain or Britain, all of which happen to be the homeland of many of its citizens. We may be brothers under the skin, or even sisters,' she added, 'but we most sincerely believe that all men are created equal.'

'Hear, hear. I do most heartily agree,' Benjamin Blake surprisingly said. None the less Hester regarded his sparkling eyes with suspicion. Was he making fun of her national pride, which was admittedly a new experience for her? She had always first and foremost thought of herself as a South Carolinian. But now she was thinking ahead to a wider world when America would be free and one country in its own right. A time when the laws and fancies of Britain would be of no account. Right now she would so love to prick that infuriating British self-assurance which this man carried in abundance, along with his undoubted charm.

'Nevertheless,' he was calmly saying, accepting a rocking-chair at the invitation of her aunt, 'I can no more control the affairs of war than you can. And for the moment America's position grows stronger. I trust you will not hold my country against me for its attempt to hold on to its dearly beloved ch—er—brother.' As he returned Hester's challenging gaze she felt a shiver run through her. As pleasant as it was startling, it hardened her resolve to be rid of him. Such a man under her roof would be a positive danger to her equilibrium.

'And what is your job in this war of kin against kin?' asked Aunt Kizzy, straight to the point as usual, asking the very question Hester had so longed to ask since she first set eyes on him.

Benjamin Blake hesitated before answering, and Hester guessed his embarrassment. He might pretend a sympathy with their cause but he was British born and bred and therefore their enemy, without any doubt. His answer was a long time in coming and when it did come it confirmed her worst fears. 'I ship guns, as a matter of fact.'

'Guns?' Hester could not contain her horror.

'They are unfortunately necessary in wartime,' said Benjamin, a barbed note in his voice. 'Someone must supply them. I run regular trips between the American coast and Liverpool.'

Hester regarded him with a cold eye. 'You admit to being a gun-runner and still ask us to allow you accommodation in our house? You certainly do not lack impudence!'

Benjamin laughed out loud. 'I have been called many things in my time but never impudent. I think I rather like it.'

'I did not mean it as a compliment.'

'Hester, do sit down. You make my head ache with your quarrelsome manner,' said Aunt Kizzy, flapping her mittened hand and Hester was at once filled with contrition.

'Oh, Aunt Kizzy, I'm so sorry.' She went to kneel by her aunt's knee and, casting an accusing glance up at Benjamin Blake, she said, 'The fault must be yours, Mr Blake. You have a most disturbing effect upon us both.'

It was a second or two before he answered and when he did his words were accompanied by a slow smile as if he knew some great secret. 'Yes, I can see that I do,' in such a way that Hester went hot and cold all at once, from the tips of her still bare feet to the top of her tousled head.

'And now, Mr Blake, that we have settled the war issue,' said Miss Kizzy calmly, 'perhaps you would be so good as to tell us a little about your background. And Hester, what a tumble you do look. Go upstairs and freshen up, do, and on your way ask Susy to bring us more lemonade. I declare it gets hotter by the minute.'

'Oh, but. . .' Hester was most unwilling to leave this little circle. Besides, everything was going wrong. It should be Benjamin Blake who was being shown the door, not herself.

'Hurry now, before I die of thirst.'

Hester had no option but to get to her feet, and, excusing herself, walked away down the length of the porch to the screen door, aware every step of the way of Blake's eyes upon her.

'She's a good girl,' said Miss Kizzy, missing nothing of Benjamin's interest in her niece's movements, which were a mite fetching to a young man, no doubt, despite the dreadful old dress that had long since given up any pretence to fashion. 'And she do mean well, despite her exuberance, which quite tires me out at times, I don't mind telling you. But she is young. She will learn tolerance in time, as I have.'

Benjamin laughed, but not unkindly, and the old lady began to feel a warmth towards him. 'I quite like her liveliness. To be perfectly honest with you, ma'am, I find the milk-and-water girls back home exceedingly predictable. I doubt you could ever accuse Miss Mackay of that.'

Miss Kizzy chortled with delight and her pale eyes fastened shrewdly upon him. He was certainly handsome, and well dressed in a sharply cut coat of pale grey with silken lapels, and whoever did his linen knew their job for it was snowy white in the extreme. He reminded her of a young Englishman she had once known when she was a girl, a man she might well have married if things had not gone amiss between them. 'The one thing you can predict about Hester is that whatever you may want her to do she will do the exact opposite,' said Aunt Kizzy with a smile. 'Though to be fair she is not quite beyond persuasion and will always listen to reasonable argument. But come now, Mr Blake, no more prevarications. If it's rooms in my house you are wanting, for yourself and your men, you must offer me some credentials. At the very least I would wish to know your origins and how long you intend to stay.' She raised finely plucked brows in enquiry and waited.

Benjamin did not hurry with his answer. He always favoured careful thought when faced with a tricky question. Susy brought out the lemonade and Miss Kizzy poured a glass for each of them, placing a twist of lemon and cracked ice brought from the ice house in each. Benjamin drank his with obvious gratitude and had his glass at once refilled. 'The warm climate and humidity of South Carolina is markedly different from rainy Liverpool.'

'You'll grow accustomed,' smiled Miss Kizzy, adding more ice to his glass. 'Just take life a mite slower, that's the secret. You won't find anyone rushing around here in the South.'

Nor had he expected such an odd welcome. His one thought as he had stepped off the ship yesterday morning was how quickly he could complete his transactions in Charleston and be on his way. There were matters he wished to attend to before returning to Liverpool so perhaps his mind had been wandering when the carriage bore down so swiftly upon him but it had certainly taken him by surprise. And, to find his aggressor in the form of a fiery young Southern miss who, if he was not mistaken, kept a very evident but delightful sense of humour not quite so well hidden as she imagined, the prospect of spending time in this port no longer palled. But he had no wish to repeat last night's experience of staying in a seaman's hostel— overcrowded and malodorous in the extreme. He had resolved to find more salubrious accommodation in the city with someone who could put this endless war sufficiently from his mind so as to offer a non-military Englishman refuge. And the obvious first choice had to be Hester Mackay, for more reasons than one. Even as he thought of her with renewed appreciation she re-entered the piazza and he felt a strange tightness in his chest as he watched her walk towards him. Gone was the harum-scarum child. In her place was a sophisticated young miss with sun-kissed brown hair done up in a mass of curls on top of her pert head. A dress of cream organza had replaced the rough cotton. It floated and clung to her slender waistline, billowing out most becomingly to show a provocative hint of trim ankle above the shapely feet clad in matching slippers which were most certainly not meant for chores such as chicken-plucking. A ball of unexpelled breath lodged in his throat and he began to see even more attractions to life in the colonies than had occurred to him previously.

'Mr Blake is about to tell us his life story,' said Miss Kizzy in her direct manner. 'So pour yourself a lemonade, Hester, and try not to interrupt.'

Benjamin looked helplessly from one to the other. The story of his life was the last thing he wanted to give for it would undoubtedly result in his being thrown out on the street by these unconventional but none the less upper class Charlestonians. 'I doubt you would find it of any interest, ma'am,' he asserted. 'My origins in Liverpool were, shall we say—unpretentious, and my prospects poor. I decided to seek my fortune, as many have done before me, on the high seas and take my chances with the war in this new, exciting land of yours.'

But Miss Kizzy was not so easily satisfied. 'But what of your mother, your father?'

Benjamin sighed. 'I'm afraid I have no recollection of either.'

'Then who raised you?'

Again Benjamin hesitated, and, looking from one to other, said, with just a hint of desperation in his voice, 'I was brought up by an aunt.'

'As I was,' said Hester. 'What an odd coincidence.' And, not quite meeting her gaze, Benjamin agreed.

'And where were you educated?' Miss Kizzy asked. 'I hear there are some fine schools in England. Let me see. Was it Eton? Rugby?'

Benjamin Blake gave a short, sharp laugh and, getting to his feet, walked over to lean casually against the porch rail, turning to smile at the two ladies and showing every ounce of his devilish charm. 'You could say that my education was founded in life. There are many fine schools, even in Liverpool, but I was forced to work from a very early age.'

'Was your aunt troubled by her health, that she could not support you?' asked Miss Kizzy.

Benjamin smiled, rather thinly, Hester thought. 'You could say that.'

'How dreadful.'

'However,' Benjamin blithely continued, not wishing to overplay his hand and seeing he had won some of their sympathy—the last thing he wanted was to make them curious about him, 'I made it my business when I grew from a boy to a man that poverty would never again be a problem. I made myself more than enough money to set out on this new adventure, where I will double my fortune, Miss Kizzy, with or without the war. You may depend upon it.'

'And how do you intend to do that?' Hester asked, intrigued despite herself, and longing to ask a dozen questions to fill in the gaps Benjamin Blake was so obviously leaving in his story.

Again that quirky grin. 'The war cannot last forever. And then, who knows? There is bound to be an increase in trade since America has many raw resources. I have a fine ship and a knowledge of the seas. I can transport any product anywhere in the world. In short, I intend, Miss Mackay, to become an American.' He leaned back against the rail and folded his arms across his broad chest. 'If you will have me.'

He did not have long to wait this time for his answer. After a short, stunned silence, Miss Kizzy got abruptly to her feet and jerked her folded fan at Benjamin. 'I like your spirit, young man. You're more'n welcome to stay. Show him up to the blue room, Hester, and stop that pouting. Get on with it, girl. Fiddle-de-dee, do I have to do everything around here?'

CHAPTER THREE

BENJAMIN BLAKE followed Hester up the staircase that spiralled through the heart of the house, its balustrades glistening white and the mahogany rail smooth and highly polished beneath his hand. The contrast of this house to the row of tenements where he had been born and survived his early years—hardly termed living— could not have been more marked. But those days were long gone and he had no wish for them to be picked over by a curious child and her straight-talking aunt. The less they knew, the better, and he put the problem resolutely from his mind.

His interest at this precise moment was more with the curve of hips that swung so beguilingly before him, the narrow waist so artfully emphasised by the softly flounced folds of the skirt beneath, and the proud column of soft white neck with its bob of curls above. But he could not help but smile as he wondered what this vision's reaction would be if she knew she was about to harbour a convicted criminal in her pretty home. Would she scream and throw a fit? Sock him in the jaw more like, if her previous behaviour was anything to go by. More pragmatically, Benjamin realised, she would most certainly show him the door. Which would be a pity.

Had he not been the reformed character he had so carefully devised for himself he would already have been planning ways of dallying with this treasure when they finally reached the upper floor. As it was he restrained himself with commendable aplomb as Hester threw open the door of a small but airy bedchamber in the furthest corner of the third floor of the house. It amused Benjamin considerably that she should deposit him as far from the family as deemed possible. And it was evidently not the blue room her aunt had recommended for the bed-hangings were in a soft, if faded pale green.

'Very charming,' he said, with a decided twinkle in his blue eyes. 'I do appreciate your trust in me and I promise not to abuse it.'

'No doubt you will wish to rest now,' said Hester coolly. 'Most folks do in the afternoon.'

'Do you?'

'Yes.'

His eyes ran lingeringly, and regretfully, over her. 'Then I must do likewise though I feel bursting with energy.' His eyes left her in no doubt how he would like to spend that energy and she edged quickly to the door.

'Perhaps you will wish to collect your baggage later?'

'Would you have any objection to my borrowing your driver?'

Hester very nearly told him to take his devil cheek and whistle for a carriage but he was lifting her hand and opening the clenched palm and she couldn't quite catch her breath.

'I like to have financial matters clear from the start,' he was saying, getting out the roll of notes he'd produced earlier, and pressing her fingers around it. It felt very solid in her hand.

'Supper is at seven-thirty,' Hester informed him, rather more meekly and then, trying to rally her shattered self-possession, 'I trust that meets with your approval?'

'I shall look forward to it. What more can I say?' Blue eyes sparkled and she squirmed with fresh embarrassment.

When she had devised her scheme for their financial salvation, if it had occurred to Hester for one moment that she would be compelled to take into the house an enemy of her own country she felt sure she'd just as soon have starved. She could not imagine what had come over Aunt Kizzy to agree to it. Benjamin Blake was undoubtedly a highly suspicious character and nothing that happened over the next few days changed that viewpoint. He proved most successful at revealing little of his past, and what he did tell them was, to Hester's mind, unconvincing. Whenever the subject was raised he shied away from it or framed his answers in such a way that told them nothing. He was evidently the master of prevarication and without question was withholding some dark secret from them. Hester resolved that one way or another she would discover it.

Six of his men—and a decidedly brown, decrepit-looking crew they were—came to occupy the remaining three rooms on the top floor. They sat on the satin sofas in Aunt Kizzy's drawing-room and ate at the long mahogany table in the dining-room. And Hester waited upon them. She did not always do it with any excess of charm. And when she heard them talking of the war and adversely commenting on the methods of fighting adopted by her fellow countrymen, which she could not fail to do as she handed round the soup or meat course, she positively bristled with pent-up frustration.

'Would you care to dine with us?' Blake asked on one occasion when she was hovering overlong at the task of serving ham and celery soup. Hester was quite put out.

'Oh, no, indeed. That would not be at all correct.' But a subdued twinkle in his blue eyes almost made her change her mind. It might well be pleasant to enjoy an intelligent conversation at dinner with an attractive male for once. Very determinedly she shook her head and he laughed, that deep rich sound which sent odd little ripples of emotion up her spine.

'It was only that I thought perhaps you might wish to contribute.'

'Contribute?' Why must he look at her in quite such a challenging way?

'To the discussion which appears to have you riveted.'

Hester froze. 'If you are implying that I was deliberately eavesdropping I do assure you I would never dream. . .'

'Of course you would not,' he said smoothly. 'No more than I would.' And he held her gaze for a long moment until, unable to help herself, she laughed too, remembering the incident in the general store.

'I could not help but overhear some of it,' she admitted, setting down a dish of fried chicken pieces, 'including your opinions on the skills of the American rebels.'

'And they do not coincide with your own?'

'Indeed not.' Hester pushed up her chin in defiance. 'I have always thought it the height of folly for a soldier to dress in a red coat and walk in a straight line with a hundred others directly towards the enemy. Seems to me that makes him a prime target. At least the American army is more cunning.'

'Or cowardly, sneaking from tree to tree, depending upon your point of view. The British expect their enemy to run from the awesome band of red encroaching upon their territory, or fight them like gentlemen on equal terms. They are unaccustomed to the erratic tactics of farmers.'

Hester bridled. 'And what of King's Mountain?' she taunted, acutely aware of the interested stares of the assembled men as they chewed on their chicken legs and mopped up their gravy with biscuits, missing nothing of this exchange of heated words. 'The frontiersmen felled your Loyalist troops in rows, and blasted their leader, Major Ferguson, from his proud white horse in less than half an hour. Was that the work of ignorant farmers?'

'I did not call them ignorant,' said Blake mildly, but the wide mouth tightened dangerously. King's Mountain was a sensitive issue which had kindled fresh heart into the American army and sent Cornwallis into a scurrying retreat, his men subsisting on turnips and Indian corn throughout the winter months. The only consolation being that the patriots were suffering equally from lack of food, ammunition and pay.

'But it has happened again, has it not, at Cowpens and at Guilford Courthouse?' said Hester, with pride. 'Do not think, Mr Blake, that because I am a woman I understand nothing of the progress of this war. Almost the entire British force under Tarleton's command was either killed or captured and no Southerner would shed a tear for that scoundrel, not after what he has done to the people of Charleston.'

'And what of your own Benedict Arnold, who turned traitor for the lure of gold? Is he not a scoundrel of a worse kind?'

Hester tossed her head and the curls jounced with the heat of her fervour. 'I would have no truck with traitors, from whatever side,' she said, in her determined southern drawl. 'Nor with anyone who does not give himself heart and soul to the cause of his country.'

Blake's eyebrows rose in speculative enquiry. 'A harsh judgement indeed. Let us hope that none you care about falls short of your high ideals.'

'My brother did not. He died fighting for his country, which is a more worthy cause than shipping guns to those who pay the highest price.'

A dull stain of colour crept along his high cheekbones. 'I may never attain the hero status of your brother but I said nothing of selling to the highest bidder. That is your own interpretation run riot, as it appears so often inclined to do. Let us hope that our respective governments can find a solution to this issue before too many more lives are lost,' he said coldly and returned pointedly to his meal.

'You mean for America to surrender,' Hester cried, regretting the withdrawal of his goodwill in the argument yet resolved to win her point. 'Well, she never will. Washington has every faith in our ability to win and beat the scurrilous English,' she said, plumping her fist upon the table in emphasis. The men stopped their chewing to regard her in silence for a moment and for the first time in their presence she felt a prickle of unease.

'Take care, Hester,' said Benjamin Blake in dangerously low tones. 'This is that very same scurrilous enemy you entertain at your table, and they do not take kindly to insults.'

'From savages,' added one brawny man, wiping his greasy chin with the back of one hairy hand.

Hester looked at him with disdain and then handed him a napkin. 'There are savages,' she said crisply, 'and then there are savages.' Whirling upon her heel, she marched from the room, the sound of raucous laughter resounding in her ears.

For the next few days Hester managed to avoid the disturbing presence of Benjamin Blake by sending Susy in to wait at table while she confined herself to kitchen duties.

She knew she should feel grateful for the extra money coming in, which ensured they all fed much better than they had in months. And their debts were rapidly diminishing at the general store, a state of affairs which brought Hester great relief, though surprisingly Carter Lois had been less enthusiastic. Nevertheless, Hester was determined to continue paying regular sums off her account, which she hoped to clear entirely by Christmas at the latest. So it would not be in their best interests to cause friction with their paying guests and have them go elsewhere, for in all fairness Hester had to admit that, despite their differences of opinion over the war, they were little trouble. The men ate every scrap put before them, made no undue noise at night and even removed their caps in her presence.

Settling herself beneath the crinkled pink blooms of the myrtle tree with her endless mending one evening, she tried not to allow herself to think about how life would be without the presence of their leader, one Benjamin Blake, in the house. However much she might preach her patriotism, and her indifference to him, the very sound of his footsteps on the stair sent her heartbeat scurrying. Musing over the reasons for this quietly to herself in the softness of the evening as she plied her needle in and out of a muslin petticoat, Hester had to admit that he seemed an essentially relaxed and sociable character for all he was English. Though at times she had caught a darkly brooding, thoughtful look upon his face which she had a strange longing to banish with teasing smiles of her own. And when he laughed and joked with his men, even joining in their songs on the piazza before retiring, she found herself creeping from her maidenly bed to twitch aside the lace curtain and stick her head over the window-sill to watch and listen unobserved.

At least she sincerely hoped she was unobserved, for not for the world would Hester have Benjamin Blake know of her interest in him. Which was partly her reasoning behind sending Susy into the dining-room. The further Hester kept herself from his probing gaze, the better. It was simply her misfortune that the first man she'd really found herself reacting to happened to be British. Not that it mattered a jot, she told herself firmly, so long as he did not know of it. But she could not resist idly considering how their relationship might have developed had they not been on opposite sides in this conflict. The very thought made her heart beat faster. He might well be a mite brusque and a touch arrogant but there was a delicious humour in those heavenly eyes, and even, rather surprisingly, a compassion in evidence when George had been mentioned, as if he understood the loss of a dear one. And he spent a good deal of time talking to Aunt Kizzy, much to the old lady's delight, so he couldn't be all bad.

'Aha, the elusive Miss Mackay,' came a soft voice in her ear and Hester jumped so fiercely that she pricked her finger and cried out in her distress.

'Now look what you've made me do,' she said mournfully as a bright spot of scarlet spread upon the white muslin.

'I do beg your pardon,' murmured Benjamin, instantly contrite. 'Perhaps I may be permitted to buy you a replacement?'

Bright flags of colour flew to her cheeks. The very idea of an Englishman buying her underclothing was too unspeakably embarrassing for words. She rolled the petticoat into a tight ball and thrust it deep in her sewing basket. 'It will come out perfectly well if I soak it in salt water,' she said demurely. 'It was simply that you startled me with your creeping about. Do you have to behave in quite such a clandestine manner?'

Benjamin laughed. 'Why, Hester, how delightful you are. I had not realised that I was *clandestine* at all. What a very splendid description. I wonder what it means?' His grin was quite disarming but Hester refused to respond to it. Though now she had deprived herself of her sewing it was difficult to know quite what to do with her hands. She folded them together, the fingers lacing and unlacing in her lap.

'Did you wish to speak to me about something in

particular?' she prompted. 'I was about to go in, as a matter of fact.' She half rose from her seat.

'What nonsense, this is quite the most tolerable part of your southern day. I assure you, you are quite safe from me if not from these damnable mosquitoes. Shall we sit in the gazebo for a moment before they eat us alive?'

She allowed Benjamin to lead her down the garden and seated herself beside him in the white fretworked gazebo, though it was quite against her better judgement. She consoled herself that they were still in full view of the rear of the house so it was all quite proper, even though it was doubtful any of the family would be in that vicinity at this particular time of day.

'I wanted a word with you, Hester.' He stopped, and his eyes looked down into hers with a sweetness she found startling. 'You do not mind my calling you Hester? Only I have found all Americans so friendly, I've quite got out of the habit of saying Miss and Mister. And in these last weeks, staying in your beautiful home, I've come to think of you as a friend.'

'H-have you?' she said, clearing a sudden constriction in her throat. 'N-no, I do not mind in the least.' She had always hated her name. Until now. It sounded so much softer, so much more beautiful and less plain and dull upon his tongue. Whatever was the matter with her? She must pull herself together. 'What was it you wished to discuss?' she asked, and a sudden kernel of fear was born within her. Was he about to tell her that he was leaving? And, though she knew it might well be unpatriotic, she knew also that it was the last thing she wanted. Or would he perhaps tell her how much he admired her and, were it not for the war, would beg leave to court her? And how would she react if he did? He had certainly chosen a romantic setting. With her heart in her mouth and her hands neatly folded, she waited with breathless anticipation for him to speak.

'I wondered what preparations you have made in the event of open conflict taking place in Charleston? Do you have anywhere else to live other than this house?'

Hester stared at him in dismay. 'Anywhere else? Open conflict? What are you saying?'

Blue eyes regarded her steadily. 'That this is a war, Hester, not simply a verbal exercise. And in war there is combat. People get hurt, even killed.'

'I know that.' Her voice was sharp with disappointment. The war yet again. How she hated it.

'Then I repeat. Have you nowhere else you can go? This house is beautiful, yes, but very close to the seafront. Have you never considered how dangerous that might be?'

She could only shake her head, mesmerised by his concern.

'Then it is time you considered alternative arrangements.' He moved closer to her on the bench and her heart gave a little skip of pleasure at his nearness. 'Surely you have other family?'

'There is no one but Aunt Kizzy and myself now that—that George is gone.' It was still hard to think of him as dead. 'But it is true that we do have another house, an old plantation house way out west.'

His interest was almost tangible. 'Then you must go to it, at once. Where is this plantation?'

'In North Georgia, near the Savannah River, about a half-day's journey from Atlanta. But none of our family has lived there for years,' she protested. 'It will be too horribly damp. I have no intention of taking Aunt Kizzy to such a place, nor of leaving our home. Besides, I cannot believe we will be in any more danger here.'

Benjamin gave something very like a snort of derision. 'You Charlestonians will never accept disaster until it is staring you in the face.' Taking her shoulders, he gave her a little shake. 'Will you not believe me? There is every possibility of a naval attack from the French, possibly in these very waters.'

'The French are on our side. I do not fear them.'

'But their cannon will take lives irrespective of what side they are on,' he sharply rejoined, but Hester had heard enough. It was not at all what she had wished to hear from him and she would listen no more. She was on her feet, glaring fiercely at him.

'If the French come, well and good. If they do not, we will win without them. But I'll not run, not now, not ever, Mr Blake.' But as she turned to go he caught her very neatly by the wrist to hold her captive for one long heart-stopping moment.

'I want nothing dreadful to happen to you, Hester Mackay. No matter what happens, you must be kept safe. That is absolutely imperative.'

She gazed at him startled for a fraction of a second, then, brushing his hand aside, flew into the house. He watched her go with a mixture of sadness and admiration and a deep sense of failure. Why was it that every time he tried to talk to her it went wrong and they ended up quarrelling about this dratted war?

By August reports were coming through that Cornwallis had once again moved to the coast, this time Yorktown near the mouth of Chesapeake Bay. Charleston relaxed in the summer heat. Used to the presence of its invaders by now, many felt relief that the main thrust of battle seemed to be moving away from South Carolina and they were no longer troubled by the girlish-faced but sadistic Tarleton, who had been responsible for so much savagery during the British siege.

Hester was far too busy to consider the war. All her time was devoted to housekeeping and cooking, not normally her favourite occupation but if they were to have bread in their mouths it had to be done. She had never worked so hard in all her life and wondered sometimes how long she could go on.

'You need not do all this for my sake,' Aunt Kizzy said more than once as she watched Hester and Susy struggle with wet sheets. 'There are still funds enough in the bank and I have my small annuity.'

Hester sighed. 'Prices have risen, Aunt Kizzy. You are not so well-off any more.'

'But you could marry that nice Carter Lois and be spared all this. Why have you not told him you will?'

'Because he hasn't asked me, for one thing,' Hester said, rather more sharply than she'd intended, and far from accurately. 'Besides, this is not the time to be thinking of marriage while the British dither over where the next battle will take place. Benjamin might well be right, and it could be in our own backyard.'

Aunt Kizzy fanned her flushed face with her fan as she rocked idly on the piazza. 'Mr Blake really is quite a pleasant young man, don't you think?' she said. 'Reminds me of a young man I once knew. He was a British officer, Andrew Fitton, I believe his name was. Ah, so long ago. But he was so fine and dandy, and so anxious to marry me.'

Hester couldn't help but giggle as she smoothed out the corner of a sheet. 'Oh, Aunt Kizzy, I don't know how many beaux who were eager to marry you you must have had when you were a girl. New names seem to crop up daily.'

'At least I put some effort into it, girl, which is more than you do. Fiddle-de-dee, you mustn't let the war spoil all your fun.'

The same argument was used the very next afternoon when Caroline and Beattie Ashton came to call.

'Why, we haven't seen you in simply ages,' mourned Caro, accepting a cup of lemonade with a delicately

outstretched little finger. The war might force her to
wear outmoded dresses but it was important to retain
ladylike behaviour. 'You never come to our card
parties any more and we haven't seen you at a dance
in months.'

It quite defeated Hester how anyone could continue
to enjoy themselves when young men were dying, but
then human nature was largely a puzzle to her, particularly in the guise of this pair of delightful but empty-
headed sisters. 'I have been very busy looking after
Aunt Kizzy.'

'And your guests?' added Beattie slyly. 'We've heard
tell that one of them is mighty good-looking.'

'Is it true that he is a pirate?' gasped out Caro,
unable to hold back her curiosity any longer and Hester
almost choked.

'I very much doubt it,' she said.

'Then *who* is he? Do tell all.'

Hester was at a loss. Even after almost three months
staying in her house, she knew little more about
Benjamin Blake than that first day when he arrived, or
rather had foisted himself upon them. She had once
daringly rifled through his belongings while changing
his bedlinen but they had proved to be disappointingly
sparse. 'He comes from Liverpool, I believe,' she said,
as if she did not care if he came from the moon.

'Do go on, Hester,' ordered Caro, eyes shining
gleefully. 'You are far too noble. There must be some
meaty mischief you have learned about him.'

'I know nothing,' Hester replied, rather heatedly.
Really, what a gossip Caro was becoming. 'Nor do I
wish to know.'

'Tch, what a tale,' chuckled Aunt Kizzy from her
favourite shady corner. 'Hester is bursting to know all
about our mysterious visitor but he, rogue that he is, is
even more adept at avoiding telling her. I, however,
managed to elicit some facts.'

'Oh. What are they?' breathed Beattie and Caroline in unison, and, abandoning Hester, went to sit at Aunt Kizzy's feet, which was a great boost to the old lady's vanity for she did so love to be the centre of attention. Hester resolved not to demean herself by doing likewise and stayed very firmly where she was, though she did hope that Aunt Kizzy would not whisper too quietly or she would not hear a word.

'Benjamin Blake lived in a tenement of very poor houses close to the docks at Liverpool. He has not a relative in the world now that his poor sick aunt has departed this life. However, the young Benjamin vowed never to be poor again and set about making his fortune.'

'How?' The two girls were held spellbound, their eyes stretched wide.

Here Aunt Kizzy was on shaky ground. In her several attempts to converse with Blake about his background she had been little more successful than Hester, but not for the world would she admit as much. 'Why, how else but by buying and selling things?'

The two girls' faces dropped. 'You mean like Carter Lois at the general store?'

'No, no, indeed not,' tutted Aunt Kizzy. 'He is a positive old woman and will never amount to anything grand.'

'Then why on earth do you wish me to marry him?' gasped Hester, getting up and going to her aunt after all.

Aunt Kizzy looked startled. 'I did not say you must marry him. I said you *could* if you wished.'

Hester looked at her, aghast. 'I distinctly remember your asking me why I had not promised to marry him.'

'Tch. Promising is of no account. Fiddle-de-dee, I promised any number of young beaux when I was a girl, and married none of them.' The two girls gave a light laugh followed by a short uncomfortable silence.

'But I could have done, oh, my, yes, indeed,' Aunt Kizzy vehemently maintained and obediently the girls agreed, not wishing to spoil the old lady's fantasy. Then, more quietly, her eyes glazing slightly with memory, 'It was only that the right one never did ask. A problem that is difficult to overcome in certain circumstances.' Again a small silence in which the girls exchanged doleful glances, followed by a sigh of resignation. They understood the agony of that problem only too well. 'And if this war carries on much longer, you girls will likewise be left on the shelf as surely as poor Hester. It doesn't do to be too fussy, you know.'

'If anyone were to ask my opinion,' came a low, deep voice from the door, 'I would venture to suggest that someone not quite twenty was very far from the proverbial shelf you all dread so much, and that, whoever she chooses to marry, it should definitely not be Carter Lois.'

CHAPTER FOUR

'Why, Mr Blake, how you startled us,' cried Aunt Kizzy into the ensuing silence. 'Do come and join us. We would be delighted to hear your opinion.'

Hester watched in disgust as Caro and Beattie, in a froth of pastel pink and blue, flew across the porch to capture the bemused Englishman and almost frog-marched him back to the cosy corner.

'Oh, do tell us all about yourself, Mr Blake.'

'You must come to one of our parties.'

'Do you dance?'

'We are *desperate* for partners.'

'When do you think the war will end?'

'And what are the English ladies wearing this season?'

'Goodness! What a deal of questions. I know not which to answer first,' he laughed, and as the sisters fussed about him with cushions and lemonade, both of which he refused, his eyes slid sideways to meet Hester's. Seeing her scowl, he threw back his head and laughed out loud, which made her scowl all the more. 'If you hold that expression too long, Hester, you will be in no danger from Carter Lois, or anyone else for that matter.'

'Fiddle-de-dee, haven't I told her so a score of times?' agreed Aunt Kizzy.

'Oh, take no notice of Hester,' pouted Caroline, anxious to regain the handsome stranger's attention. 'She does like to see the gloomy side of everything. And she will never come to our little gatherings.'

Benjamin frowned mockingly at Hester. 'Dear, dear, Hester. You are becoming quite the recluse. How can you hope to find a beau if you never go out? I do hope that is not my fault.'

'Not at all. I have no wish to attend dances and such while our boys are fighting.'

'How very noble of you. But are not some of these affairs intended as fund-raising events to finance food and clothing for your boys?' He made it sound like an accusation and Hester was stung beneath the truth of this.

'Y-yes, but. . .' Drat the man. Had he forgotten their straitened circumstances? How dared he rub in their penury even more by adding guilt to their suffering? Then, as if he had read her thoughts in her expressive brown eyes, he turned to the sisters and sketched an elegant bow.

'I'm sure Hester has simply been too busy. I shall make a point of seeing we *both* attend your very next function.'

Caroline sighed with pleasure. 'Now do tell us all about yourself, Mr Blake. Is it true that you carry gold bullion on your ship?'

'I'm sorry to disappoint you, but I carry nothing half so fascinating. Only boring things like cotton, tobacco and sugar, I'm afraid.'

'And guns.'

He glanced up at the sound of her voice. 'And guns. Thank you, Hester, for reminding me. Though I confess I prefer not to think of this war more than I have to.'

'Oh, so do we, do we not, Beattie?' echoed Caro rather breathlessly and her sister nodded in silent agreement, as was her wont. 'And you will come to our next party, will you not? It is so vexing but Papa will not let us have a proper ball until the war is over. When do you think that will be, Mr Blake?'

'I'm sure I don't know, but I believe sooner than we think and hopefully by Christmas. I have to say that the English grow pessimistic and no longer know how to win the war. The result is that nobody is doing anything very effectively. If none of those great British generals is keeping watch on de Grasse, they might turn round and find him not only on their doorstep but in their best parlour, as it were. The English have always underestimated the strength of the French navy and certainly that would be a mistake where Admiral de Grasse is concerned. If Washington is half the man I think he is, he will not hesitate to take advantage of the British indecisiveness.'

'You sound as if you want the Americans to win, Mr Blake,' said Caro, fluttering her eyelashes, and Benjamin smiled.

'It would never do for me to admit such a thing. Suffice to say that there are many British people who consider this whole war a waste of time. Hester is reluctant to understand my attitude and I can see that someone of her high ideals would find it hard to trust an Englishman, even one who claims neutrality.' He smiled up at Hester where she stood, stiff and solemn, against the porch rail. She did not respond to his smile, except for the tiniest flip of a heartbeat.

'And yet transports guns?' she tartly reminded him yet again, in case he had forgotten.

Benjamin gave a deep, protracted sigh. 'Someone has to. To make my position absolutely clear, I am not against the necessity for war in its rightful place, so long as the moment to put up arms and start talking is recognised. I believe we are rapidly reaching that point now.'

'Oh, I do hope you are right,' said Caro. 'I hate it.'

'So do I,' wailed her sister. 'It quite spoils all our fun.'

'Where did you leave your carriage?' interposed Hester, wishing to have done with this inane conversation and be rid of the doting twosome. 'I shall walk with you to it, for I feel in need of some fresh air.'

'Why, if you insist, Hester. But the carriage is only at the door.' Caro slanted a provocative glance across at her quarry. It wasn't often she met a man quite so delight-fully attractive as this one and she made her resentment of Hester's unneighbourly reluctance to share him very plain. 'We did think that you might at least invite us to supper. Glory, Hester, you can't keep this delicious man all to yourself. Wouldn't be fair, now, would it?'

'You flatter me, Miss Caroline,' smiled Benjamin and Hester ground her teeth together in silent frustration. The very thought of Caro and Beattie let loose among Blake's band of rapscallion crew sent her into a positive sweat.

'I doubt that would be at all suitable, in the circum-stances,' she said. 'Mr Blake and his crew like to dine early, before they go out carousing or whatever it is they find to do of an evening.'

'Boys will be boys,' trilled Caro, simpering, and Hester felt sure she would be sick at any moment.

Smiling with excessive and unnatural delicacy, Benjamin lingered over each proffered hand, much to their owner's delight. 'Then we must make it some other occasion, Miss Caroline, Miss Beattie.'

'Oh, yes, indeed,' they said in twittering unison, bobbing rather foolish curtsies which made them look, in Hester's opinion, rather like a pair of fairground dolls dangling on a piece of string.

'And be sure to invite me to that ball, the very moment your papa allows it.'

'You mean you will still be here when the war is over?' gulped Caro, pink-cheeked with delight.

'Indeed I shall,' he said, very seriously, lifting his gaze to Hester's. 'I intend to be here a long while yet. At least until we have found a suitable husband for Miss Hester. I should hate to be held responsible for her being left upon the shelf simply because she is forced to stay in and play house.'

The two girls giggled and fluttered their hands. 'You are really quite outrageous, Mr Blake.' But Hester very firmly put a stop to the conversation by marching the exuberant pair out to their carriage, her cheeks burning with mortification. Within seconds she was back on the porch, where she found Benjamin in a positive huddle with Aunt Kizzy.

'And what was all that about?' she challenged, while a part of her mind registered twin spots of colour high on Aunt Kizzy's cheekbones and the way she broke guiltily away. What had the pair been discussing? Herself, no doubt.

Benjamin, however, glanced up in an attitude of mild surprise, a slight frown marking his high forehead. 'All what? I was merely being polite and accepting an invitation kindly offered. I meant nothing at all by it, so you have no reason to be jealous.'

'Jealous?' Hester could hardly believe her ears. 'Jealous of those two buzzing bees? Never.'

'I agree you have nothing to fear from that pair,' said Benjamin, lounging back in the rocker and propping one heel on the porch rail so that his long legs stretched out right in front of her, and for a second she was quite dazzled by the rippling of thigh muscle in fine white breeches, and the shine of polished black boots before she had a proper hold upon herself.

'Why should I be jealous at all?' she said, acutely aware that she was losing her grip upon the conversation, which always seemed to go in the direction Benjamin Blake decreed.

'Why, indeed, when you are quite the prettiest belle in the whole of Charleston?'

Aunt Kizzy's low-throated chuckle did little for Hester's rising temper. With commendable effort she cooled it with an indrawn breath, while deliberately avoiding the mischievous glint of Blake's smile.

'I was not in fact referring to my own looks, or lack of them. Nor of Caro and Beattie's breathless adoration of you. Heavens, they worship every creature in breeches. The sooner they are married off, the sooner their poor over-strained parents can relax and enjoy their declining years in peace. My issue with you, Mr Blake, as you are only too aware, is that I object most strongly to your interfering in my life and passing comments on matters which do not concern you.'

'Interfere? Good lord, I never intended any such thing.' He looked so comically insincere that Hester had great difficulty in suppressing a gurgle of laughter.

'I think you did,' she reiterated calmly, exaggerating her slow southern drawl. 'It really is no concern of yours who or when I choose to marry.'

Pushing down his lower lip in a parody of a sad clown, he succeeded in making her want to laugh all the more when really she should remain cross. 'I was merely agreeing with your aunt that it does not do to be too choosy, though I take the liberty to *disagree* about the recipient of your favours.'

'You have no right to take such liberties, particularly since I never asked for your opinion on my future plans.'

'That is unquestionably true, and most remiss of you, for my opinions, as your dear aunt will verify, are always worth having,' he said with a bland charm not lost on Hester.

'Nevertheless,' she said, striving to maintain a stern expression, 'I will make my own decisions, thank you very much.'

Benjamin Blake adopted a puzzled frown which was all too mendaciously false. 'Are you saying that you *do* in fact wish to marry Carter Lois? I was under the impression, when I accidentally eavesdropped upon your conversation on that notable day when we first met, that that was the last thing you wanted. What can have changed your mind? Surely desperation has not set in quite yet? I cannot too strongly recommend you not to rush into such a madcap enterprise as marriage with Mr Lois.'

Hester had a strong urge to slap his self-satisfied face, but, remembering the last time, she resisted. He was perfectly capable of returning the compliment. Were it not for the interested observation of Aunt Kizzy, who sat rocking and oddly smiling, she would very decidedly tell him what she thought of him. In fact, she decided to do just that anyway. 'Would you mind, dear aunt, leaving us alone for a moment? There are some matters which Mr Blake and I would perhaps be better discussing alone, if you have no objections?'

Aunt Kizzy was on her feet with an alacrity quite remarkable for one with a heart defect. 'Why, of course, dear Hester. I have no wish to play gooseberry, I'm sure.' And she scurried from the porch in her noiseless slippers as Hester swung afresh upon her adversary. But he cut in before she could speak.

'How very flattering that you should wish to be alone with me,' said Benjamin Blake with a wry smile which stoked Hester's warming temper all the more.

'Let me make this perfectly plain to you once and for all, Mr Blake. I am not in the least interested in you, or your opinions. My life, and what I choose to do with it, is my own affair. I shall live in which house I choose. Attend or not attend whatever social function I think fit, and marry whom I wish to marry when I consider the time is right for such a move. I would be obliged, therefore, if you would keep your nose out of my affairs. Do I make myself clear?'

'Abundantly, but it is not at all true.' As Hester attempted to unravel this remark he continued blithely,

'Your interest in me is only too obvious. Why else would you search my room?'

Hester was at once bathed in blushing confusion. It being quite impossible for her to deny it, she sank down upon the adjacent rocker and stared at him in mute despair.

'Did you find anything of interest?' he asked, and Hester was almost certain she noted the slightest edge to his question which hinted at a deeper concern for her reply than was at first apparent by the way he nonchalantly creaked back and forth in the rocker.

'Nothing at all,' she said, squirming with embarrassment, and as she heard him expel a long breath continued hurriedly, 'I dare say it was quite wrong of me but my curiosity was only fuelled by your obstinate refusal to be open and honest with us.'

To her complete astonishment, Benjamin Blake gave a shout of laughter. 'So I am to blame for having my room turned over by those sweet, inquisitive hands, am I? Hardly seems fair. I shall take more care in future not to goad you into such a dreadful practice again.'

Recognising his teasing tone and knowing she deserved it, she could not prevent her tightly pressed lips from turning up very slightly at the corners as she shafted him a sideways glance from beneath her lashes. 'The situation will not arise again, I promise. And it was not at all premeditated. I simply peeked at one or two items while I was changing your bedlinen.'

He nodded sagely. 'Ah, well, if you only peeked— and while you were changing my bedlinen—then I dare say I must forgive you. Besides, how can I resist such a charming smile?'

She glanced at him again to check if he was funning her but the expression in the hooded blue eyes seemed genuine enough, if holding a challenge she dared not identify.

Then, without warning, Benjamin Blake swung out of the rocker and lifted her to her feet, his long, tapering fingers fastening themselves very firmly to her shoulders in a manner which could neither be escaped nor ignored. She dared look no further upwards than the tanned square jaw, mere inches above her head. The heat from his long, taut body swept over her so that her heartbeat ricocheted around her ribcage like the gunfire at Cowpens.

'Have you looked at yourself recently?' he asked, in an oddly gentle tone.

'Why should I? I am aware of what I look like,' she managed, trying desperately to stop the trembling in her stomach from spreading to her limbs where he might sense it.

'Are you?' He straightened the frilly mob cap she had donned for her morning chores and quite forgotten to remove during the long busy day. Then he rubbed a forefinger along the side of her nose and showed her the motes of dust he'd removed. 'But there is worse,' he said, and to add to her mortification he held out her arms, forcing her to step back a pace while he openly appraised her. 'Apart from the dowdy dress, which would do better as a dish mop, you have grown thinner of late,' he coolly pronounced, without any degree of compassion. 'Despite all the money being brought into this household, despite the good food prepared by Susy, and of course yourself, I see little evidence of it in you.'

'I—I am perfectly well,' Hester resolutely declared, wishing he would stop roving his shrewd-eyed gaze over every inch of her person. She could feel the rosy flush it created right from her burning cheeks, down through her pulsating stomach to her tiny toes curling tightly in her slippers.

Hands back upon her shoulders, he gave her a little

shake instead of the respite she'd prayed for. 'What are you doing with all the money?'

'It is none of y——'

'It is very much my business,' he growled, 'if it makes my landlady as scrawny as a stripped willow wand and twice as pale.'

Hester, sunk in gloom, dropped her gaze to somewhere around his shirt collar, which was open on this warm evening to reveal a pulse beating in the hollow of his tanned throat. She had a sudden and unquenchable urge to kiss it, and, shocked at this unexpected weakness in herself, she tried once more to wriggle free. Benjamin Blake, however, held her fast, his fingers tightening around her arms like a whiplash. She found herself fastened even tighter against the masculine hardness of his chest, which interfered greatly with her breathing.

'Where has all the money gone?' he patiently repeated, his voice carrying an authority it was hard to resist, despite its softness. 'Paid it to that damned shopkeeper, have you?'

She did not answer and he shook her again.

'Damn you, Hester. I didn't pay you over the odds in order to line that rapscallion's pocket. It's growing fat enough at the British expense. That money was meant to make life easier for you, and for Aunt Kizzy.'

'Aunt Kizzy is fine, thank you very much,' she finally flung at him. 'I need no help from you to look after my kinsfolk, so there.'

'Don't be petty, Hester, it doesn't become you.'

'I had accounts to settle. It's my money and I'll use it as I please,' she retorted, and valiantly tossed back her head to meet him eye to eye, defiance shining in hot brown eyes. 'Debts incurred through a long starvation brought about by the British occupation, if you recall.' She almost spat the last words at him. 'Tarleton bled us of everything he could, forcing prices up, making it impossible for us to manage.' Her lips curled. 'And yet he felt he had the prerogative to help himself to whatever soft delights the South has to offer wherever he chose to sample it. It seems to be a British tendency to plunder and ravage. Is that what you thought you were paying for? Well, I'm sorry to disappoint you. Though should you choose to, I doubt there would be anything I could do to prevent you but I swear you would not enjoy it.'

For a second she thought he would fling her to the ground but then his shoulders sagged, his chin lowered and before she knew what was happening she found her feet had left the ground, her small body lifted and pinioned against the hardness of his broad chest, his lips hard upon hers.

She had never been kissed before, not even a fleeting experiment beneath a mistlebough. Benjamin Blake took and explored virgin territory as if it were his right so to do. And the effect of his invasion was cataclysmic. She held no defences, had prepared no counter-attack and possessed in her own body a traitor to her cause. Instead of fighting him off, she clung fast to the solid strength of his neck. Instead of gathering a broadside ready to repulse him at the first opportunity, she felt perilously close to surrender. And when he removed his lips from hers to savour the sweetness of her throat and burgeoning breasts she protested only regret, wanting their return. She dared not open her eyes, drugged as they were with this explosion of unexpected happiness, in case it would vanish as swiftly as a dust storm in June. When he set her down upon her feet again she swayed as if she would topple over and he held her for a long silent moment before finally relinquishing his hold.

When she opened her eyes, he was gone. And so disturbed was she by that kiss that she was forced to work excessively hard the next few days to keep her mind from dwelling upon it.

'Put your glad rags on.'

'I beg your pardon?'

Hester was sitting on the back step polishing the silver, her hands encased in soft white cotton gloves. Susy was preparing supper, Aunt Kizzy was dozing and she had believed the house to be empty of her guests for once. Now here was Benjamin Blake proving her to be wrong, and, embarrassingly, finding her engaged in work yet again, as no Southern woman liked to be found.

'Did you forget about the invitation?' He waved a gilt-edged cream square of card before her eyes and, easing her aching back, she let her gaze travel upwards to take in the surprising appearance of its bearer.

Here was a very different Benjamin Blake from the one she was used to seeing. Often, around the house, he had taken to wearing simple breeches and loose cool shirts, dazzlingly white, either open-necked or tied with an equally pristine stock. When he went out he often donned more formal attire but never so immaculate as he looked this evening. The jacket and breeches were of deep gentian blue very closely touching the colour of his eyes. The froth of white at his neck, the double-breasted waistcoat in palest blue watered silk and the glistening buckles on his shoes which looked suspiciously more like gold than brass set her heart thumping with astonishing verve.

'Caro and Beattie's invitation,' he reminded her when she did not reply. 'For the supper party? It is this evening.'

'Oh.' She had taken not the slightest notice of the invitation, propping it with the rest which she had likewise ignored somewhere behind the teapot on the mantelshelf.

'We did promise,' he continued, pursuing his argument with the patience one employed with a rather dim child. 'If you recall.'

Now he mentioned it Hester did recall some talk of it on that afternoon on the piazza, almost a week ago. She should have realisd Caro would not give up in her pursuit of a new man, particularly one as handsome as Benjamin Blake, for all he was English.

'I'm afraid it is quite out of the question for me to go,' she said, deliberately removing her recalcitrant gaze and fixing it firmly on the silver teapot she was polishing.

'Why?'

He was blunt almost to the point of rudeness, she thought. 'Because, as I have explained previously, I will not socialise while there is a war on. I have more important things to do than play cards, sip lemonade and make foolish tittle-tattle with empty-headed girls,' she said, rather ostentatiously.

'What were you thinking of wearing?' he continued, as if she had not said all of that. 'I'll have Jonas bring the carriage round in half an hour. Will that give you sufficient time?'

'I've just told you. . .'

He gave her a lazy smile. 'And I have told you. An evening out from time to time will do you the world of good. Even soldiers at the front relax occasionally and there is nothing to gain by playing the martyr.'

Hester gasped. 'I am not playing the martyr.'

'Half an hour, then.' And, turning on his heels, he set off in the direction of the stables, calling over his shoulder, 'And don't be late. I hate unpunctual women.'

'Well, really.' Hester dropped the half-cleaned tea kettle, flung her polishing rag at an unsuspecting lilac bush and very nearly tipped over the precious cleaning fluid as she bounced to her feet. 'Do not think you can order me about,' she called after him in her most prim voice. The echo of laughter floated back over the garden paths and, nonplussed, she found herself giving serious thought to the idea. How long it was since she had dressed in a pretty gown! Even longer since she'd danced in the arms of a gentleman, handsome or not. Her brown eyes gleamed softly at the memory of sweet music on softly warm evenings, the sparkle of chandeliers and a bouquet of ballgowns prettily swirling. Of course this was not a proper ball as such. Even so, a card party, a social get-together with long-neglected neighbours would not be unpleasant. And there just might be a little music and perhaps a sedate gavotte would not be too unpatriotic.

She was ready five minutes early. Her dress of pale pink silk with its lavender overskirt, though no doubt a year or two out of date, was still pretty. She had refrained from filling the low neckline with a draped shoulder-scarf, choosing instead to fasten a simple pearl necklace, which had belonged to her mother, about her neck. The pleated hem-line in matching lavender gave a tantalising glimpse of trim ankle and shoes of black silk in which she knew she could dance all night if need be without them pinching a bit. Her hair she had brushed until it shone and Susy had coiled it in long curls beside each rosy cheek.

'I would have been happy to wait an extra half-hour for such a transformation,' Benjamin told her, his eyes warmly admiring, and she found herself flushing at his obvious sincerity. Offering her his arm, he led her out to the waiting carriage and handed her into it. As they settled back upon the cushions he turned to her with a roguish smile playing about his sensual mouth. 'And now we must see what Charleston thinks of us.'

'Of us?'

'Of you and me. At least of me. How will they rate me, do you think, as a possible beau?'

She stared at him bemused. 'Beau?'

'Isn't that the word you southerners use for a candidate male in the marriage stakes?'

She went hot and cold all over. 'I didn't know you were considering marriage. To whom?'

'Oh, that is not quite decided.' And before she could question him further he begged Jonas to step out quickly for they had no wish to miss too much of the jollities.

Hester sank back into the corner of the chaise, all her high spirits dissolved in a miserable speculation as to which of that vexing twosome had caught his eye and how he dared to use her as an excuse to accept their invitation in order to see them again.

CHAPTER FIVE

CARTER LOIS could not believe the evidence of his own eyes. During the past year and a half he had asked, nay, almost begged Hester to come out with him on any number of occasions. Always she had had an excuse. Too busy. Aunt Kizzy would be left alone. And of course it was much too unpatriotic to enjoy herself with the poor boys dying at the front. And now here she was, not only rigged out in the prettiest dress in the room, or at least it seemed so on her softly feminine figure, but hanging on the arm of that darned Englishman. And the way she looked up at him, trying not to let him see how he fascinated her. But Carter could see it, and by the look of them so could the rest of the assembled company. And that did not entirely meet with their approval.

He began to circumnavigate the long room, keenly observing the reactions of his friends and neighbours as Hester introduced her new partner. Here a nod, there a smile, and the usual polite bow, but in the eyes a quizzical astonishment. A sense, almost, of outrage that Hester Mackay should have the gall to walk into their midst with her hand on the arm of the enemy. However many here present still nurtured a soft spot for the British, this was evidently all too much for them to stomach and Carter watched with satisfaction as people drew away from the pair, as if they would be contaminated by their nearness. Some guests actually turned their backs and refused to be introduced at all. Colonel Barker for one. That old roué could only tolerate the English if they were blonde and dressed in a demi-gown.

A smile came upon Carter's lips and he moistened them in readiness, for he intended to speak to the couple. He could hardly wait for the opportunity of giving that gent a piece of his mind. Carter thought he had very neatly made sure Hester was beholden to him, and it would be a very short step to have her depend upon him entirely. But he certainly had no intention of having his carefully laid plans spoiled by this nonsense of a friendship growing between Hester and a pesky Englishman. That wouldn't do at all. Making a sharp detour to avoid being accosted by Mrs Winborough, he thrust his way through the melting crowd and placed himself directly in the couple's path.

'Good evening, Hester. I was sure I must be dreaming when I saw you drift through that door looking so lovely, no one would imagine there was a war on. Can that be Hester? I thought. Never, and looking so radiant, you just wouldn't believe.' He smiled at her, but his pale eyes stayed bleak and cold and Hester, for no reason that she could fathom, shivered.

'Is there any reason why she should not accept an invitation?' asked Benjamin, in his quiet voice, which did not disguise the underlying strength in it.

'No, indeed. No reason at all. But when she has been so stubbornly determined to spend this war in her kitchen, you must have used blasting powder to get her out of it.'

'That is not my style.' And it was Benjamin's smile now which crackled with frost. Hester, looking from one to the other of them, quaked at the vibrancy which split the air between them.

'Mr Blake believes the war will soon be over,' she gabbled, for some reason she could not explain suddenly riddled with nervousness. Coming into this delightful but eminently American drawing-room had not been easy to say the least, and now she felt adrift in a sea of disapproval, warring against an uncalled-for desire to defend her action. Why should she not come to a party if she wished to? And if she should choose to come with a guest, albeit an Englishman, whyever not? It was Caro and Beattie who had invited him, after all.

'My, my, and there's me thinking I'm in the heart of things in Charleston and know every piece of news that's worth hearing and I never did hear tell the war was almost over.' Carter's sarcasm, not usual in him, made Hester wince, but Benjamin was less perturbed.

'The trouble with war is that it is all too easy to start but exceptionally difficult to stop. It must be done with delicacy and precision and a considerable degree of intelligence.'

'Something the English lack,' rejoined Carter Lois with a smirk. 'This one will not end until the English are ready to admit defeat. They haven't won an effective battle in months yet won't give in because they are afraid of losing face.'

'It is a common enough flaw on both sides,' said Benjamin. 'Frankly, I believe it will take an absolute battle before either the British Government admits its loss of a colony or the emerging American nation abandons its fight for freedom and independence.'

'Something it will never do. As I would never give up something that belongs to me, not without a fight.' The statement was made in Carter's usual toneless style yet with an edge to it that was disturbing. It was perfectly apparent to them both that Carter was no longer referring merely to the war.

Hester sensed an inner struggle in Benjamin Blake not to retaliate since he was a guest in this house, in this land. Desperately she searched her mind for a way out of the impasse which had sprung up between the two men but before she had managed to form any words she heard Benjamin's icy reply.

'Before you engage in a defensive battle, you have

first to establish ownership.' Very pointedly he took Hester's hand and replaced it upon his arm, then, giving a slight bow, a wry smile twisting his lips, he continued, 'Besides, in some matters, a little competition can be a good thing, do you not think so? I certainly thrive upon it and have no objections to a rival.'

Hester stared up at him in astonishment. Competition? Rival? What was he talking about? Surely he could not mean herself? But by the way both men's eyes swivelled in her direction, making her cheeks flame, it would seem that was exactly what they meant. Carter's face was a picture of outrage while Benjamin's was blandly smiling, eyes sparkling with mischief.

'I believe we have embarrassed her,' said Benjamin with mild good humour, but as he was about to lead Hester away seemed to bethink himself. 'Ah, yes, I recall what it was I meant to say to you, Lois. This money which Hester owes you seems to be taking an unconscionably long time to diminish. Is there some particular reason for that?'

Carter Lois reddened as he foundered for words. 'If it is any business of yours, which I doubt, the sum was a mighty big one and what with the interest on the loan, you know, it ain't likely to disappear quickly.'

'Interest?'

The flush deepened. 'It is normal business practice to charge interest on a loan.'

'To one's friends?' One dark brow rose in enquiry before crashing down to join its mate in a thunderous line. 'I suggest you put the loan on hold for a while. Hester, if you haven't noticed, is practically starving herself in order to repay it, not to mention working her fingers to the proverbial bone.'

Hester gasped. 'I am perfectly all right.'

'And whose fault is that? You are the one who

brought her the extra work, not me. I was quite happy to wait for my money. I told her so. Did I not, Hester?'

'Yes, I do recall the terms under which you were prepared to waive repayment of the debt,' interposed Benjamin before she could speak. 'But, in view of Hester's difficult circumstances, I think we should agree to no more repayments until the war is over.'

'Er——'

'Splendid. I'm glad that is settled.'

With a grunt which might well have expressed a wish to send Benjamin Blake and his interfering ways to lower quarters, had he not mumbled it so incoherently, it was impossible to be sure, Carter bowed stiffly to Hester and informed her in clipped tones that of course he would be happy to wait as long as need be for repayment of the debt. Hadn't he always said as much? Whereupon he stormed off across the room, large feet slamming down on the polished boards in frustrated fury.

Hester turned at once to Blake, bouncing with exasperation. 'Now see what you have done. Carter has never pressed me for repayment of the debt, rather the very opposite. It was I who wished very much to be free of it. All you have succeeded in doing by your interference is leave me beholden to him and offended one of my best friends.'

Benjamin gave her a quizzical look. 'If he is the best you can do for friends, then I dare to suggest you have a severe problem.'

'How dare you? I have many friends and how I deal with them is my own affair.' Warming to her theme, she decided she'd had enough of Benjamin Blake's meddling for all his concern for her health, and she meant to tell him so, despite the dazzlingly quizzical smile he offered her. 'It was kind of you to try to help me,' she said instead, her voice soft. 'But, as I have said before, I would prefer it if you kept your— your. . .'

'Nose?' supplied Benjamin helpfully. 'Out of your business? So you said before.'

Hester stamped her foot. 'Just leave me alone. If I require your assistance I will ask for it.'

A look almost of regret drifted across his handsome features as he gazed down at her. 'Ah, but would you, though? If only I could be sure of that. Hester, you are a very sweet girl, with a spirit to be admired, and, were you to allow it full rein, a delightful sense of fun, but your judgement of character is far from shrewd. If you take my advice you will give Mr Carter Lois a very wide berth. His type of person is selfish to the core, thinking only of his own needs and giving not a thought to anyone else's. If it is true that he is building you a house on Meeting Street then I would offer that as a typical example to prove my point. It never occurred to him to ask you if that was what you wanted, as I suspect he has never properly proposed to you.'

Cheeks now truly afire at the man's impertinence, Hester drew herself rigid. 'I declare it is no business of yours who might or might not have proposed to me.'

'Has he?'

'I—I. . . There is, I dare say, an understanding between us.'

'My point exactly. You are not sure.' Taking her gently but very decidedly by the arms, Benjamin moved closer so that she could not help but brush against him, and the scent of the sea and sandalwood drifted over her from the folds of his jacket. 'Were I to propose to you, you would be left in no doubt whatso-ever about my intentions.'

A tremor ran through Hester's body at his touch and she pulled herself hastily from him, hearing his soft laugh as if in some way her discomfort delighted him. She forced her gaze to slide past him, attempting to fix it on a buxom lady, in a blue dress two sizes too small, who was attempting to importune the hostess to begin the dancing. She felt suddenly quite light-headed. The crystal chandeliers glistened like spun glass, the glow from them bouncing off the polished floorboards and the petal pastels of the ladies' dresses. What was the matter with her? The very touch of his hand upon her arm sent shafts of burning delight through her entire body. She no longer had the will to continue with this foolish argument. Her body seemed to melt and crumble beneath his touch and not for the world dared she meet his gaze for fear of what he might read in it. And on top of all that he was now making the most outrageous jokes at her expense. How she must amuse him. 'It is fortunate,' she began, rallying her depleted reserves as best she might, 'that the question does not arise.'

She had taken a mere two steps before his hand was once more upon her elbow, restraining, compelling, holding her captive. She felt the warmth of his breath against her ear. 'Do not be too sure. Life is full of unexpected turn-abouts, and I have a mind to stay in Charleston, war or no war. Besides my ambitions of getting into the cotton business, it holds certain attractions I never expected to welcome again. It is easy to forget the warmth of a woman's smile.'

Despite declaring to herself very firmly that she should ignore this comment and continue on her way to pacify poor Carter as she'd intended, Hester found herself turning back to Benjamin and now she did meet his gaze. Steady, softly blue, and profoundly searching, the shock of it set off a series of small explosions right through her. 'Have you been married before?' The question was out before the words had scarcely formed in her head.

For a second Benjamin went very still, frowned, then offered an illusory smile and, lifting one hand, stroked away a recalcitrant golden brown curl from her cheek. 'Is that what you imagine? Was that one of the questions you wanted answering when you searched my room? One day, when the time is right, I shall answer all your questions. Every one.'

She was holding her breath, sinking into him, becoming a part of that magnetic personality for she suddenly wanted, very badly, for him to answer her now. 'Soon?' she asked on a small rush of breath and he nodded.

'Very soon. I promise. When we have decided what to do about this interesting development between the two of us, Hester.'

The room stopped revolving and they were alone in the world. Just a young southern girl and an Englishman who believed he'd experienced everything life had to throw at him, reading a truth in the other's gaze which neither had expected to find. Then into the silence came the penetrating voice of Caro as she bore down upon them in a flurry of orange organza. 'Where have you been hiding yourselves, you two? Why, everyone is just dying to meet you, Mr Blake. They have never met a *real* pirate before.'

Turning smoothly, Benjamin rewarded her with a dazzling smile which stunned Hester every bit as much as it clearly enslaved Caroline. 'I hardly think that can be true, and they are doomed to disappointment. You must rid yourself of this fancy that I am a pirate, for I am certainly not that.'

'No?' Regret bit deep in the dazed voice.

'No.' And then he laughed. 'Much worse than that.'

Caroline blinked as her tiny nails clung on to his arm. 'Oh, you must tell us all, do. I cannot wait to hear.' And Benjamin allowed her to lead him away, chuckling good-humouredly as if at some private joke.

'I shall tell you no more than is good for you. As I have already explained, Miss Caroline, I buy cheap goods where the opportunity presents itself, perhaps where a ship has foundered and has to ditch its cargo. And remember, I also carry guns to fuel your enemy. I have no home and go wherever there is likely profit, wandering gypsylike from port to port. So you see how unglamorous and unspeakably leechlike I am, taking advantage of the troubles and tribulations of others.' His voice was light and bantering but Hester sensed a caustic note to it, as if there was some self-loathing of what he did, which she didn't wonder at. Put as bleakly as that, it sounded an exceedingly heartless occupation and, hearing it, she was able to harden her heart once more.

Benjamin Blake was definitely not the kind of man she wished to have any truck with. Why, Carter Lois's opportunism paled by comparison. No, indeed, she vowed, she would not be tempted by sweet talk and beguiling smiles, nor by any other fleeting physical attraction between them. The man was a rogue and apparently proud of it. Swirling about, she flounced across the room in the wake of Carter. In view of their long-term friendship it behoved her to apologise for the treatment he'd received at Blake's hand, and it would give her immense pleasure to offer it knowing how it would annoy that gentleman for her to do so.

With Caroline's boundless chattering eddying about him, Benjamin watched Hester go with considerable regret. For the first time in their burgeoning relationship he had felt a softening of her attitude towards him. Somehow, instinct told him that Caro's intervention had interrupted what could have proved to be a very important scenario in his life. Despite his resolution never to become embroiled with a woman again, he had felt himself grow almost fond of Hester Mackay. He had excused the feeling thus far by telling himself it was no more than a mature concern for a young person in difficulties, almost paternal, certainly nothing more than that. But ever since he'd been tempted to kiss her on the porch that evening he'd begun to doubt his own excuses. And merely the touch of her against him now had confirmed it. Whatever it was he felt for Hester Mackay, it was certainly not paternal, and it was a dratted nuisance. He'd best put a stop to it at once before she started getting any romantic notions, or once more his life would become unhinged. He must have been mad to promise just now to tell her all about himself. What could he say? How could he inform this innocent, trusting, sheltered young woman that she entertained a convicted criminal in her home? So long as the problems of that charge hung over him, however false it might be, there was no future for himself, or any woman, not even the delectable Hester Mackay.

'You can hardly hold me responsible for something Mr Blake said,' Hester protested, quite reasonably, she thought. 'I shall continue to pay off the money I owe you, week by week, as I have been doing these last months.'

'There is really no necessity for that, Hester.'

'Nevertheless it will make me happier to do so.'

Carter's hand was upon her arm. 'It would make me happier if you did not shut me quite so firmly out of your life. You can clearly find time for Mr Blake, then why not an old friend? You sure don't accept my invitations but you're ready enough to accept his.'

Hester shot him a glance filled with guilt for there was some truth in his accusation and Carter had every reason to feel slighted or hurt. 'I—I really cannot explain why I did accept. Somehow this evening had been arranged between Caro and Benjamin and I found myself obliged to come.'

Carter did not miss the use of Blake's Christian name and he cast Hester a quick assessing look. The man clearly rode roughshod over her and the poor girl was bewitched. If he was to put a stop to the damage he'd best act quickly. 'Then at least allow me to drive you home. Surely you will not deny an old friend that small privilege?'

Hester's eyes widened in consternation. 'Oh, but I assumed. . .that is, since I came with Mr Blake. . .'

'He can hardly expect to monopolise your entire evening. After all, there is no understanding as such between the two of you, as there is between you and me, Hester, honey. Ain't that so? And I would welcome the opportunity to discuss details of our new house on the way. Perhaps we can arrange for you to come with me one day to view it. Don't I just want you to have the very best of everything in the whole world? And you've only to say if there's something you don't like, honey, and we'll get it changed right away.'

Hester felt hot panic rise in her breast. She would never have a better opportunity to put an end to this preposterous situation between the two of them. Benjamin Blake was right; there had been no proper proposal, and no proper acceptance so it was quite outrageous that Carter should continue as if everything were sewn up nice and neat between them. She would have to disenchant him as gently as possible, for instinct told her he could prove to be a pettish enemy if he took her refusal badly. But she would procrastinate no longer. The matter had to be dealt with at once. Not least, in her own mind, because of the strange swirl of feelings awoken in her for the first time by the attentions of an attractive male.

'I think perhaps it would be a good idea, Carter, if you did drive me home, so we can have a real good talk for once. There are some matters I wish to discuss with you.' And so it was arranged, whereupon Hester hastily made her excuses that she wished to help Caroline put out the card tables, which was not strictly true, but hurried off anyway in search of her friend.

She found Caroline head to head in a corner with

her less effervescent wisp of a sister, who was dressed in a dull yellow dress that did nothing for her pallid complexion, deeply engaged in agreeable gossip. Hester felt loath to interrupt but, spying her, Caroline jumped up and dragged her over to sit beside them on the sofa.

'Why, Hester. How glad I am you came over. What do you think? Mr Blake has been telling us such a story, you wouldn't believe.'

'Indeed?' Hester tried not to sound interested.

. 'Though I dare swear you already know that the last port of call he was in was St Eustatius, in the West Indies?'

'I know where Statia is, but I have no knowledge of Benjamin Blake's itinerary,' she said loftily.

'You don't?' Caro stared at her pop-eyed for a second, and then transferred her shocked gaze to the small wren-like girl beside her. 'I would have made certain he'd have told *Hester*, wouldn't you, Beattie?' And the loyal Beattie nodded her head in agreement, which irritated Hester all the more.

'Well, he's been relating all his adventures to us and it was absolutely fascinating. The British have closed St Eustatius as a free port because it had become a centre for contraband, don't you know? Seems all goods to and from the colonies have to be transported in British ships from British ports and mustn't conflict with goods manufactured in the so-called mother country. You know how selfish the British are. Well, it seems Statia, being in the middle of islands belonging to the Spanish, French and Dutch, was not keeping to this agreement because it claimed neutrality.'

'Do get to the point, Caroline,' said Hester, her temper sharp largely because Blake had chosen to divulge this information to Caro and not to herself.

'Oh, do listen, Hester. Benjamin says that, like St Eustatius, he considers himself neutral too because his father was Dutch and his mother Irish and everyone knows that the Dutch have been on our side all along. And, being half Dutch, he thinks that America should have been given its independence long since.'

'I understood that he didn't remember his parents.'

Caro clicked her tongue with impatience. 'He may not remember them personally but he knows of their antecedents, for goodness' sake. So, you see, Benjamin Blake isn't entirely British at all.'

Hester looked doubtful. 'He was born in Liverpool, so I think there is little doubt on that score. Besides, how can he be neutral when he is working for the British, shipping guns from England for them? He told us that himself.'

Caro pushed herself excitedly forward on to the edge of the plush sofa, her small hands flapping. 'Oh, but that must simply be a cover-up. He really is a privateer working for whatever brings him the finest profits. Isn't that too exciting for words? I've never met a real rogue of the seas before, have you, Hester?' Caro giggled. 'And such a handsome one at that; why, he puts even our southern boys in the shade with those broad shoulders and that bewitchingly wicked smile.'

But Hester was frowning deeply. 'I haven't the first idea what you are talking of, Caro. Why do you call him by such a foolish name? Rogue of the seas, indeed. He transports goods to and from England. Even I, who do not care for Mr Blake one iota, can find little fault with that. And what has all this gotten to do with St Eustatius?'

Caro glanced surreptitiously about her and, dropping her voice to an excited whisper, continued, 'Mr Blake says that it all happened back in February when a British ship of the line fired on Statia and the commander, an Admiral Rodney, took possession of over a hundred merchant ships, various property, produce such as tobacco, rice, sugar, brandy and *gunpowder*, and whole warehouses just full of arms and ammunition. The whole amounted to some three *million* pounds. And Hester, listening to Mr Blake tell us this tale, do you know what came to be perfectly obvious, not only by the hints he let slip but also by the expression on his poor face?'

'No one can be quite neutral in a war, Caroline, and it is foolish of you to imagine they can. If Mr Blake has been up to some clandestine tricks such as selling stolen coffee or whatever, merely for extra profit, then he deserves to be hounded by the British. Personally I hope they catch him.'

'Oh, but it was far more dreadful than that.' This, from the usually silent Beattie, served to stop Hester in her tracks.

'If you do not come out with it at once, Caro, I shall tear my hair out with frustration, and yours too, I shouldn't wonder.'

Caro, unperturbed by such a horrendous threat, continued with her tale.

'Mr Blake admitted that his ship was among those carrying gunpowder from Holland. And that would be for the *American* forces, would it not? He had to run it up the coast to escape capture, but doesn't that just prove that he is not our enemy at all? There now, what do you think of that?'

Hester sat as if someone had turned her to stone. It was as if the foundations of her world had slipped from beneath her and she dared not move for fear of falling. Yet what possible difference could it make to her whether Benjamin Blake sold gunpowder to the Americans or not? But it did. It mattered very much indeed. Her voice, when she found it, was scarcely above a whisper. 'What kind of man, Caro, sells gunpower to the enemy of his own country? The shipping of arms by someone who declares themselves to be neutral is against the law, certainly the British law to which he is subject. Therefore, Benjamin Blake is likely to be charged with——' She stopped as the awful truth dawned. 'With treason.'

Caro stared at her, wide-eyed. 'Oh, my. I hadn't thought of that. But he says it happens all the time, that half the merchantmen and privateers don't know what shipment they carry. And we know he carried other contraband; he admits as much,' gabbled Caro, bright blue eyes fading slightly with this new worry. 'He says the merchantmen were only trying to earn a living through difficult times and when Rodney attacked Statia many innocent people were robbed of their livelihood. I thought it sounded great fun to think of him as truly on our side and not our enemy at all.'

'It isn't fun, Caro, not if Benjamin Blake is a traitor to his own country.'

'Oh, my,' wailed Caroline. 'You don't think they'll hang him, do you, by his lovely, lovely neck?'

Hester sat rigid on the sofa as if she were stuck to it with the horror of this new discovery. She felt shockingly, unpredictably sick. Yet she really shouldn't let it concern her whether Benjamin Blake were traitor or no, whether he were entirely or only half British. As Caro so rightly said, it happened all the time on Statia, known as the Golden Rock for its cache of goods stored there free of customs duties. 'Free ships, free goods', wasn't that the cry of the so-called mercantile neutrals? And so long as they did not supply arms to one side which would cause a military disadvantage to the other there were no rules broken, no danger to either themselves or their ships. But if what Caro said was correct, then Blake had broken those rules. He was not a free neutral at all, nor was he a loyal associate of the British navy. He was a mercenary of the very worst kind, a traitor to his own land. Never, no matter what the provocation or special circumstances concerned, could Hester feel herself able to condone such an act, or ever care for such a man.

CHAPTER SIX

THE three girls sat staring at each other for some moments in numb, contemplative silence. Surprisingly, it was Beattie who was the first to speak.

'I feel awful sorry for poor Mr Blake. It can't all be his fault and he does seem to have such bad luck, what with one thing and another.'

'If you mean because no one would give him accommodation when he first arrived and then was foolish enough to walk in front of my carriage. . .'

'Oh, I didn't mean about that,' said Beattie, almost animated for once. 'Anyway, walking in front of your carriage proved to be a piece of good luck, didn't it? Since you later offered him a room. No, I mean about his being held in prison.'

The silence which followed this statement was stunning. Hester felt as if there could be no breath left in her body. But before she could even venture to question this astonishing remark Caro chipped in with the unabridged version.

'Oh, fiddle-de-dee, you know how easily the British do charge people. It seems that when he was just a boy poor Benjamin, whose parents apparently disappeared to foreign parts when he was quite small, was frequently half starved, as you know.' Hester did not know, but she held her tongue on that score. Benjamin Blake and Caro had certainly had a heart-to-heart.

'He was caught stealing apples from a market stall,' Caro continued, in a doleful voice, 'and spent three whole months in a rotting gaol cell, would you believe? Isn't that just too terrible for words? How cruel the authorities are out there. I do declare, the sooner we

84

Americans break free of those old-fashioned principles, the better.'

Relief washed over Hester like a cascade of sparkling water. For one moment she had imagined she was about to learn Blake had committed some crime even more terrible than treason, dreadful as that was. But it was only a childhood prank carried out by a lonely boy, and punished, as people were in those days, unnecessarily brutally. Thankfully, folk were growing more enlightened in these modern times. Hester actually found herself laughing, and the other two were joining in as if sharing a huge joke. The relief was so enormous, she felt almost light-headed.

'It's a good job we've never been given similar treatment here,' Hester chortled. 'From the number of apples I scrumped as a child I'd have spent my whole life behind bars.'

'Me too,' squealed Caro, and the three girls doubled up with laughter, clutching each other in delight.

'Hester, honey, isn't it time we were going? It's past eleven and I have to open the shop early in the morning.'

Hester glanced up at the sound of Carter's cool voice to find him stolidly waiting beside her, his hat and gloves already in hand. For a moment a prickle of irritation flickered over her at his intrusion. She did not have a shop to open in the morning, and, having resolved to put the problem of Benjamin's alleged treason down to Caro's excessive imagination, she was just beginning to enjoy herself. But remembering the apology she owed Carter, and the problem she still had to solve regarding their odd relationship, she merely smiled and got to her feet.

'As you wish, Carter. I'll get my wrap.'

But as they made their departure through the stair-hall they came face to face with Benjamin Blake himself.

Taking in the picture the pair of them made, with Hester standing in her neat, precise way, her gloved hand on Carter Lois's arm, Benjamin felt an unexpected rage storm through his body. She looked so young and vulnerable. A trio of soft brown curls had escaped the strict confines of her bonnet to lie forlornly upon her brow and there was an air of confusion, almost of panic clouding those frank brown eyes. It was as if she was not quite sure how she came to be there but was bravely resolved to carry her duty through to the end.

'Hester?' Benjamin offered a polite bow but did not trouble to hide the puzzlement in his tone.

While he'd been attempting to fob off the overcurious friends of the empty-headed Ashton sisters, this small-minded storekeeper had captured Hester once again. Benjamin might not want her for himself—for heaven's sake, hadn't he had enough of doting females?—but that did not mean he wanted Lois to have her. On the contrary, the man was a barbarian. Benjamin did not ask himself how he would have felt had she been with any other man, if he would have minded any less.

'What is this, Lois? I was under the impression that I would be driving Hester home, since we share the same house.'

These simple but true words brought high spots of angry colour to Carter's flat round face. 'There is no necessity for that. I always drive Hester home. Tonight is no different.' And, nodding to Hester with a smile, he continued, 'If you are ready, honey?'

Not daring to look at Benjamin, Hester swallowed hard and gave a quiver of a smile. 'Of course, Carter, whatever you say.'

With a glint of triumph in his pale eyes, Carter Lois led Hester past his rival and out to the waiting carriage with a great show of satisfaction and without a backward glance. But if he thought he'd won this little contretemps he would soon be disenchanted.

Whirling upon his polished heel with all the ferocity of a southern hurricane, Benjamin Blake tendered swift farewells, collected his hat and gloves and called Jonas from his below-stairs card game in a voice which demanded instant obedience.

'Miss Hester has been taken home. Jump to it, Jonas, I intend to follow.'

'Yassir, I'se ready,' cried Jonas, bringing round the chaise with more speed than he normally exhibited, though even then it was too slow for Benjamin's liking and he chafed and fumed the whole time for Jonas to hurry. Captain was stirred from his doze with a sharp, 'Git along there,' helped by a smart tap on his ample rear by Benjamin as he flung himself aboard.

Of one thing Benjamin was certain. Carter Lois was up to no good, he was sure of it. He didn't trust him with Hester for a moment and was furious with himself for allowing Lois to whisk her away from his protection. There was something decidedly fishy about the man and Benjamin intended to discover exactly what it was. He could do that at least.

Hester did not feel at all relaxed, acutely aware of Carter's oppressive silence beside her in the small chaise. It was quite dark and the arms of the live oaks rustled eerily in the wind, swaying their wreaths of Spanish moss like phantom manes high above their heads. It was cloyingly warm and she removed her wrap, folding it neatly upon her lap while she searched her mind frantically for a way of introducing the subject that bothered her so much. Their betrothal. Try as she might, she could not recall the moment when it had actually come about. Surely he had not, in so many words, asked her. Rather had always said that he would ask her, one day. Nevertheless, Carter spoke constantly of an understanding between them. The situation had to be clarified. She cleared her throat.

'Carter? This question of our betrothal.'

She felt his body grow taut, instantly alert. 'Yes?'

She swallowed. There was no turning back now. 'I wondered if we might discuss it?'

He pulled at once on the reins, drawing the horse into the side of the road where a low bridge crossed a creek. Hester took no note of where they were, her mind completely engaged upon her problem.

'Sure, honey. I've been waiting for an opportunity to talk with you.' He turned to her with such excitement upon his face that she almost quailed from continuing.

'I've been trying to recall. . .that is, I wondered when it was that you actually. . .? The fact of the matter is, Carter, I do not at all *feel* betrothed to you.' Hester could, however, feel her cheeks burning with embarrassment. This was even more dreadful than she had feared.

'I can understand that,' he said.

'You can?' Hope sprang within her.

'Of course. It is this dratted war. Everything is so topsy-turvy. Once that is over, and I believe it will be soon, life will get better and you can stop trying to take all the responsibility for your dear aunt, which you shouldn't have to do, being merely a woman, and leave all of that to me.'

'Oh, but——'

'No buts, Hester. I shall not hear of anything different. Why, you don't think I'd leave poor Aunt Kizzy all on her lonesome, do you? What kind of a man do you take me for? Wherever we make our home, she is more'n welcome to share it.'

This conversation was going all wrong. 'Oh, but that wasn't what was on my mind.'

He smiled softly at her, and the smile was like a leer in the green darkness. 'I understand perfectly, don't you fret. All young ladies are eager for that special day. Mebbe it's my fault that you feel so lonely and hard done by, neglecting you the way I do for my store.' Hester tried to interrupt but he waved her to silence. 'No, no, don't deny it. I know how obsessed I get with the darned thing, but it's our future, don't you see? One day it will be the finest store in the whole of Charleston. And once the British pay me what they owe me, I don't mind telling you, Hester, I'll be a wealthy man.'

'But Carter. . .' She must say it, she must, but how?

'Why don't you come out tomorrow and cast an eye over our new house? It ain't no more'n four walls at the moment, but any day now I'll have enough for a roof and then you'll see it'll be done in no time. Mebbe if you sees it you'll feel more affianced.'

It had to be now. With her hands screwed tightly together, Hester closed her eyes and said in a voice that came out as a thin croak, 'I don't *want* to marry you.'

But Carter must not have heard her for he was still talking. 'Meeting Street is going to be the up-and-coming place, I'm sure of it. I was thinking of having a two-tiered portico on the front done in white Portland stone. I shall naturally employ the very finest carver. And all the fireplaces must be marble, don't you think? So elegant.'

She tugged upon his sleeve. 'Carter, did you hear me?'

'Sorry, honey. What was that you were saying? Oh, sure, I know you're impatient for our wedding but I wouldn't dream of asking you to live over the store, though it ain't a bad place by any means. Plenty of space for a family man.' He winked at her most outrageously, and she felt suddenly sick as she saw a new expression dawn in his eyes. 'Are you saying you don't want to wait for the house, honey?'

'No, no, what I meant was. . .'

And as she floundered for words there came the sound of thundering hoofs behind them.

'Now, who can be driving their team so hard?' murmured Carter, shifting round in his seat to look back along the track. 'Why, I believe it is your carriage, Hester. I can see Jonas driving.'

'Mine? Driving at that pace?' She was on her feet, jumping down from the chaise at the same moment as Jonas reined in the sweating Captain to a lathering halt and Benjamin Blake himself leapt from the carriage to reach her in two long strides.

'Hester. Are you all right?'

She gazed at him in astonishment while her heart set up a drumbeat that seemed to echo the length and breadth of the road in the darkness.

'Why, of course I am all right. Why should I not be? And what are you doing here?'

Benjamin was breathing deeply, and gazing down at her as if he had never set eyes on her before. For a long moment he seemed lost for words. 'Jonas was anxious. We saw you heading out of town, away from the direction of East Bay, and we wondered if perhaps you were in trouble, or lost.' Then he glared up at Carter Lois, who was still sitting with his hands on the reins and a bemused expression on his face.

'We're entitled to enjoy an evening drive, I suppose, without asking your permission?' said Carter, rather petulantly.

Choosing to ignore this remark, Benjamin bestowed his glare upon Hester, his usually benign expression replaced by a scowl of such murderous intent that her whole body trembled. 'Were you aware that he intended driving you to this deserted creek?'

Hester at last gave proper attention to their location. The track upon which they were stopped was wide and dusty, the rails of the wooden bridge crumbling and broken. And beneath it slid a black expanse of swamp water in which there were no doubt alligators lurking in the reeds. She shivered. No, indeed, she had not been aware of any such thing. So occupied had she been planning what she should say to Carter, she had given no attention to their direction at all. But the thought of admitting as much was another matter. And to Benjamin Blake of all people, after what Caro had told her this evening. Why, what right had he to criticise anyone? She tossed her head and pursed her lips into a tight rosebud as if to say, I have no need to answer to you.

Watching her, Benjamin found himself entranced by the fleeting expressions that had come and gone across her piquant face. He almost wanted to laugh out loud, so transparent were they. Dismay, despair, and now an almost childlike defiance. The knowledge that she had made a mistake all too clearly writ upon it but coupled with a stubborn refusal to admit as much.

'Well?' he asked. 'Are you going to answer or no? What would Aunt Kizzy think if she knew you were gallivanting all over the countryside at this time of night?'

Hester gasped. 'It really is none of your business what I do, or what you imagine Aunt Kizzy might think. I was perfectly safe with Carter. We were only— only——'

'Only what? Seems to me that any gentleman worthy of the name would never take advantage of a young, unchaperoned lady in this way.' His icy glare was returned to Carter Lois in full measure, who at once felt compelled to step down from the carriage.

'Here now, just a minute. I've no intention of taking advantage of anyone, least of all dear Hester. And I'll have you know that she and I are affianced and so a chaperon is not strictly necessary.'

It was as if Carter had put touch paper to gunpowder.

'Not strictly necessary?' echoed Benjamin and even the horses shied in shock at the sound. 'Are you quite without sense, man? Until a young lady is safely ensconced in wedlock a chaperon is a must.'

'Really,' gasped Hester, growing quite flustered. 'There is no need to take such a scolding tone, Mr Blake. Carter was only driving me home.'

Benjamin whirled about, dark lowering brows completely hiding the blue of his eyes, which was perhaps just as well considering the ferocity reflected in them. 'Driving you home? He was doing no such thing. He was driving you to a quiet, lonely spot for his own nefarious purposes.'

Hester stamped her foot very loudly upon the wooden boards of the bridge. The sound of it echoed across the water and the trees seemed to moan in response. 'I'll not have you talk about me in such a way. I would never allow him to do such a thing. We were simply so busy talking that we quite forgot the direction. I am sure it is as innocent as that, Mr Blake. And furthermore I'll have you know that I'll not be *ensconced* in anything, unless I have a mind to be, least of all matrimony.'

'You'll do what's good for you and like it,' barked Benjamin, surprising even himself by the anger he felt. But someone had to say these things to her, for she was a danger to herself with her unconventional ways. What on earth had possessed her to allow Carter Lois to drive her out here? 'Marriage is the only safe haven for a woman in this dangerous world,' he said sternly.

'Stuff and nonsense,' she retaliated, her cheeks growing scarlet with rage. 'I am perfectly well able to look after myself and need no man fawning about, proving himself a nuisance. Why, I know of some husbands who do nothing but drink and spend money. What kind of haven can they offer a girl?'

'Exactly,' said Benjamin as if she had proved his

point. 'Therefore every young lady must take particular care to keep herself free from scandal and select a husband with care.'

'Which is what I intend to do,' cried Hester, stamping her foot again. 'When I am good and ready.'

'Hester, honey, pray do not allow your temper to get quite out of hand,' simpered Carter in her ear.

'I've already told you that Carter Lois is not the man for you,' said Benjamin coldly, speaking as if Carter were not there. 'Why do you so stubbornly set your mind against what I tell you? You don't even like the man, let alone love him. Throw yourself away on a fool like that and you'll regret it for the rest of your life. I'd marry you myself sooner than see you do that.'

'What was that?' intervened Carter. 'Hester, what is the fellow saying?'

'Oh, shut up, do,' she cried, and so startled had she been by Benjamin's outrageous remark that without thinking what she was doing she slapped a hand at Carter, pushing him away from where he hung over her shoulder.

Perhaps she caught him off balance, or the push had more strength in it than she'd realised but the next moment he was rocking on his heels, arms flailing like a windmill before he disappeared backwards, swallowed up by the darkness. It was the sound of the splitting fence rail followed by a loud splash which brought Hester from her paralysis.

'Oh, my goodness, he's fallen in!' She flew to the rail to peer anxiously down into the blackness, expecting any moment to hear cries of agony as some passing gator took a bite at poor Carter's skinny legs.

'I believe it would be more accurate to say that he was pushed,' said Benjamin, finding great difficulty in keeping the laughter from his voice.

'Well, don't just stand there. Do something. Perhaps

he can't swim. He'll drown. Oh, my, I never meant to push him in. He just gets on my nerves so.'

Fortunately for Carter, there were no alligators cruising the swamp at that precise moment, nor was the water deep enough to drown in, but it was certainly muddy. And as he was pulled dripping from the quagmire there were no offers forthcoming to drive him home. Poor Carter had to swallow his dignity, along with several pints of stagnant swamp water, and tend to himself. The buttercup-yellow seat cushions of his sporty little carriage never fully recovered. And neither did Carter. It was a slight, on top of everything else which had occurred that evening, he was unlikely to forget.

'Why do you always hit one when you are angry with the other?' Benjamin and Hester were sitting alone in the kitchen sipping a soothing cup of hot coffee. Aunt Kizzy had indeed been waiting up for Hester, concerned by the lateness of the hour and of course had insisted upon a full explanation. Shamefaced, Hester had told her the sorry tale.

'I know I shouldn't have done it, Aunt Kizzy. It's just that he—oh, I don't know. He's so very proper. Always telling me what I should and shouldn't do.'

'And not accepting you for what you are, a woman with a mind of her own,' put in Benjamin.

'Precisely. But I feel so guilty. I shall have to call and apologise. Oh, dear, that was the first time he'd worn that new grey coat.'

'I shouldn't worry, he can well afford another,' said Aunt Kizzy. 'Wish I'd been there to see his silly face. It must have been a picture. Why, even as a child he never did know when to hold his tongue.' And, chortling delightedly to herself, she went off to bed.

Now Hester looked stunned by Benjamin's question. 'Do I?' she asked. And then remembered how she had slapped Benjamin's face when Carter had irritated her at the store that day, and now, when she'd been angry at Benjamin, it was Carter she sent flying into the swamp.

'I do seem to, don't I? Oh, my. And poor Carter looked so surprised.' And then she was laughing, a joyous sound that lit the dim kitchen with light and her young face with a new radiance. Benjamin caught his breath. He had never seen her look quite so carefree before. She laughed with a freshness he found intoxicating. The wide mouth dimpling delightfully at each corner, unselfconsciously revealing the prettiest pearl teeth he'd ever seen. He had a sudden and acute longing to kiss each dimple, to taste again the remembered sweetness of those soft lips, only this time lingeringly, giving himself time to explore their charm. How lovely she was. If only he had met her before, long ago, in that other life, before he'd been made bitter by life's tricks. But no. He could not imagine this delightful, honey-skinned girl in the back streets of Liverpool. What was he thinking of? She was but a child and he must guard against being too moved by her natural, easy manner. That way led to emotional disaster.

He stood up abruptly. 'I must say goodnight. Since Aunt Kizzy, your delightful chaperon, has now retired, it would not be proper for me to remain alone with you in this kitchen.' Because he didn't trust himself and what he might do.

'Oh, Benjamin, don't be a silly goose. I know that I am perfectly safe with you.' She was still laughing up at him, brown eyes wide and candid. And strangely Benjamin felt something close to disappointment in his heart. Why should she feel so safe with him? Because she thought him too old for her? Too staid? Because she believed him to be a respectable English gentleman? Or because she simply didn't think of him in that particular way at all? None of these reasons brought him any pleasure at all, and left him feeling oddly depressed. 'I feel absolutely wide awake after our adventure so stay and talk for a while. Besides, you haven't finished your coffee.'

Reluctantly, Benjamin sat himself down again, glad suddenly of the wide scrubbed kitchen table that stretched between them. There was something so amiable and approachable about her that he found himself relaxing, smiling into her eyes. He wanted to stay. And for the first time in years he felt the urge to talk of his problems to a woman.

'Did you enjoy yourself this evening?'

Her eyes kindled joyously. 'Oh, yes, I did. Thank you for making me go, Benjamin. You were quite right, I was becoming a positive recluse and an absolute bore.' She wrinkled her small nose most becomingly. 'I'm not sure that quite everyone approved of you, though.'

He smiled. 'Probably not. Does it worry you?'

A small silence, a lowering of the eyelashes and then a light laugh as they flickered open again. 'No, why should it? But you certainly seem to have gotten on well with Caro,' she added, rather bravely, and held her breath as she waited for his response.

'There is nothing in Caro which could possibly cause offence,' he said, and Hester chuckled. With relief? Caro might not be overly bright, but she was extremely pretty and had a natural inclination for flirting which Hester sometimes found rather vexing.

'Did she tell you of our conversation?' Benjamin quietly asked.

'A little.'

Benjamin rubbed the flat of his palms over the table, feeling the smooth sanded surface of the old pinewood. 'She is a mite too easy to talk to.' Then he looked directly at Hester. 'Though not half so engaging as yourself.'

Hester wasn't quite sure whether to take this as a compliment or not. 'I suppose you find me more amusing,' she said with a slight pout, thinking of her outbursts of temper which he had so shamingly witnessed. 'I have seen you laughing at me, frequently.'

Benjamin chuckled. 'Not at all. You must forgive me if I gave the wrong impression but I only laugh with people, not at them, and only then with people I like.'

Hester looked at him with a directness he found at once beguiling and unnerving and he had an almost irresistible desire to bare his soul, to lay his whole life before her. 'Do you like me?' she asked, in a voice as soft as a child's, and he reached across the table, taking her hand and squeezing it gently between his own.

'I do, indeed, Hester. I like you very much.'

Perhaps it was her own sweet innocence which permitted her to ask the next question, or else it was that certain degree of intimacy which was only present in the dark loneliness of the night that gave her the courage.

'Why did you say that you would sooner marry me yourself than see me wed to Carter?'

'Because I don't think he is right for you,' Benjamin quietly replied.

'But isn't that rather an extreme remedy?'

His hands were now stroking her wrists, so slender and fragile, he hardly dared touch them in case they should snap in his fingers, yet their warm silkiness made him acutely aware of her as a desirable woman. Perhaps he was wrong to try to shut women entirely from his life. Because one apple was bad, it did not mean the whole barrel was rotten. And life at sea had grown increasingly unsatisfying these last years. It flashed upon his mind that life with Hester, here in

Charleston, would not be an unpleasant one. Quite the contrary.

'Perhaps so. But it is rather an interesting thought, is it not? One which might be worth exploring if the time ever becomes more propitious. And now I really think you should go to bed, little miss. I can see your eyelids positively drooping.'

'I am indeed tired.' She drew her hands from his and they felt at once cold and bereft. She offered a shy smile. 'Goodnight. And thank you again, for everything. It was kind of you to be so concerned for my safety that you should bring Jonas and come after me in that rather dashing way. I do appreciate it even though it was quite unnecessary. It shows what a very kind and caring man you are, but then I never really believed all Caro said about you.' And, covered with confusion at her daring, she fled up the stairs.

Less than ten minutes later, Hester lay in her bed with the sheets tucked up to her chin and her mind filled with the events of the evening. She was quite sure she would not sleep a wink from the excitement of it all, but it seemed only moments later that she was waking to the sound of birdsong, her face bathed in warm morning sunshine and an unaccustomed happiness about her heart.

CHAPTER SEVEN

FOLLOWING that evening, their relationship seemed to move on to a different footing. They were far more relaxed in each other's company and for some reason Benjamin did not go out quite so much. He seemed content to sit on the porch with them, perhaps reading a newspaper or book, or playing gin rummy with Aunt Kizzy, generously allowing her to win more games than her playing deserved.

And as Hester surreptitiously watched him she was all too aware of his eyes frequently upon her. Often when she glanced up from her embroidery or mending she would find his blue eyes fixed upon her face, which would then flush as she hastily dropped her gaze back to her work.

It was Benjamin now who brought the glasses of lemonade, and his whole aspect seemed to be more open and friendly. Had the idea not appeared so entirely ridiculous, Hester would have imagined that it was a deliberate ploy on his part to improve their relationship. It was almost as if he wanted her to think well of him.

Hester had gone the very next day to Carter's General Store and tendered her apologies, which had been grudgingly accepted, but she had refused point blank to visit the house on Meeting Street.

'I am not ready to talk of marriage,' she had said very determinedly. 'I don't even want to think of it at this stage.'

Carter of course blamed Benjamin for what he termed Hester's 'change of heart', refusing to accept that she had always felt this way, and they had had a little spat upon the subject.

But more and more Hester found herself questioning how she felt about Benjamin Blake, and about his enigmatic remarks on the possibility of a marriage between them 'when the times were more propitious', whatever that might mean. Could he have been serious, or was it simply one of his jokes, at which he was adept? The idea was, of course, quite absurd. Yet if the dreams which haunted her sleep and left her bleary-eyed the next morning were any judge perhaps it was not so impossibly foolish as she might pretend. And despite the sleeplessness, and the doubts and puzzles over his comments, despite all that nonsense Caro had told her she felt unaccountably content.

It was a contentment, had she known it, which showed all too clearly in her face. Benjamin had watched it grow there with interest and satisfaction. How pretty she was in repose, he often thought, as he watched her bend to her sewing. And he had noticed a softening in the face whenever she looked at him these days. He hoped that did not mean that she was growing too fond of him. The last thing he wanted was to hurt her and yet he did not feel free, either physically or emotionally, to give himself to another woman, even one as delectable as Hester Mackay. It would be better if he kept his distance. A stab of regret pierced his heart and he recoiled in surprise, then smiled at his own foolishness. Not so startling a reaction, surely, for she was attractive, no doubt about it, and had a certain beguiling charm. He liked a woman with spirit and if things had been different, if he had never. . . But enough of that. Should he find other accommodation? No, she would only be insulted and in any case he was comfortable here. But perhaps he should make the situation clear to her.

He smiled as she puffed and fanned herself in the

heat, or pushed back a damp tendril of golden-brown hair that had stuck to her brow. And often he would have the urge to smooth it back for her for she sometimes looked so tired.

'You work too hard,' he told her one evening.

She looked up at him in surprise. 'Indeed I don't. Susy and Jonas do the bulk of the work. I am well taken care of.'

'I'm not undermining their efforts, none the less you do work too hard. Today you have cooked, tended the garden, done some shopping, taken part in Caro's latest charity function, and, if that pile of mending is anything to go by, been busy ever since you returned home. Where does so much mending come from?'

Hester leaned back in the rocking-chair with a small sigh. 'You tell me—much of it belongs to your men. It seems to grow with a life of its own.'

He looked shocked. 'I did not know they were piling it all on to you. I'll speak to them first thing in the morning.'

She was at once eager to protest. 'Oh, no, really, I don't mind. I'd much rather be busy than bored. And they have so many more important things to do. Besides——' and here she smiled that quick wide smile he was growing almost fond of '—I can ply the needle with more skill than they, for all they are seamen.'

Benjamin laughed. 'You probably have a point there. Seamen they may be, needlemen they are not.'

'Where did you meet them?' she idly asked, picking up the needle once more and giving her attention to a button.

'I took them on at Liverpool, by the docks. I accept they are a pretty grim-looking bunch and for some of them it is their first time at sea. But they are loyal and hard-working. Most of them, anyway. I had a ship needing a crew in a hurry, and they needed work.' He paused, seeming to consider something very seriously as he stared down at his boots. 'Hester. . .'

'Yes?' She glanced up at him.

'Nothing.' And he was striding from the porch, the screen door swinging closed behind him.

Hester was astonished. 'Now whatever brought that on? Why did he leave so suddenly? Did I say something wrong, Aunt Kizzy?'

The old lady grunted. 'I reckon he has something to get off his chest, but don't pay no mind. He'll come out with it in his own good time.'

And there were other things to think about. A fleet of ships, possibly bearing a British flag, had been sighted heading north. Speculation was rife. Could it be Rodney searching for de Grasse, who was supposedly on his way to New York? In fact the Admiral's health had demanded he return to England, taking two of the British warships with him, which were to prove a serious loss in the battle that was to follow. Nor would Rodney enjoy his visit home since judgement awaited him there in the form of legal actions from the merchants of St Eustatius. But before he left he did dispatch a message to Clinton in New York to tell him that de Grasse was, in fact, heading for Chesapeake. And, while a combination of miscalculations and bungling paralysed the British forces, Washington was marching his men down through New Jersey to meet up with de Grasse, who had already arrived in Chesapeake Bay, unnoticed by anyone.

All this information was given much later, of course, to the Charlestonians, together with the longed for news that de Grasse did indeed defeat the British navy with twenty-eight ships and three thousand men. Less than a month later, on October nineteenth at Yorktown, the British leader, Cornwallis, surrendered. By the following spring political heads would roll in England and, though not until the Treaty of Versailles in 1783 would England unreservedly concede the victory, a victory it most certainly was. America, with the help of her French allies, had won. Jubilation spread. And if it was to take months before the last of the British could finally leave, it was somehow much easier to live with a defeated people than with a conquering victor. Life could at last begin to return to normal.

And for a time life was indeed better. There was a gaiety in the air, a feeling of freedom, and Hester and Benjamin joked and laughed together as if they had discovered a new joy in each other, as indeed they had. They took to taking a regular daily walk or drive, often down to the riverfront, where he would tell her about the different ships in the harbour.

'Do you see, that one is loading cotton from the cotton factor's warehouses. It's bound for Liverpool and the new factories of northern England.'

Hester cast a sideways look at him, her heartbeat increasing its momentum at the fear which had suddenly been born in her. 'And one day soon you will be on it,' she said, but the lightness in her voice did not fool either of them. Benjamin looked down at her and his gaze was shrewd, probing, seeming to seek out her soul, her innermost feelings.

'The British all plan to be gone by next winter. But I have no plans to accompany them at this moment,' he said, and Hester was so relieved, she gave a little hiccup of laughter.

'I'm glad to hear it.'

'Are you? Why is that?' His voice was soft, almost caressing.

'Oh, I've grown used to having you around. My, but Aunt Kizzy and I will not know what to do with ourselves when you and your men leave.'

'I dare say you will find other guests to fill your delightful rooms, or else a fine young man to marry.'

Their glances locked and held for a long indescribable moment that seemed to go endlessly on. Hester could not even catch her breath for it lay as solid as a cannon-ball in her ribcage.

'It would have to be the right young man,' she said with a soft smile.

'And you have not met him yet?'

Silence. Hester's mind raced. What could she say to that? Had she met him? Was Carter the one? She shuddered inwardly at the thought. Then who? 'Perhaps I too should see something of the world,' she said flippantly. 'I have always longed to see England.' But even as her tongue prattled on her eyes were fixed upon Benjamin Blake and as realisation dawned perhaps it also registered upon her expressive face, for he seemed to stiffen and turn from her, jerking away his body as if avoiding the possibility of her reaching out and touching him.

Hester felt as shocked as if he had slapped her. For a moment they had seemed so close that she had felt able to express her regret at his possible departure, as she would with any friend. But in her thoughts had come the realisation that she did not think of him in that light at all. She did not want him merely as a friend. She loved him. There was no question about it, and with a dawning horror she suspected he had guessed as much and the revelation was not welcomed. For some reason she had overstepped some invisible mark, a mark he did not wish her to cross. Desperately she tried to think of something to say which would reinstate their closeness, but she felt rejected and unwanted so the solution eluded her and she could only allow him to lead her back along the bay as if everything were the same between them. Yet she knew that for some inexplicable reason it never would be.

But later than evening, after Aunt Kizzy had retired for the night, Benjamin stayed on the porch with

Hester, as had become their habit. To her amusement, Hester had noticed that Aunt Kizzy had taken to retiring earlier and earlier as if she had no wish to intrude upon them. And this particular evening she had gone to bed almost as soon as supper was over, declaring she was exhausted, having spent an hour closeted with her man of business.

And now, in the softness of the Southern darkness, Benjamin began at last to talk.

'There has been something on my mind for some time, Hester, that should be said, perhaps before it is too late.'

Hester's hands stilled and she set aside her sewing. It was too dark now in any case, but she regretted the loss of the occupation. 'That sounds dreadfully serious,' she said with an attempt at a smile, but Benjamin was not smiling. He was not even looking at her. His eyes were fixed somewhere out in the middle distance, or perhaps way back into his life.

'Perhaps it is. Or perhaps I am worrying unduly.' He drew in a deep breath. 'If this hurts you then I apologise in advance, for it is the last thing I intended.'

'I understand.'

But she did not. She did not understand at all. What was it that troubled him so, that made him look so grim?

'There was once someone—someone in my life. We had grown up together and so were good friends, used to each other, at least I thought that was the case. Her name was Sarah. I did not think of her as a woman, if you can understand that.'

'I think so.'

'But that was not so for Sarah.' Benjamin got up from the rocker to stroll restlessly down the garden path and Hester was obliged to follow him. 'Her fondness for me grew to a level beyond friendship.'

Hester held her breath. What was he trying to tell her?

'It became almost obsessive. I could go nowhere without Sarah tagging on behind. Whatever I did, she watched me. Wherever I walked, she followed. She tried to pre-empt my every need, handing me things I had never asked for, buying me things I did not want. She would even stand outside the door of my home for hour upon hour, waiting for me to come out. It was unnerving.'

Hester felt herself grow tense. 'It must have been difficult.'

Benjamin turned to face her and even in the half-light the grim, almost angry expression upon the planes of his handsome face was only too clear. 'Never could I allow that to happen again. She should have married Stefan, who loved her, but she was obsessed by me, with catastrophic results. Stefan took it very badly and has borne me a grudge ever since. I could never risk a recurrence of such uncompromising devotion for it very nearly destroyed my life, Hester, do you see? A person must be allowed to live his or her own life without let or hindrance, make his own decisions and mistakes, and not be pushed into a corner simply out of pity.'

She saw only too clearly. He was telling her not to grow fond, not to fall in love with him. But it was too *late*. He was telling her that he ran from England to escape this Sarah, and would run from her if she too was foolish enough to try to capture his love. And he was telling her that on no account must she attempt to follow him to England when the time came for him to leave. That was the invisible line she had crossed earlier as they had talked down by the harbour, and he had seen the dawning love for him written in her face. But, much as she might wish it otherwise, whatever damage had been done to him in the past, he was making it abundantly clear that he wanted none of Hester's help now to mend it.

She was trembling so much, she was sure he must be aware of it. Her palms felt clammy and a pain had sprung up at the sides of her temples.

She must not let him see that it was too late. Only the residue of her pride could save her. She managed a sympathetic smile. 'Poor girl. If you did not love her in return it must have made her most miserable. That is partly the reason I am constantly trying to disengage myself from Carter Lois, for I have no wish to hurt him, but it is so difficult for he is a very determined gentleman.' She was gabbling, saying anything at all to avoid the pressure of possible silence in which her true feelings would be laid naked, exposed to his censure. Not for one moment dared she risk that.

'Carter Lois is a different problem, but you are right to keep away from him. You are shivering, Hester. Are you cold? How thoughtless of me to keep you talking out here simply to get an old worry off my chest.'

He slipped his coat about her shoulders and the pain of nestling into a garment which still carried the residual warmth and male scent of his body was almost the undoing of her. She said not a word as he led her back through the knot of box-edged paths, past the old kitchen where Susy prepared most of the meals safely away from any danger of setting fire to the house, and back up the steps of the piazza.

He placed his hands gently upon her shoulders and his touch almost scorched her through the thick cloth of his jacket. 'Forgive me if I said it all too clumsily. But you are young, and vulnerable to the presence of a newcomer in your home. We are friends, I hope, Hester, but you must not read more into it than there is, nor hope for more than there can ever be.'

He could not have been plainer. Hester snatched the

jacket from her shoulders and, thrusting it into his hands, she gazed at him unseeing through tear-blurred eyes. 'You need have no fear on that score. I can do nothing about my youth, but my vulnerability, as you call it, is quite another matter. For your information, Mr Blake, I am well able to take care of myself and would not dream of inconveniencing or embarrassing you in any way. Goodnight to you.' She fled into the house, to her bed, where she poured out all her misery and despair into a balled-up kerchief and a yielding pillow which would tell no tales on the morrow. And at breakfast she was able to serve Benjamin his eggs and biscuits without a tremor.

Caro and Beattie held their celebration ball, which was declared a great success by everyone—except, that was, for Hester. The pair were, as ever, overdressed in yards of ice-blue frills, and Hester felt positively dowdy in her cream organza with its cinnamon trim at least two seasons old. It certainly did not inspire Benjamin to ask her for more than one dance, and as they whirled and side-stepped and swung about he appeared distracted, as if he were more interested in everyone else rather than herself. Which no doubt he was, since he had made his feelings on their relationship only too plain.

Sometimes she would catch his eye across the room and her heart would leap, startling her by its intensity and the sharp pain it left in her breast. But then his eyes would seem to glaze as if he were looking straight through her, deliberately avoiding her. The disappointment she felt was keen. Did he have to make his dislike of her quite so obvious?

Even Carter was absent, having been called abruptly out of town on a private business matter, or so she understood. Hester thought this most odd, since he had no business affairs outside of Charleston so far as she knew, and no family either. She would most definitely take the issue up with him when he returned. It was all most intriguing and not a little vexing, for tonight Carter's presence would have helped to soothe the balm of her rejection.

Benjamin did not even request a ride home in the carriage. Handing her into it, he merely nodded his head in an abrupt kind of way.

'I'll say goodnight here, Hester, if I may. And don't wait up for me. I shall sleep on board ship this night, for I must pack a few things for some business I need to attend to and will be away for a few days. Pray give my good wishes to your aunt and promise her I shall return to even our score as soon as possible.'

'Very well,' Hester replied, but there was a stiffness in her voice, a bleakness. The prospect of the next days without his presence was too awful for words and the aching void of how life would be when he had gone opened up before her. 'I take it you do not require any food, since you have given me no notice of this absence?' she said coldly, and he looked up at her in sudden concern.

'I'm sorry, Hester. I didn't mean to be inconsiderate. This matter has arisen unexpectedly. I do assure you I will return with all speed. Do not trouble about packing any food. Stefan, my bosun, who is coming with me, will see to all of that.' So he did not need her in any way at all.

'I see.' There was a small, uncomfortable silence and then Hester tapped on the carriage door. 'Drive on, Jonas. Goodnight to you, then, Mr Blake.' And he was forced to step quickly back as Jonas clicked the horse awake and the carriage wheels rolled forward.

She did not turn to wave, nor even look back at him, though she could see him in her mind's eye standing forlornly in the road. She clicked her tongue with impatience. Forlorn indeed. Why should he be? Sleep on board, he said? For all she knew he might well be off on some assignation, which men did all the time, didn't they? The thought brought her out in a cold sweat. Yet it had nothing whatever to do with her. For one mad moment she wondered if perhaps the assignation were with one of the Ashton sisters. An elopement perhaps? Now she was drenched in uncomfortable heat. Surely not; the prospect was too terrible for words. She was allowing her imagination to run riot simply because she had spent a dull, lonely evening.

She decided that she would insist Aunt Kizzy come with her to the next social gathering, then at least she would have some company. But Aunt Kizzy seemed to be withdrawing into herself and this was causing Hester consternation. It was most unlike her. Hester had almost made up her mind to call in the doctor when the matter was brought to a head by Aunt Kizzy's falling down the porch steps one evening, resulting in a bad ankle sprain. Dr Livesey was called in at once and Hester waited anxiously for him to finish strapping up the injured limb before begging a quiet word with him.

Dr Livesey had been the Drayton family practitioner for years and was a valued friend. Hester knew that any advice he would have to offer would be of the very best. 'I will be down directly, Hester,' he said, smiling kindly at her, and tugging at his grey moustache whiskers as she had seen him do countless times. 'I'd first like a word with your good aunt.'

Hester nodded and, kissing Aunt Kizzy on the cheek, softly admonished her. 'Now, Aunt, do allow Dr Livesey to look at your chest. You have been sounding decidedly wheezy lately.'

'Stuff and nonsense,' declared the stalwart old lady, yet without her usual conviction, and a small crease of worry deepened on Hester's brow.

'Please, for my sake,' Hester wheedled as she saw

the old lips thin into a stubborn line. 'I'll wait in the library, Doctor, and don't allow her to bully you.'

Eyes twinkling, Dr Livesey laughed. 'I've been coping with Kristina Drayton's idiosyncrasies for more years than I care to recall, young lady. You need have no fear on that score.'

But later, when he joined Hester in the library, there was not a trace of laughter in the old grey eyes. Even the crinkles, caused by years of screwing up his eyes against the sun or to peer into his patient's mouths, eyes and ears, seemed without their usual curl of good humour. Suddenly filled with foreboding, Hester flew to the wine table.

'Would you care for a small Madeira, Doctor? Or a port?'

'Port, if you please, Hester. Though I dare say I shouldn't.' He set down his leather bag on a tapestry chair and, drawing in a deep sigh, flopped down upon the sofa. 'How long has Kristina been like this?'

Hester almost dropped the decanter. It was one thing to imagine that something was wrong with Aunt Kizzy, but quite another to have it so swiftly confirmed, and before she had even had the chance to ask Dr Livesey to investigate her suspicions.

Hester handed him the glass. 'If you mean without her usual show of spirit and fire, I would say almost a month, I think.' Hester sank down into a low armchair as if her legs could no longer support her. 'It's hard to say for sure. But that was the reason I wished to speak with you. I've been wondering whether to call you.'

'I rather gathered it was something of the sort. One look at your aunt told me that she was not herself.' He took a sip of port. 'But the devil of it is, Hester, I can find nothing physically wrong with her.'

Hester almost breathed a sigh of relief until she realised that that didn't help at all. Something *was* wrong, she was sure of it.

'She says her appetite is good, what do you say about that?'

Hester shook her head. 'She is saying that simply to put you off. She does no more than pick at her food, stays in bed late in the morning, which is most unlike her, never takes up her embroidery and is too listless to even take her evening stroll, which she has always enjoyed.'

'Do you know of anything worrying your aunt? Sometimes, when a problem weighs too heavily upon the mind, it can have this debilitating effect. Has she spoken of any worries to you?'

'No.' Hester shook her head.

'Have there been any unusual occurrences, letters in the mail, or unexpected visitors?'

Hester fell thoughtful. 'No, indeed. None that I can think of. There are rarely any letters for either of us these days, not now that—George is dead.' There, she had said it. No prevaricating with the doctor.

'You don't think she is grieving for him still?' Dr Livesey asked, sympathy in his voice. 'It can sometimes overtake us when we are least expecting it.'

Hester blinked back a sudden pricking behind the eyelids. 'We both do badly miss George, for all he was a bundle of nerves when he was here, always worrying about things unnecessarily.' Hester smiled reminiscently. 'Aunt was always telling him to eat up his grits, because they would make him fit and strong and cool his blood, which she maintained would stop his fidgeting and those constant attacks of panic he was prone to.'

Dr Livesey looked thoughtful. 'Yes, George was indeed always highly strung, but your aunt never appeared to be that way.'

'Perhaps you are right, Doctor, and she is merely suffering from his loss, from not having him to fuss over.'

Draining his port glass, the doctor got to his feet. 'If this is the case then you must endeavour to occupy her mind. Try to encourage her to maintain a normal routine.'

'I will.'

'And I would not advise you to leave her alone, Hester, not while she is in this frame of mind. I know you will not, for you are a good girl.' He smiled roguishly at her and for a second Hester saw a glimpse of the young Jasper Livesey. 'Too good in some respects. What are the young men thinking of around here? You should have been snapped up long since. Now see you look after her, and don't cross her in anything. She must be thoroughly coddled.' He grinned. 'Does us all good once in a while.'

'Oh, I will. Indeed I will, Doctor. Have no fear.'

And Hester was true to her word. She had Susy make all Aunt Kizzy's favourite dishes, most of which returned only half eaten to the kitchen. Hester read to her, told her all the latest gossip, even sang to her, for she had a sweet, tuneful voice. But Kristina merely lay in her high bed, sightlessly staring up at the ceiling. She scarcely spoke and sometimes hardly seemed to be breathing. The doctor called regularly but he could throw no more light upon the matter. December came and with it the prospect of Christmas, a time she usually loved, yet she showed no interest in it whatsoever, and when Hester tried to discuss the coming celebrations Kizzy retorted with a surprising sharpness, despite her weakened state, 'Poppycock. There will be no Christmas celebrations in my house this year.'

Hester was shocked. 'But, Aunt, we always celebrate Christmas, and this year, with the war over and all, I thought we could make a special effort to bring in the festive cheer.'

But Aunt Kizzy only turned her face to the wall and mumbled something about who did she think was to pay for it all, which puzzled and hurt Hester greatly for hadn't they lived well enough from the moment they'd taken in Benjamin Blake and his crew? Concern in the household grew, for nothing anyone did was right, nothing brought a smile to the old lady's withered face, and not a visitor from outside the family, other than the doctor, was allowed in to see her.

And then one morning the door banged open and Benjamin strode in, bringing a gust of welcome fresh air with him.

Hester ran down the wide stairs to greet him, the joy she felt at sight of him lighting up her whole face, her slippered feet seeming to fly from each step. Watching her, Benjamin experienced a peculiar tightening of his chest muscles and knew a familiar quickening of the pulse. So he was not so immune to her charms as he would like to imagine.

'Oh, Benjamin.' And then she was in his arms, pouring out her woes, in desperate need of comfort, and Benjamin was stroking her hair, kissing the tears from her cheeks and promising her that all would be well now that he was home.

'I will speak to your aunt, and try to get to the bottom of it. And while I do so I would be grateful if you would put on a pot of coffee, for I am parched.'

'Oh, yes, of course.' Hester ran to the kitchen, and with a sigh almost of resignation Benjamin climbed the stairs. He rather thought he knew what ailed the old woman, and it seemed to him that there was only one possible solution, a solution he had tried to avoid facing for some considerable time.

Less than half an hour later, his worst fears confirmed, he was back in the library watching Hester pour coffee, her face a wreath of anxiety. When the coffee was set before him and the cream added with, he noted, a trembling hand, she left her own cup untouched and sat, rather abruptly, upon a chair opposite to him.

'Did she tell you?'

'Not willingly, Hester. But I guessed and so she had no choice but to come clean.'

Hester's brown eyes widened. 'And?' What could it be?

Benjamin took a sip of the dark, scalding coffee, playing for time. And all the while he looked deep into those lovely brown eyes. Perhaps there would be compensations for such a heroic gesture as the one he planned. And certainly the alternatives did not bear thinking of. He was unwilling to admit it, but he knew with a certainty that brought at least some kind of peace that he could no more walk away from these people and leave them to their troubles than he could cut his own throat. And they did have troubles. More than they realised. If he was careful, he saw no reason why they should ever learn of his.

He set down his cup with excessive care. 'I am afraid the problem is largely financial. Your aunt has been visited by her man of business, who has informed her that she is, in short, penniless. That this house is no longer hers since it was mortgaged some time ago to pay for numerous debts. Now that the war is over, these financial considerations must take precedence over sympathy and the result is that you have both been given notice to quit.'

CHAPTER EIGHT

'ARE you telling me that we are about to be thrown out into the street?' Hester cried.

'Not quite so dramatic as that, but you have the nub of it, yes. Hester, I think you had better prepare yourself for the whole sordid tale.'

She straightened her back with characteristic determination and though the small, blunt chin beneath the wide mouth protruded with a strength of will to be admired there was raw fear in the soft brown eyes. 'Is there worse to come?' What could possibly be worse than hearing that she had just lost the roof over her head?

Benjamin took her small, cold hands in his. In any other circumstances the gesture would have warmed her. Now it merely confirmed the severity of what was to come.

'The house was put on mortgage some years ago by your brother, George, in payment of a gambling debt.' When she would have interrupted he shushed her gently, placing one chiding finger on her lips. 'Let me finish. George, according to Lawson, your aunt's man of business, had a weakness. He loved gambling and spent much of his time so engaged in the basements of friends' houses. It got out of hand of course in the end, and he took out a small loan. And then another to try to win back his losings. He didn't succeed, naturally. Disaster followed disaster until he was driven to using the house as collateral for a further loan. At just nineteen and not come into his inheritance, he persuaded your aunt of his intention to re-open the plantation and grow cotton. She admits to signing a paper she scarcely read, which evidently proved to be a hefty mortgage on the property which would one day have belonged to George. As it is, the amount has grown with interest over the years and is now quite beyond her. After he disappeared, presumed dead, and with the war still on, Lawson did not have the heart to call in the debt. But now. . .' He left the sentence unfinished but Hester did not now rush to fill the ensuing silence.

Her mind was too shocked to form a single sensible word. She felt as if the pressure in the top of her head would lift it off at any moment. George, a gambler? *George*? But he was always so retiring, almost timid, even nervous.

Benjamin got up and began to pace the hearthrug. 'I had heard rumours, so it was not difficult for me to elicit the truth from Aunt Kizzy, though she too had believed in him implicitly.'

'Rumours?' Hester was instantly on the alert. 'What rumours? I have heard none.'

'No reason why you should. Your friends were loyal enough to protect you. You should be grateful for that.'

'Caro,' said Hester in a tiny broken voice. 'You heard all of this from Caro, didn't you?' She couldn't bear to think that her dearest friend had known this awful truth and said nothing about it.

'She laid the foundations, that is true. Don't think too harshly of her, Hester, for she only told me so that I would be in a position to help, should the worst come to pass.'

'As it has.'

'As it has.'

There was no sound in the room beyond the ticking of the small grandmother clock against the wall.

'And George gambled, you say?' She still could not believe it.

'I'm afraid so.'

'Someone must have led him into it. He was so—so shy. No, not shy exactly, but certainly quiet. An introspective kind of person.'

Benjamin considered this for a moment. 'Perhaps gambling was his way of relaxing, of expressing a need to feel fulfilled. It was probably not, at first, a major problem. But later it became an obsession, and, having used up all his allowance and borrowed more from your aunt than he should, he felt he dared not ask again.'

'I would have helped him.' There was agony in Hester's eyes, and she brushed away the tears that had slid down her cheeks with an angry gesture.

'Inevitably.' His voice was so matter-of-fact that she would have liked very much to hit him. Her world was crumbling about her and he spoke in a dry, expressionless tone as if it were of no account. 'But even your generosity would have run its course in the end. Brother George became hooked on the excitement of it all, and terrified of admitting to either of you that he had lost a small fortune. And so he made the gambler's classic mistake of borrowing to try to win it back. In the end I suspect he ran away to war to avoid you all.'

'He was merely weak, and made rash decisions. You said so yourself.'

'Obsessions do tend to have terrible consequences.' His eyes had glazed again, and Hester knew he referred not merely to George's weakness. 'He was a fool.'

She thought of her brother, tetchy, highly strung, weak-willed and lacking in financial judgement, yet he was her beloved brother. She could not, would not stand by and hear him insulted. She opened her mouth to protest.

'What am I to do?' It was softly spoken, scarcely above a whisper and not at all what she had meant to say. But it was wrung from the heart.

Benjamin seemed to collect himself and offered her a smile which in the circumstances warmed her not at all. Even when he spoke his voice was cold and seemed to come from a great distance. 'There's only one answer that I can see. You must marry, Hester, with all speed.'

Her eyes flew to his and her lips quivered as she spoke. 'Marry? Whom? Carter?'

'Good lord, no. I can't put my finger on it, but I'm convinced the man is a rogue. No, there is only one man you can marry in my estimation. Whether you like it or no, it has to be me.'

'You?' The word shot from her mouth like a bullet and he pulled a rueful face. It was the most human expression he had worn during the entire half-hour's discussion.

'I did not expect quite so much shock and horror, though I'll admit I'm no great catch. But you'd fooled me into thinking you were not entirely indifferent.'

Hester at once dropped her gaze, shielding her eyes with the droop of dark lashes. Sensations swamped her. How could she begin to sort it all out? So recently he had made it abundantly clear that he was not only totally indifferent to her but warning her, strongly, not to grow fond of him. And now he was offering for her. How could she possibly believe in him with these constant changes of mood? Yet in the circumstances, if common sense prevailed, how could she refuse him? And did she want to?

She lifted her eyes to his. 'But you do not love me.'

He looked surprised, then seemed to consider for a moment. 'That is true,' he said at last, with a frankness which cut through her pride like ice, despite it being softly tendered. 'But there are many reasons for marriage, and there is no reason why we should not grow used to, even fond of each other in time. Most people in marriage do, or so I'm told.'

Hester was rallying. 'And you would gain the cotton plantation you have always wanted. I take it we have not lost that as well?'

It was unkind, and he twisted his eyebrows wryly at her before answering. 'The plantation safely remains in the family. And yes, I dare say I would be more willing to work it than yourself, and supply the money necessary to refurbish it. But I beg leave to be corrected.'

He waited for her reply, but she merely chewed upon her lower lip for they both knew she could never cope alone with Rhapsody Creek. At last she said, 'I could sell it.'

'But the sale of it would not buy you a like house in Charleston. And if we each gain something from the alliance, then there can be no feeling of being beholden, can there? We can each of us keep our pride intact.' It was a fair comment for which Hester was suddenly supremely grateful for she had not thought of it in that light. But this was her marriage they were discussing, and he sounded so matter-of-fact. She had expected, hoped there would be some sign of romance when this great day dawned. But if she was to be denied such joy by practical necessity then she must make the best of it.

She met his gaze directly. 'If this is to be a truly businesslike arrangement, a marriage of convenience, then we must deal with every likely problem. What about Aunt Kizzy?'

For the first time Benjamin smiled. 'I do not see your Aunt Kizzy as a problem. But what she does is entirely up to her. She can come with us to Rhapsody Creek, or she can stay here. I will buy back the mortgage of course.'

Hester gasped. 'You can do that?'

'I can do that. Money, you see, is not a problem. We can call it payment in lieu of your plantation if you like.'

'But if you have such a fortune you could buy any number of plantations,' Hester declared.

'But that would not help you, would it? Nor your aunt. And don't ask me why I wish to help you,' he said coolly. 'Because I do not know. Perhaps I wish to feel heroic. Or perhaps I merely long to become an American. I certainly have no wish to return to England.' He leant two large tanned fists on the arm of her chair so that he could look closely into her face. 'But you are wrong in one respect.'

'And what is that?' She was beginning to see a future again, and it was not so disagreeable as she might have expected. But something in Benjamin Blake's probing expression gave her pause and she caught her breath in her throat.

'We may be making businesslike arrangements, which is perhaps sensible in all marriages with or without the element of love. But this is not, Hester, and never will be, simply a marriage of convenience.'

And now the held breath was spiralling through her head, turning, she was sure, into fizzy bubbles for she felt quite light-headed. 'W—what do you mean?'

'I mean that I am a man, like any other man. I am willing to come to your aid for the reasons stated, but if you agree to become my wife it will be in the fullest sense of the word. I will be generous with you and you will want for nothing in the way of dresses and furbelows and such. I'll purchase and refurbish both your homes, and work your plantation to add to both our fortunes. I will care for your straight-talking aunt and save you from the odious Carter Lois.' He paused, and, coming to stand over her, she felt his gaze slide over the fullness of her high breasts, down over her flat stomach to the neat little hands clasped tightly in her lap and on to the small feet placed together on the carpet. Likewise his voice slid like cool silk over her skin. 'But you are an attractive woman, Hester. And in return for such generosity I want a wife. And children.' A pause while he allowed her to digest this. 'Is that agreed?'

In truth she would not have expected anything else. She knew little of such matters, having been suitably sheltered by Aunt Kizzy, who as a maiden lady naturally never mentioned the subject. But Hester was sure it wouldn't be quite so dreadful as all that, or how else were all these babies born? That was another thing she should find out about. How *were* babies born? She had heard whisperings behind hands, of jugs of hot water, binding strips, and wrung-out towels for the mother-to-be being carried to the birthing-room. But what these were all for, and how it all came about, was a little hazy. Perhaps Caro would know. However, there was no reason to worry about all of that today. Today her dreams were coming true. In a roundabout way maybe, but, after all, George was dead and no longer hurt by life's troubles. She and Aunt Kizzy, however, still had a life to build. The war was over, spring would come soon and a new beginning beckoned. For herself, the prospect of life with Benjamin Blake was far from unpleasant. For didn't she love him? And oh, yes, she would make him a good wife.

She was on her feet, gazing shyly up into his eyes.

'You won't be sorry, Benjamin. I promise I will do all I can to make you happy.' And taking herself, and him, completely by surprise, she reached up on tiptoe and kissed him, very firmly, upon the cheek. He smelt of fresh air and pine woods and for a fleeting moment she wondered where he had been these last few days but then it was gone as his arms came around her and he was swirling her around, laughing uproariously and lifting her off her feet.

'You'd better, little one, or you'll be the most expensive wife any man ever acquired.' And he kissed her very soundly in return, though with not a sign of any passion in it, much to Hester's disappointment.

When he set her on her feet again her face was flushed with happiness and her hair was tumbling down, the pins falling to the floor. And as he picked one up and handed it to her there was an odd look in his eyes. He watched her for a long moment in silence while she hurriedly restored order then he made for the door and his laugh now sounded forced and brittle.

'I think perhaps I should go and speak with Aunt Kizzy. What if she will not give her blessing?' But there was a sparkle in his eyes and Hester thought again what an enigma he was. Did he want to marry her or did he not? Oh, but she would make him love her, she was sure of it. A gurgle of happy laughter bubbled up through her, taking the tension from her body.

'I think there is little danger of that. I believe she has had her eye set on this match for a long while.'

Benjamin chuckled, a natural sound, joy to her ears. 'I think you may well be right.' Then, taking both her hands, he kissed each one tenderly. 'Then we are agreed?'

She smiled at him, joy shining in her eyes. 'We are agreed.'

As he opened the door he turned, and there was the slightest frown puckering his brow. 'Oh, just one more thing. I would prefer there to be no further questions concerning my life in England. Let the past be dead to us both. Can we agree on that?'

After the smallest fraction of time, Hester inclined her head. 'So be it. Let the past be dead.'

A small buggy was driving through Asheville, its butter cup-yellow seats somewhat marred from ineffective scrubbing. It was heading east for Charleston but, despite a journey of almost three hundred miles still ahead, the driver did not intend stopping longer than was necessary to change horses and grab a bite to eat. Carter Lois was in a hurry and intended driving all night if necessary for he had no intention of dallying any longer than was strictly necessary. This didn't feel safe country in any case for a man to be travelling all on his lonesome. Besides which, he'd never intended being gone more than a day or two, and it must be getting on for three weeks now. But then this whole journey had been unexpected from start to finish.

When he'd received that oddly worded message from old Joe, half Cherokee, half Spanish, who wandered the Blue Ridge mountains with more freedom than most people dared, Carter had been reluctant to act upon it. He would very much have liked to treat the whole thing as a hoax but curiosity in the end had won and he had headed west as quickly as he could harness the team.

'Rhapsody Creek. Meet me there. And don't come empty-handed,' was all it had said but Carter had recognised the writing. Hadn't he seen it on more IOUs than he cared to remember? He'd given a good deal of thought to that last sentence. What did it mean? In the end he had settled for money, a few clothes, and ample supplies of food. He'd been proved right for George Mackay had been close to starvation.

The two old friends had met on the wide empty drive that led up to the tall house with its white porticoed front and Carter had been at once shocked by the hollow-eyed, sallow-cheeked appearance of his old card-playing buddy. Later, after they had both eaten their fill and drunk from the whisky flask Carter had brought, George told his tale. And all the time he talked, he nibbled at his finger-ends, and plucked imagined bits of cotton from his clothes.

'Didn't die of yellow fever,' he said at last. He spoke in short, blunt sentences as if talking was difficult. Perhaps, after so much time spent alone, it was. Carter listened with careful patience, not wishing to risk flustering George. He'd always had an unpredictable temper. 'All my buddies were dying, going down like flies and I sure as hell wasn't letting that happen to me. So I upped and ran as far from that danged camp as I could get.'

'Where did you go?' Carter watched him with open curiosity. What did he want? Why had George sent for him and not for Hester?

'I fled to Cherokee.'

'*Cherokee*?'

'It's OK. The Indians were friendly. Joe was with them and he vouched for me. Anyway, it was the safest place to hide. I stayed in a shack by the Fontana Lake for a long while, don't know how long.' He bit on his fingernails for a moment. 'Always meant to go back, y'know. Wait till the worst of the fever is over, I thought. Not worth risking life and limb for. But then the longer it went on, the harder it was to make up my mind to it.'

'I can imagine.'

'War's a terrible thing.' The young lean face, prematurely lined, the lips cracked and flaking, looked oddly lost and forlorn. George licked his lips nervously. 'Never expected it to last this long. Thought it'd be an adventure, y'know?'

'I know,' said Carter, for once sympathetic. He too had thought the war would bring adventure and even a fortune, but the debt owed to him by the British was still unpaid and he had begun to wonder if it always would be.

'Tried to screw myself up to going back. Then I'd turn sick as a dog.' His eyes widened, eager for understanding. 'Not out of fear, you understand? I just—just hated the waste of life, the stink of rotting corpses, the smell of disease and the sight of grown men crying for a scrap of food. I'd had enough. Couldn't stomach any more.'

Carter said nothing. This was a part of war he'd managed to avoid.

George coughed and the sound echoed hollowly beneath the green canopy of Spanish moss under which the two men walked. He looked edgily about him, eyes round and bloodshot as if he hadn't slept in months, as probably he hadn't. Carter shivered, telling himself it was only because the sun never struck through the Spanish moss to reach this cold driveway.

'There was an Indian girl, Silver Wing. She stayed with me for a while, till she had to go back to her tribe and marry the man her father had picked out for her.'

'Did you love her?' Carter bluntly asked.

George shrugged. 'There could be no marriage between us. I came home, to Rhapsody Creek. It took days, but I made it in better shape than I would have without Silver Wing having fed me so well. Guessed the army wouldn't think to look for me here.'

'Surely you realised they'd take you for dead?'

'In saner moments I did.' The red-rimmed eyes looked furtively about him again, down the long drive that stretched ahead beneath the hanging live oaks, out over the reed-filled swamps and the pretty creek beyond to the overgrown fields which had once harvested cotton. 'But it's hard to stay sane all alone out here.'

Carter was none too happy with the atmosphere either. He decided he preferred the town, after all. Once he got a hold of Hester, he'd make her sell this place. They had reached the wide front steps and here the pale December sun warmed them, recharging Carter's optimism. 'Well, there's no need to stay any longer. You can come home with me in the buggy and I'll grill you the thickest steak you ever did see.'

But George was making him sit on the wide white stone slabs. 'No, no, hush, or else they'll hear you.'

'Who?' Carter jumped and looked about him. 'Indians? For God's sake, they won't scalp me, will they?' His eyes dilated in terror.

'Not Indians. Don't you listen to a darned word I say? The army. I deserted. When they catch me they'll string me up for sure.'

Carter was thunderstruck. 'Never. The war is over, George. You can come on home now.'

'I can't ever come on home.' George grasped Carter by the lapel of his fine coat and pulled him close, his foul-smelling breath making Carter reel. 'War over or no, they'll have me. Don't you see that? It's regulations. I gotta stay here. And you've gotta fetch me more food. I can't live on Indian rice forever, no more'n I can till these fields, else some Nosy Parker will sure as hell see someone is living here. You gotta keep your mouth shut and your eyes open, Carter. I must stay till it's well and truly blowed over.'

'When do you think that will be?'

'When the English leave. They started this war and it won't be over till they go. Then the army will leave Carolina and Georgia for good and I can come back to Charleston. Leastways on a visit. Got some problems in Charleston too, remember? Till then, have to stay holed up here. No one must know. You must keep silent.'

'You're mad. Someone is sure to find out.'

It was the wrong thing to say. A look of such maniacal fury flooded George's face that Carter almost fled in terror at sight of it. It was a pity in a way that he didn't for the next instant they were grappling together, George lunging, tearing Carter's hair, beating his face to a pulp, grasping his throat in a choking grip as Carter desperately tried to fend him off.

'OK. OK. Have it your way.' Carter was gasping for

breath, sure that he was about to choke to death, his vision glowing red with the beat of blood in his temples. 'I swear it. I won't tell a soul.' The deathlike grip slackened and Carter coughed up half his dinner in the grass.

When he felt human again, helped by a swig of the whisky, he dared to ask one more question. 'What about Hester?'

George met his gaze but said nothing for a long, long time. At length he spoke, his voice oddly quiet. 'You going to marry Hester?'

Carter smiled. 'If I can.' He didn't say, 'If she'll have me.' He rather took it for granted that in the end she would. 'As soon as some accounts are settled and I have the funds, we'll arrange the wedding.'

'We'll tell her then.'

'I beg your pardon?'

'We'll tell Hester after you and she are married.'

'But why? She's your sister, for God's sake. She thinks you're dead, and so does Aunt Kizzy. They've grieved for you. Buried you even.'

There was no expression in George's hot eyes. 'Good. Then I'm safe. Not a word to Hester till after you and she are wed. Don't want no feeling of misguided honour and duty messing up the issue. She thinks I'm some kind of dead hero, let her go on thinking it. Once the fuss has died down, we'll start getting this place back in order. They won't be watching me then.' George gazed about him, a look of possession so strong upon his face that Carter suddenly had grave doubts about selling Rhapsody Creek.

Living alone here in the wilderness these last two years had clearly turned poor old Georgy's mind, and who could wonder at it? Maybe it would be better for all concerned if he were left out here. Who wanted a mad brother-in-law about the place, anyway? He certainly gave Carter the creeps.

'I ought to be getting back.'

George looked sharply at him. 'You only just got here. Did you bring some cards?'

'Yes.'

A look very like relief crossed the old-young face. 'We'll have a game or two. Hope you brought more whisky; I'm sick of that Indian stuff. Come into the dining-room. It ain't got no food in it but it has a plenty big table. Want to talk some more to you about this plantation. About how I aim to make it pay. Need more money. We have to think of a way round that.'

'We?'

George ignored him. 'And about Hester. Maybe she needn't ever know about me.'

Carter stopped short and, grabbing hold of George, stared at him. 'Whyever do you say that?'

The once beautiful eyes narrowed, taking on a wily, cunning look. 'Things mightn't be too wonderful back home either. Gotta lot of debts, y'know.' He pushed the great doors shut, sliding home well-greased bolts. 'Happy here. Don't want Hester telling me what to do. Nor Aunt Kizzy organising me. Intend to find myself another squaw and settle down here. Like it. Peaceful.'

The two men walked together through the high arched hallway of the old mansion, the smaller, thinner man walking with a slight limp but with a surprising agility.

'There is one possible way of raising the necessary funds,' said Carter as George began to deal the cards with a dexterity born of long practice. The fingers barely paused as the voice rasped out a sharp query.

'How?'

'It's a long story, but it concerns a certain newcomer who has insinuated himself into Charleston, and into your sister's home,' said Carter, a grim smile playing about his moist lips. He'd always known it would pay to keep his ear close to the gossip-mongers. Now he believed he had just the lever he needed to settle things very nicely for all of them. All, that was, save for one Benjamin Blake, with whom he most definitely had a score to settle. From the moment of his arrival Hester had had eyes for no one else and Carter was not prepared to stomach that state of affairs for much longer. 'He happens also to be an Englishman.'

George tore his eyes from his hand of cards for one whole second, all his senses alert. 'Go on. I'm listening.'

And by the time the long night of card-playing was over they'd thrashed out a plan, of a sort, which had benefits for both of them. And as long as everything went smoothly, and there was no reason why it should not, they would both have more than enough funds to set them up for life.

George would have the plantation, and money to buy as many negroes, cotton and seed corn as he wanted, not to mention whisky and squaws, should he desire them, though Carter suspected most of George's share would soon disappear in his unabated passion for gambling. He would place a bet on two raindrops on a window if the stakes were high enough. As for Carter's share, well, he would have Hester, naturally. Plus a substantial sum to recompense him for the slights he had suffered at Blake's hand, not to mention the tardiness of the English to pay their debts.

So now, halfway home, he scarcely tasted the food set before him at a wayside eating-house. His mind was entirely taken up with his plan. As far as he could tell it was absolutely foolproof.

CHAPTER NINE

HESTER believed she must be the happiest person on earth. Aunt Kizzy had made a miraculous recovery the moment she heard the news. Caro and Beattie had hurried straight round, insisting on helping to plan the wedding, and Susy had never stopped cooking for two whole weeks, or so it seemed.

Christmas had passed by in a blur and now Hester stood beside Benjamin on the soft green turf of Aunt Kizzy's wide lawn, promising to love, honour and obey him for the rest of her life. Oh, and she would, with joy in her heart. She saw the years of happiness stretching ahead of them and she felt sure that her heart would burst, it was so full. Even now he was smiling down at her as he placed the ring upon her finger, his handsome face with that familiar crooked smile and the eyes crinkled against the sun, so that Hester couldn't be quite sure she knew what secrets they held. But she didn't care. Nothing mattered but the fact that Benjamin Blake was to be her husband. He would never leave her now, never sail away to the cold grey shores of England.

Not once since the revelations of that dreadful day had she thought of the reasons for their marriage. She put that firmly from her mind. It was enough that it was taking place. 'Let the past be dead,' he had said, and Hester was happy enough to let that be the case. Poor George's mistakes and follies could be safely set aside as part of that past, and need trouble them no more.

'A toast to the bride. Three cheers.'

Then everyone was whooping and laughing,

exchanging kisses and slaps on the back. The band struck up a merry tune and wine flowed, and overflowed. And now Benjamin was reaching down and kissing her softly on rosy lips. It was done. They were man and wife. Nothing could spoil that now.

She was certain that she recognised in his guarded glances an appreciation for her appearance. Her dress was the very finest that the three girls, stitching furiously together long into the night, had been able to fashion. Made of stiff cream silk with a tiny starred stripe woven into the fabric, the gown fell open at the front to reveal a matching skirt edged in pleated cream cord. And around the neck was a modest vandyke collar in sheer white lace, a matching flounce of which edged each elbow-length sleeve. And pinned into the tiny waist of the tightly laced bodice was a pink rose, one of the last of the season. The full skirt swirled out to reveal tiny satin pumps as Hester danced and danced in Benjamin's arms till her feet throbbed.

Perhaps it was her imagination, but she believed that he held her closer than was strictly necessary, surely proving that he liked her more than he had so far admitted. Or was he simply trying to give an impression to the assembled company of a normal, happily married bride and groom? She pushed the doubt from her mind. Benjamin Blake was not the kind of man to strike poses or keep up a pretence for the sake of neighbours. And when his chin came down to brush against her hair, making her heartbeat catapult, she was sure of it.

'Are you enjoying yourself, little one?' he murmured.

'Oh, yes.' She looked up, directly into his eyes, and she saw them widen, as if in some way she had startled him. As indeed she had. Benjamin had been unprepared for how completely her love would be revealed in that simple gesture, of how vulnerable it would make her appear, as if all the darkness had been wiped clean from her mind, leaving her face looking younger than ever and shining bright from some inner sun. But he should have known she would do nothing to mask the truth of her feelings. Didn't her ready temper show she was not one for vacillation? She took after the aunt in more ways than she realised.

And as he pulled her closer into his arms he found he liked the feel of her firm round waist within his grasp. He enjoyed the fresh scent of her silken skin and he could hardly tear his eyes away from watching the multitude of emotions which chased each other across those entrancing lips. Laughter, joy, quivering insecurity and sometimes pouting femininity.

The effect of all this upon his own equilibrium was unexpected and the first stirrings of desire for her surprised him. Hester Mackay was not perhaps a beauty in the accepted, classical sense of the word but she had a rare quality that held a promise of greater worth than superficial appearance. Marriage with her would be no penance but deep in his heart he held a regret. For a moment the sadness of this fact revealed itself, unknown to him, in the harshness of his expression as he experienced an impulsive longing to be able to offer her more of himself. If only he had met her before he had sealed up his heart in the black hole where it now resided. Fleetingly he wondered if her bright young charm might ever nudge it back into life, but at once abandoned the idea as too fanciful. He watched the smile slide from her face and readjusted his own expression to its more usual circumspect appearance. The responsibility for her happiness suddenly weighed heavily upon him. He hoped he would not live to regret taking it on.

'Are you bored with dancing? We can stop if you wish,' she said, rather hastily. But in her efforts to please him Hester saw the very opposite effect in his gesture as he at once pulled away from her to gaze fiercely down into her face.

'Do you always intend to do as I wish? Now that would be too boring for words,' he drawled.

She had said the wrong thing, not for the first time, but it was time she learned better. Hadn't he made it abundantly clear how he abhorred adoring females? Lifting her chin higher, she replaced his hands upon her waist.

'If I do it will be a new experience; Aunt Kizzy says I'm as selfish as a cat.'

And the frozen moment which might well have ruined the entire day melted into open laughter so that Hester too was giggling, clapping her hand to her mouth in agony.

'Oh, you mustn't make me laugh. Don't, it is most unbecoming and in the very worst of manners.'

But he took no notice of her protests, whirling her into the hectic steps of the dance all the faster. 'Why should we not laugh, Hester? This is our wedding day and we cannot always be bound by fashion.' His eyes sparkled down at her, a dangerous mischief in their shadowed depths. 'Perhaps this night I will bring you further joy. If we cannot laugh together it would be a sorry parody of a marriage, would it not?'

She was gasping, her hand flying to her burning cheek. What was he saying? It was most improper. How on earth was she to reply to such teasing? But it was night now, and soon they would be alone. What then?

'Hester, are you quite well?' called out Aunt Kizzy from a gold-encrusted sofa where she and several other matrons were viewing the proceedings. 'You look rather tired and a touch feverish.'

Hester gladly called a halt to catch her breath. 'Nonsense, Aunt, I am perfectly well.'

Kristina beckoned Hester over with a single finger so

that she could whisper in her niece's ear, 'It is almost midnight. Our guests will be wishing to depart but they cannot do so until you and your new husband have retired. I'm not well versed in such matters, but do you think—that is, I wondered if perhaps. . .?' Now it was Aunt Kizzy's turn to take on a feverish glow, but Benjamin saved her blushes.

'I was only saying as much to my wife just now. Pray excuse us, for it has been a long, tiring day. I am sure she is ready for a rest.'

But if they thought they would escape so easily they were mistaken. Amid much teasing and jocularity, and the throwing of rose petals and tossing of stockings, the bride and groom were finally left in peace, seated side by side in the huge canopied double bed.

Benjamin lay back upon the soft downy pillows, his hands clasped behind his head, and gave a soft chuckle. 'You look as if you are waiting for Armageddon.'

In truth Hester felt rather as if she were. She sat stiff and cold and wished herself anywhere but in this uncompromising, thoroughly embarrassing situation. What on earth had possessed her to imagine it might be fun? What was one supposed to do to please a husband? She wished she had had someone to ask. . .to talk to. . . But there was no one. Certainly Caro and Beattie had filled in some of the gaps but their own mother had prepared them with little better care than dear, ignorant Aunt Kizzy, so the whole procedure was still largely shrouded in mystery. It all sounded dreadfully uncomfortable.

But she was all too aware of the vibrancy of this male presence in her bed. She could feel the pressure of his warm thigh stretched out alongside her. It filled her with unease and a strange, unwilling excitement. Was that quite normal?

'Won't you lie down, Hester? I cannot spend the entire night viewing your back, delightful though it is.'

Very carefully, first making sure that her new night-gown was well buttoned up to the chin and neatly spread right down to her bare feet, she lay back upon the cold, clean sheet and placed her head alongside Benjamin's. She dared not turn to look at him, but she could feel his gaze riveted upon her. Very firmly she pulled the top sheet up to her chin. Never, in all her life, had Hester Mackay been more scared. The feeling was new to her and though a part of her resented the fact another, less disciplined part wondered if it might be a prelude to an exciting discovery. Yet how could it be, for hadn't she learned her lesson? Beyond everything she must remember not to show Benjamin how she truly felt. She must never suffocate him with obsessive love as that other girl, Sarah, had done so long ago. It was essential that, whatever happened this night, she keep her cool dignity intact.

'I suppose we had better begin with a kiss,' he sardonically remarked and Hester felt herself shiver right down to her toes. Did that mean he wanted to kiss her, or merely wished to perform his duty? She remembered an earlier, stolen kiss and grew warm with anticipated pleasure.

But when his lips touched hers there was nothing of that earlier excitement present in it at all. His lips were cool and dry, pressing hers with a touch too light for passion, and too strong to arouse any erotic response. She was disappointed. Or was it perhaps her fault? She felt so ignorant, and Benjamin did not seem inclined to help her.

'Not exactly earth-shattering, was it?' he drily asked when it was finished and Hester swallowed her misery, clutching all the tighter to the sheet. She could feel the heat of his body beside her, and above the hem of the sheet she could see the bareness of powerful shoulders. Was he wearing anything beneath, she wondered? Oh, my. She tried to edge herself further along the bed away from him.

'Do stop fidgeting, Hester. How can we make love if you will not keep still?'

She could feel a ball of tears growing in her throat. Was this then what all the fuss was about? Was this where love got you? A cold exchange of kisses? It all seemed horribly clinical. Hester waited with bated breath to see what would happen next, how this necessary act of marriage might be accomplished.

To her complete astonishment, Benjamin propped himself on one elbow and, taking the sheet in his hand, peeled it from her grasp and flung it from the bed. Hester's heart stopped dead in the middle of a beat. She had never seen a naked man, not in the warm, living flesh, and she was hard put to know where she should look. Perversely her eyes refused to obey orders for modesty, wanting only to devour every lean, tanned line of him as he lay beside her so beautiful, so strong, and richly masculine in every toned muscle.

'Who chose this nightgown?' he asked, his icy blue eyes scanning the starched figure, so stiffly aligned that she might well have been waiting for her funeral pyre.

Hot brown eyes turned to meet his, a hint of outrage in them. 'I made it myself. It is the very best lawn, edged with handmade lace. Don't you like it?' She longed for him to replace the sheet, sure he must see that she was trembling.

And unexpectedly Benjamin chuckled, a deep throaty sound that vibrated through her with a resonance that thrilled. 'You look like a delightful school-girl dressed in her mother's gown. It is at least six sizes too large for you.'

Hester flushed. She'd been well aware of that fact, but Caro had assured her that a voluminous nightdress would be necessary, in the fullness of time, so best to make it a useful size from the outset. Thankfully Hester did not explain this far-thinking thrift to Benjamin.

'And, since this is your wedding night,' said Benjamin with soft emphasis, 'quite unnecessary. Why don't you take it off?'

Rebellion flared. 'What on earth are you talking about? It is December, I shall freeze to death.'

That soft-throated chuckle again, followed by the light caress of his hand smoothing over her cheek, down one shoulder and coming to rest upon her stomach, where it interfered very seriously with her breathing. 'I very much doubt it. Shall I help you?'

To Hester's entire shock and utter horror his hand went to the hem of her gown and began to slide it up her legs. In pure panic she slapped his hand away. 'What are you doing? Leave me alone.'

Benjamin shrugged, but ceased the action. 'Very well. Take it off yourself. I shall turn away if it will spare your maidenly blushes but that nightdress is not sharing our bed this night, of that you can be quite certain.' He pulled himself from the bed with the agility of an athlete, and Hester watched, mesmerised, as he strode away from her across the bedroom to gaze through the window out into the dark night. His legs were long and straight, finishing in tight round buttocks. And above the tapered waist flared a muscular back and wide powerful shoulders. Taking in every detail of his perfect body, Hester felt an unaccustomed burning deep down in her stomach. 'Are you done?' he asked, still with his back towards her.

'No, no. Wait.' Hester was out of bed in a flash. She quickly removed the offending nightgown and, grabbing the sheet, wound it around herself in its place. In less than a second she was back on the bed, sitting up tight and straight like a Buddha waiting patiently for deliverance. 'You can turn round now.' She was quite unprepared for his reaction. He took one long look at her then burst out laughing. It had a hard, brittle sound to it and for some reason she felt quite unable to respond in kind.

'For God's sake, that's even worse. I thought we had an agreement. Really, Hester, put aside this nonsense and start to behave like a real wife.' Benjamin laughed again, only too aware that he hurt her but unable to avoid intuitively hardening his own carefully protected resources.

But to Hester, in her current vulnerable state of highly wrought nervous energy, it was an insult too great to endure. She glared at him, fury cascading over her like a hot summer tide. 'What would you have me do? How am I to *know* what to do? How many times do you think that I have been wed, Mr Benjamin Oh-So-Clever Blake?' She was on her feet upon the bed, almost shouting in her misery and disappointment, desperately fighting back the tears which spilled traitorously over her trembling lids and slid down hot, flushed cheeks. She had never felt so humiliated in her life before and it expressed itself as hot molton fury. 'What is it exactly that you *want*?' she cried.

'I want you to behave like a woman,' he growled, eyes half closed as he watched her slender body writhing with insidious anger beneath the thin sheet. It had slipped from one shoulder somewhat and he could see the tantalising curve of rounded breast. There was a pounding in his head, in his loins that he could not entirely control. 'And not a stiff, pathetic child. You are mine, Hester Mackay. Never forget it.' He reached for her but she jumped aside, neatly evading his grasp.

'But you told me yourself that you had no wish for an adoring wife.'

'I said obsessive.' He moved closer to the bed, his lips tightening involuntarily as he saw her hips sway with impish perversity. If she was deliberately taunting him, she was succeeding very well.

'And what, pray, is the difference?'

'You know damn well. Come down from there, Hester.'

Again she evaded one lean hand as it flicked out to grasp a corner of the trailing sheet. 'Love is love. Seems to me it is as simple as that.' And as complicated, her mind echoed the thought. 'But I do assure you, Benjamin Blake, husband mine, that you are in no danger from me. I'll stand by our arrangement. I'll be your wife, but love. . .?' She threw back her head and made herself laugh. It was all an act but he must not know that. Hester gambled on the fact that if he felt himself safe from the threat of her developing love he would at least be friends with her again. 'You can forget it.'

But her performance was carrying her along on a tide of its own, and she no longer knew what she did, nor why she did it. She was acting now by pure instinct, anger and frustrated emotions scorching through her body, trying to banish the coldness he had printed there with his touch. 'That is altogether a different matter. You cannot *buy* love,' she taunted. 'It has to be given to you as a precious gift, and you'll not get such an offering from me, Benjamin Blake, while you treat me with such arrogant callousness.' That would show him. She wanted to hurt and humiliate him as he, in a different way, had hurt and humiliated her by turning her precious wedding night into a cold, heartless process, which she could not tolerate.

'This is what you *bought*,' she cried, and, tearing off the sheet, she stood before him pink and naked. The tears were rolling unchecked down her cheeks now and dripping in cold plops on to her uptilted breasts.

She saw how his eyes devoured her and for one fragment of a second knew the awesomeness of power over him. Then one arm snaked out and he had her by the waist, pulling her towards him.

'Damn you, Hester. Damn your eyes, woman.' Then she was somehow beneath him on the bed and his mouth was on hers, taking it with a fierceness that shot through her with molten excitement. And his hands were where hands had never been before, and she did not care. It did not even occur to her now to wonder what she should do, or how she should behave. She found that she knew already by some mysterious form of magic, or that her body must have learned the art in some previous life. And, forgetting her vow of dignity and discovering it to be neither uncomfortable nor clinical, she gave herself to him with an abandoned wantonness that astonished and thrilled her. Even that first piercing pain was a joy to cherish. She became a part of him, a part of the rhythm of the earth and when some of the passion was assuaged she felt herself wrapped in a sweet tenderness, a lingering exchange of sensation that reached right into the heart of her. Could it be that Benjamin wanted, through the very act they had enjoyed together, to protect her against the harsh realities of the world? Certainly there was no coldness in him now. He cradled her in his arms and wiped the dampness of tears from her cheeks.

After she had fallen asleep, Benjamin lay for a long time watching that face, so childlike in repose. Yet the woman he had just taken had had not a touch of the child in her. She had given herself to him delightfully, unselfishly, excitingly and the results, as far as he was concerned, were shattering.

She was not the first woman he had enjoyed. But in the darkness of that first night, as he honestly examined his own reactions, he began to wonder if perhaps she might be the last. For what other woman could equal the magic he had experienced this night? She must surely be unique for him to have responded with such joy and satisfaction. And as sleep finally dragged down his eyelids he muttered to himself, even in half-sleep,

'But do not mistake this feeling for love, Benjamin, old boy. You are still immune to all that. Just count your blessings without too many questions asked. There's no law says you can't enjoy your own wife.'

In the morning Hester was surprised to find he was still there, stretched out beside her, his face boyish in the smoothness of sleep and his fingers still interlaced with hers. She dared not move for she wanted him to stay like that for a long time so that she could look her fill of him, feast her eyes on her beloved, but with a jolt she found the blue eyes were open, and smiling. With a little hiccup of relief she very daringly kissed him on the nose. His deep laugh was a delight.

'You are insatiable, Mrs Blake.'

Hester pouted. 'What does that mean?'

'Come here, I will show you.' And he did, every bit as deliciously as he had done the previous night. Hester was certain her heart would explode with happiness.

'About last night,' Benjamin was saying, again in his favourite position, propped on one elbow so that he could gaze down upon her.

'What about last night?' She dared hardly think of it without blushing. Had that wanton hussy been her, Hester Mackay? The experience had been shattering. Not even Caro could have any conception of how love really was. Nor could it be explained to her.

'My behaviour at the outset was heartless and cruel. I was unwilling to allow myself to relax so deliberately hurt you.' He seemed to hesitate. 'I'm not sure that I can explain, Hester.'

Quickly she put her hand to his mouth. 'You don't have to, Benjamin, it doesn't matter. It was difficult for both of us, in the circumstances. Let us forget it.'

He took her hand away and absent-mindedly caressed it with the ball of one thumb. 'I insisted we forget the past, but I suppose I am still haunted by it.'

'By Sarah?' she softly asked, and he jerked an eyebrow by way of answer.

'We are wed now, Hester, man and wife. And, though it might simply be an arrangement which suits us both in the special circumstances, yet I feel I owe it to you to be more open and honest. A husband and wife should have no secrets from each other. Yet it is difficult to. . .' When she wisely made no comment he quietly continued, and there was a bitter sadness in his eyes that cooled them to shards of ice. 'You must realise that there never can be love as such between us, Hester. All this. . .' He waved a hand to indicate their two partly entwined bodies, the rumpled sheet. 'It is a pleasant diversion between a man and a woman and you delighted me even more than I expected.'

Her flush of pleasure was cooled by the sharp pang of disappointment. Was that all she would ever be to him? A pleasant diversion?

'The truth of the matter is, I am incapable of love. My heart is dead, cold, finished, all my emotion used up. Can you understand that?' The bleak, harsh words cut through her, scarring her with real pain.

'I—I'm not sure.' And then more quietly, 'Because of Sarah? What happened to her? Can you tell me that, Benjamin?'

The silence which followed her question was so intense, she was sure she could hear their twin heartbeats. And she had plenty of time to regret her question as she saw the tightening of Benjamin's jaw, the flare of nostrils and the narrowing of eyes to slits of pain, or fury, she wasn't sure which.

'She died.'

Two words. No more. But enough to change her life, had she but known it. Shock ricocheted through her and she wanted to turn her face away, to avoid seeing the raw pain in his face. He must have loved Sarah after all, yet for some reason refused to acknowledge it. She wanted him to turn to her for comfort yet knew he would not. Benjamin Blake was not the kind of man who could gain his strength from others; he kept it within him, an inner reservoir which he would drain and refill in his own way. She was not permitted to offer even sympathy.

'However much I might have suffered, Stefan has suffered more. I robbed him of what was rightfully his and no matter how hard I try I can never make that up to him.' And, without further explanation, Benjamin was flinging himself from the bed, striding across the floor, picking up his clothes as he went. 'Enough of this. One night married and we have broken our pledge. Sarah is dead. George is dead. Let that be an end of both issues.'

Hester was sitting up in bed, golden-brown hair tumbling about her shoulders and spilling on to the firm curves of her young breasts. When Benjamin turned to look at her he very nearly returned to the warmth of her embrace, but something—guilt perhaps—stopped him.

'I am going out,' he said, his tone clipped and cold.

It was on the tip of her tongue to ask where he went, to say simply, 'I shall come with you.' But she knew she could not. That also would break the rules by which this marriage had been agreed. She must not follow him, or question him, or put any hold upon him, as the poor dead Sarah had done. However painful it might prove, she must let him go his own way. And so she said nothing. Merely stared at him, her eyes as expressionless as she could make them as she tugged up the sheet to cover her breasts.

Benjamin saw the gesture and almost sneered. 'It's all right. I'll leave you in peace now.' And he strode from the room, carrying his clothes with him, deaf to her cry of protest. Yet he hated himself. He was giving her no chance and he knew it. She had asked him last night what he wanted of her. He wished he knew. If he did not want Hester Mackay's love, why had he been so disappointed that she had said nothing in response to his revelation just now? What had he wanted from her? That she should leap from that damn winding sheet and call to the heavens that the past didn't matter, that she wanted only him and would follow him to the ends of the earth if need be? That was the very thing he had told her not to do.

It didn't make sense. For, though he did not want the responsibility of trying to make her happy he had taken it on. Though he said he wanted to bury the past yet he allowed it to haunt him. And though he declared he did not want her love he ached for it. It was a weakness in him that he must make every effort to eradicate. For, even as he had declared he was being open and honest with her, he had held back the most important, the most dangerous fact of all.

When Carter Lois heard the wedding had taken place he knew a desolation and anger so complete it almost finished him. Without Hester, what was the point of working so hard in the store? Without Hester, how could he face the rest of his life?

And why had he lost her? She had been stolen from him by that sour-faced Englishman. A smile now curled the thick lips, though the pale eyes remained as cool and impassive as ever. He had learned enough from Benjamin's own man to cause considerable damage. But this turn of events might mean a slight adjustment to his plans, for now he wanted more than Blake's money. Simple blackmail was not enough. He needed rid of him for good and all. Surely not impossible in the circumstances. For his own reasons, Blake's bosun, Stefan, had suggested he reduce Blake to penury or dispatch him to the mountains and the Indians. But he could play the game from both sides, could he not?

Wasn't he an expert on games of chance? There were plenty of British still in town, though some left every day, and they owed him a favour. There was no time to be lost. He would put this new plan into action first thing in the morning.

CHAPTER TEN

As LUCK would have it, Carter found Benjamin with little difficulty down by the quay at early light. He was superintending the loading of goods on to his ship and Carter could not resist a feeling of envy as he watched the more powerful man swing a rope to one of his crew with an ease born of long practice and supreme fitness.

Carter came up behind him. 'Might I have a word with you?' He did not intend to waste time. The sooner the position was made clear between them, the better.

Benjamin swivelled round in surprise. 'Carter. A word, you say?'

The flat round face remained impassive. 'If you can spare a moment from your chores.'

Benjamin gave a wry smile. 'I would not dream of denying my curiosity the pleasure. Time for a break anyway.'

When a jug of small beer had been placed before them in the bar of the local tavern, Benjamin turned to his one-time rival. 'Well? What is it? I'm sure you have no more wish to prolong this interview than I have. If it has anything at all to do with Hester, I'll warn you to take care. She is my responsibility now, for good or ill, and I'd recommend you bear that in mind.'

'It is not about Hester,' said Carter with a insinuating quietness.

Benjamin raised dark brows. He was surprised and saw no reason not to show it. 'Indeed?'

'It is about you.' The brows crashed down in their familiar way, denting even Carter's stuffed-up courage. Determinedly he ploughed on. 'I know a good deal more about you, Benjamin Blake, than you realise. I know, for instance, that you come from Liverpool.'

'I have made no secret of the fact.' The frost in Benjamin's voice almost crackled but Carter did not heed its warning.

'I know too that you have been in prison.' Carter met his gaze directly now and there was triumph in his own eyes. 'And I know why. It was in connection with the death of a young girl. You were formally charged with her murder but apparently escaped before sentence could be carried out.'

Benjamin was breathing heavily through dilated nostrils, only his massive will-power keeping his itchy fingers off the other man's throat. 'Since you clearly have picked up this tale from someone, why are you bothering me with it?' And then more sharply, 'Presumably you learned it from one of my men?'

And now Carter pushed back the thick lips into a parody of a smile. 'Didn't you know you had a traitor in your camp? It pays to trust no one these days.'

'I don't.'

'I found it immensely interesting. I'm sure the British authorities would too. Reckon mebbe some person ought to tell them.' The air was heavy with meaning.

'You, for instance?' Again that detestable smile and Benjamin abruptly moved closer but had to be content with seeing Carter flinch. He might want to knock him from his supercilious perch and grind him to a pulp but that would solve nothing, might even be counterproductive. 'Have you spoken with them already?'

Carter slowly shook his head. 'I wanted a quiet word with you first. And don't say they wouldn't be interested just because you're thousands of miles from home. I reckon I could make sure you were on the next shipload of returning wounded and I doubt we'd have the pleasure of your company hereabouts ever again.'

148

'What is it you want?' There seemed little point in quibbling.

The smile faded and the pale eyes glittered. 'Simple. The matter can be settled to both our satisfaction for a suitably agreed sum. After all, you've made plenty of profit out of our country, so why not? And I surely deserve some compensation for the loss of my girl.'

'Blackmail?'

Carter clicked his tongue. 'Nasty word. Dare say you could call it that. But then what good is Hester to you without freedom? It would be pretty galling to dream of your delectable wife while you were in some dank cell back home in England waiting for a hangman's noose.'

'How much?' Benjamin almost spat out the words. The last thing he wanted was to give in to this worm, but it was less troublesome that way, in the long run. Carter Lois had become a danger to his carefully contrived future. When the sum was named it made even Benjamin pale. 'How much money do you imagine I have?'

'Enough for both of us, I reckon.' And George too, if you did but know it, Carter thought.

'I'll do what I can, but it will be nowhere near the sum you mention. And you must give me time.'

'Reckon you'd best think again 'bout that. Don't want any mishaps, do we? Sell your ships if need be. What good would they be to you?'

'They make me my living, you fool.' Benjamin drained his glass. 'Give me a couple of days and I'll meet your demands.'

Carter smiled. Despite the substantial size of the sum mentioned he had much more in mind. Nothing less than the demise of Benjamin Blake would satisfy his injured pride now. Then, with very little difficulty and an excess of sympathy to the bereaved widow, he could have Hester, and Blake's entire fortune all to himself. Perfect. And without even staining his own hands. But just as Carter was sinking back against the bench with a deep sigh of satisfaction he found his windpipe squeezed in an iron grip.

'Breathe one word of this to anyone and you'll regret the day you were born, Carter Lois, make no mistake about it. Nor must Hester hear of it. Do we understand each other?' He shook him the way a dog would a rat, and the round head bobbled up and down. 'Do we?'

'Aye.' It was no more than the faintest croak but it was enough.

'I'll have the money by Monday. Meet me here, same time.' Flinging the pale remnant of Carter Lois away from him, Benjamin left the tavern, fury in every pounding stride. He did not trust the man an inch but at least he had bought himself some time.

But, when Carter's shivering abated, his smile widened. It had proved much easier than he'd expected. Now all he had to do was to sit back and wait for his plans to come to fruition, and remember to brush out his black suit first thing in the morning. He must look his best when he went a-calling on Hester.

Benjamin had almost reached his ship when they fell upon him. He never saw where they came from, nor how many there were. One moment he was striding along in the morning sunshine, hot fury pounding his heart, and the next he was pinned to the ground, his mouth stuffed with coarse rags. Blackness descended in the shape of a sack yanked down over his head. He struggled, but not even his awesome strength could fight off three men. They trussed him up so tightly that breathing was the only exercise left he could take, and that with difficulty. They carried him for some distance, and his last recollection before a more permanent blackness took over was of falling. And, if the smell of salt and tar was anything to go by, into a very deep ship's hold.

* * *

When Benjamin did not return at the expected hour, Hester covered her deep disappointment by keeping busy. Less than twenty-four hours married and already he was tired of her. She believed he had gone down to the harbour early that morning but knew she dared not follow to check. And so she took supper with Aunt Kizzy just as if she had never been married yesterday on the green lawn, as if last night had never taken place. What else could she do?

She sent Aunt Kizzy to bed at the usual time and sat on upon the piazza, remembering the happy times they had spent together here as if they had taken place years ago instead of merely days. What had gone wrong so suddenly and so unexpectedly? She watched and waited, her heart aching but filled with the hope that at any moment he might appear. Finally, at close on midnight, she made her weary way upstairs to the empty bridal chamber so lovingly prepared just a short while ago, hope quite gone.

But she did not undress. She sat on the edge of the bed, thinking, and one thought kept returning over and over.

She could go and look for him. Perhaps he had had an accident. Slipped on the rocks, fallen into the sea. Why should she assume that he had deserted her? Wasting no more than a moment to tie her hair up in a scarf, and slip on her outdoor shoes, Hester was running down the dark street towards the waterfront.

Where else to begin her search but on his ships?

Systematically, and somewhat recklessly, Hester searched every one of his ships in dock. They were quite empty. She called and called Benjamin's name as she struggled to open holds and trapdoors, tripping constantly over coils of wet rope and torn nets. She had never realised how many nooks and crannies were on a ship until faced with the prospect of searching them. At length she collapsed on to a coil of heavy rope, dejection seeping through her.

She had so hoped to make their relationship grow; now she felt raw and vulnerable, as if nothing in the world were certain any more, for she was not even to be allowed the opportunity. Was he even now in some downtown bar, laughing at the thought of his bride alone at home? She shivered. Surely not. The Benjamin Blake she had fallen in love with and readily married could never be so heartless, could he?

The pink of dawn was streaking the sky as she walked along the harbour, slowing her pace from time to time to look back at the ships towering out of the morning mists. Before her were the British ships that Benjamin had shown her just a week or two ago, and for a moment she was lost in nostalgic reminiscence.

She stopped and spoke to the vast emptiness, to the panorama of ship and sail, sea and wind, feeling utterly alone in the world. 'He told me how they filled their holds with the wounded, packed as tightly as cotton bales, and I was so afraid he would return on one, one day. And then we married and I thought I was safe, but now. . .' She stopped, a prickling sensation creeping up the nape of her neck. Surely he could not be on a British warship? Had the British discovered that Benjamin had carried gunpowder on board his ship that day Statia was closed? She was already halfway up the gangplank, her mind dazed but resolute.

But almost at once she scented danger. Above her on the bridge she saw movement and was forced to melt back into a doorway out of sight. Two figures, laughing, exchanging news, as the morning watch took over from the night. They seemed to talk forever, but then one gave a cheery goodnight and went below and the dark outline of the single figure left above appeared to light himself a cigar, or pipe, before starting his pacing. Hester realised she must take care not to alert

him, though she doubted the watch would be too
efficient, since the British opinion of the American
fighting forces was so low.

On cat's feet she searched every cabin, some of them
occupied with sleeping sailors, and she was wary to
make no noise or risk waking them. She had no wish
to be caught prying on a British warship. Her heart
beat like a drum and she wondered if she would have
the courage to continue with her search and whether it
were even sensible.

Again she had to hide as the watch ambled into view
along the deck, his musket slung over his shoulder. He
sat down on the lid of a hold and Hester stifled a sigh.
She had meant to search there next.

It was then that she heard the sound. It came, she
was almost certain, from that very hold upon which the
young sailor sat. Did he hear it and give a soft laugh or
was he concentrating upon cleaning out his pipe and
packing it with fresh tobacco? Hester gave a little sigh
of exasperation. It would be light soon and her chance
gone.

She heard the sound again and her heart froze in her
breast. If they had caught Benjamin they would surely
hang him. She must do something. She looked desperately about her, and her fingers closed on a spar of
wood which came loose in her hand. She knew now
what she had to do.

Holding her breath tight in her chest, she crept
around the back of the young man, still engrossed with
his pipe, and, closing her eyes, lifted and swung the
batten right down on top of his unsuspecting head.
Perhaps her courage failed her at that last precious
second for the sailor gave out a great bellow but did
not drop obligingly at her feet. Then she was being
thrust aside as another figure entered the fray, flinging
a solid fist in the surprised face of the watch and as the

young man sprawled on the deck Hester slapped her hand to her mouth to stop herself from crying out.

'Be calm. I am Stefan, Benjamin's bosun. I saw you come aboard and followed you.'

'Where is he, do you know?' Hester grasped at his arms in her anxiety.

Had it been light enough, she might have seen the flush of guilt suffuse his cheeks. Stefan's one idea had been revenge. Sarah would be alive now were it not for Benjamin Blake and he had readily led Carter Lois to believe the worst of the man he held responsible for her death. Blake could have curbed that silly obsession of hers if he'd tried, but no, he'd always made a fuss of her. Being kind, he called it. Stefan knew different. Blake just loved having a woman worship him. And here was another poor fool. She'd soon learn the man had a heart as black and cold as granite. Running after him wouldn't help.

'You must go home,' he told her. 'No good will come of this. If the British catch us they will hang us by the yard arm. Come.' He started to pull her away but Hester resisted.

'I cannot. I feel certain he is here, in this hold. Let me get to him before he suffocates or is taken from me forever.' She was struggling fiercely with Stefan, all thought of dignity quite gone. 'I must find him, no matter what it costs me. Don't you see? I love him so. Can you not understand that, Stefan?' And she looked up into his face with eyes brimming with tears.

There was a long silence and Hester was surprised to see matching tears on the young man's cheeks. At once she was filled with contrition. 'Oh, my. I forgot. Of course, you loved Sarah. Benjamin told me. I'm so sorry.'

Stefan stared at her as if she were mad. 'Benjamin told you about Sarah? And me?'

'Only a little, Stefan. I wouldn't want you to think I

was prying. I think Benjamin is riddled with guilt that because Sarah loved him and not you he feels he deprived you of her love. But some things are beyond our control. I'm sure you realise that.' And then more poignantly, 'How simple life would be if we could make those we are close to return our love. But we can only offer ourselves and if we are refused we must learn to live with that fact.' Her small face was grim as she began to listen to her own advice.

Stefan stared at her, stunned. He'd grown to hate his one-time friend, despite the fact they had been together since boyhood when they'd met in Holland on board a schooner. He'd wanted Benjamin to die here in this God-forsaken land, preferably in an alligator-infested swamp or piece by piece at the hands of Indians. Nothing but the best for Blake. Stefan had regretted not taking the opportunity of disposing of the man himself while they were away following Carter Lois for those two weeks. He'd almost brought himself to the point of trying when they'd got so hopelessly lost in this strange country, they'd had to give all their attention to finding their way home again without getting scalped or starving to death. A man could lose himself forever out there if he were not careful. Besides, if he were truthful, it was less easy to kill a friend, even one you held a grudge against, than he had realised.

But Sarah had died. And though Benjamin had not struck the blow himself Stefan had always believed it to be murder and that Blake had escaped true justice. Now this slip of a girl was causing him to question himself, to feel guilt even for having misled Carter Lois. Why should that be? Yet he'd not expected Lois to have Blake shipped back to England. That was the last thing he wanted when he himself returned, to have the man he hated back there as a constant thorn in his flesh. He would get his old friend out of this mess and trust Lois to find a more efficient way of dealing with him. Then he would return home. He'd had enough of this land. It was too big and too dangerous.

Hester was already struggling with the hold door and, starting to sweat with fear that another watch might come, Stefan assisted, wishing fervently he'd put his own views on a stronger basis to Lois. Benjamin Blake had the devil's own luck.

Together they pulled back the door, the pale light of morning spreading its fingers into the depths of the dank hole. Hester knelt down on the edge, her eyes screwed up to penetrate the shadowy corners where the light did not quite reach, her hand to her nose to keep out the overpowering stench of rotting fish and sweet decay. A rat scuttered across the floor and she shuddered. And then she saw him, the outline of his beloved body huddled in a corner.

Stefan had seen too, and in an instant had leaped down into the hold and was wrestling with the knots on the wet rope that bound his one-time friend and master.

And later, as Benjamin climbed out of that evil hole, blinking in the unaccustomed light, without a thought for her dignity or a care for the reserve which was supposed to be an essential part of their marriage, Hester flung herself into his arms.

'Oh, Benjamin, I was so frightened. Where did you go? What happened?'

He made not a sound for a moment as he held her close, then, putting her from him, he gave her a little push, his eyes riveted on Stefan as he did so. 'Not now, Hester. Time for explanations later. We must get out of here.'

The three of them fled on feet as light as they were swift. Once safely away from the British warship, Benjamin and Stefan held a rapid and heated conversation to which Hester was not privy, much to her irritation. Stefan then kissed her hand most gallantly and bade her goodbye.

'I am glad that I met you, Mistress Blake. Your kindness and bravery have taught me much. I wish I could feel as generous as you towards others, but I cannot, even though it would be Christian charity to do so. Therefore I am returning home. I wish you well.' And on these mysterious words he strode away along the waterfront.

'Where is he going?'

'Back to England. He belongs there.'

'And you?' She held her breath for his response and it came in the form of a wintry smile.

'For better or worse, I belong here.'

'Will you tell me what is going on? Why did the British throw you into that hold? It doesn't make sense.'

'It was not the British who captured me. I believe it was your friend, Carter Lois, or at least his henchmen.'

Hester gasped. 'What can you be saying? It surely must have been the British because of your attempt at treason?'

Benjamin looked puzzled for a moment. 'Treason?'

Hester stamped her foot. 'Do not play games with me, sir. You told Caro of the gunpowder on board your ship that day, and how it was for the American forces.'

'How very astute of her. In point of fact I did not, not in so many words.' To Hester's complete astonishment and utter fury he began to laugh, here on the waterfront when she had just saved him from the jaws of death. And when he saw her fury he laughed all the more.

'I am sorry, Hester. Of course, you are right; strictly speaking it was treason and it was foolish of me to so enjoy telling my tales to your gullible friend that I confided a little too much of the truth. But the fact is that it was Stefan who stowed the gunpowder on board my ship, in my ignorance. Unfortunately for him he chose the very occasion Admiral Rodney selected as the one to clear and close Statia's harbour and so his little scheme failed.'

'Scheme for what? Why should Stefan do such a thing?' Hester asked, disbelieving.

A bitter smile. 'He bears a long-held grudge against me.'

'Because Sarah loved you and not him?' Hester was appalled. Would a man do such a thing merely for love?

'Something of the sort. He was clearly happy to see me hanged as a traitor though could not bring himself to end my life himself.' Taking Hester's arm, he began to walk her away from the ship. 'Now is not the time to discuss this. But I will admit, Hester, that there was a moment in that disgusting hold when I thought he had told the authorities that I'd run gunpowder for the Americans, and it was they who had locked me up, as you evidently did. But in our heated exchange of words just now he assured me that he did not. He'd considered it, but rejected it as too dangerous without proof.' Benjamin gave a harsh laugh that chilled her. 'And of course he was too concerned for his own skin in the end.'

Hester was almost running to keep up with him, so forcefully was he propelling her down the street. 'But you are obviously still concerned else why do we run?'

He stopped then, jerking her to a halt. But as she looked up into his face she saw the anger melt into sympathy and understanding for her fear, and, tilting her chin with one finger, he kissed her softly on the lips.

'I am not afraid of being hanged for treason or anything so atrocious for several very good reasons. It happened only the once, I was innocent, and dumped the offending matter at sea the moment I knew of it, leaving no proof with which to charge me. Besides which, if the British charged everyone who was thought to have played both sides of the field in this war, they would have no suppliers left. They do not know of my involvement, nor will they. And thanks to Rodney's blundering the British government is far too occupied facing unprecedented writs for compensation from the merchants robbed of their livelihoods. Closing the free port of Statia has cost them a pretty fortune and will go down in history as a mighty over-reaction from a jealous motherland wanting to have things all her own way. Forget it, Hester. There are more important matters to attend to.' And again he was propelling her along the road.

'What things?' She was bemused.

'We must pack.'

'Pack?'

'We must be gone from here within the hour. In these somewhat delicate circumstances I think it best if we keep out of Charleston for a while, at least until the British have all gone home.' If Carter and Stefan had really been in league over his abduction, Benjamin guessed they might indeed have stirred the British to look for him. He did not trust them one iota. 'Just in case your friend Carter has any more nasty surprises.'

'There you go blaming Carter again. You have absolutely no proof. I refuse to believe he would actively wish you injury just because of me.' Hester felt her anger rising once again as she staunchly defended her old friend.

They had reached the door of her home and, grasping her firmly by the shoulders, he swung her round to face him. 'Do you trust me, Hester? *Will* you trust me?'

She wanted to tell him that she would trust him with her life, that she would follow him to the ends of the earth. But she was annoyed with him for leaving her alone all day to worry, for keeping secrets from her when he had said he wouldn't, for blaming Carter when it was clearly Stefan alone who had caused the trouble. So instead she swallowed hard on her declaration of abiding love, and her anger, and smiled coolly at him. 'You are my husband, therefore I must obey you. You have only to tell me what to do and I will do it. Where is it you intend us to go?'

He spoke roughly, as if in some way she had disappointed him. 'To Rhapsody Creek with all speed. Pack only essentials. I'll harness a horse and leave a note for Aunt Kizzy.'

'A note? I cannot leave Aunt Kizzy without first——'

'Hester.' He matched her irritation. 'Every moment you waste arguing costs valuable time. Do you think I like to run? I don't, but it is the only way; those who have tried once will try again. Would you risk my life? Please hurry.' He was pushing her up the stairs, but she needed no further urging. From the moment he had mentioned the danger to his life she was his to do with as he willed.

Her mind racing, she started up the stairs. It would be damp at Rhapsody Creek, and nothing would be aired. They would need bedlinen. And food. 'Susy, I need Susy,' she called to him.

'No,' he bit back. 'Do it yourself. The fewer people who know where we go, the better. Fetch some clothing, bandages, food, blankets. Where do you keep the tools?'

She told him and in a moment he was gone to scratch together anything which might come in useful at the long-neglected plantation while Hester ran from chest to larder to cupboard and the pile she collected grew in the stairhall.

And as they drove from the boundaries of the city,

out on to the main westbound highway, Aunt Kizzy's sweetly innocent sleep was disturbed by a loud pounding at her door.

She stood at the top of the stairs in her dressing-gown with her hair screwed up in curl rags and her eyes puffy from sleep.

'Will you tell me what you are all doing in my house at this hour?'

Sergeant Brixham, a bluff, not unkindly man, looked very slightly nonplussed. Expecting to find a runaway convict, he was instead confronted by a grey-haired old lady, who, if his experience was anything to go by, was not half the butter-wouldn't-melt type as might at first appear.

'Beg pardon, mistress, but we are looking for one Benjamin Blake, wanted for jumping a gaol sentence in England, or so I'm told.'

'Benjamin. . .?' Aunt Kizzy hesitated only for a moment before continuing blithely, 'Blake, did you say? Don't know that I recall the name.'

The sergeant smiled. Yes, he'd been right. Canny old bird, this one. 'That won't wash, mistress, for we know that he married your niece only yesterday. Surely you can't have forgotten him already?'

'Oh, that Benjamin Blake,' said Aunt Kizzy smoothly, coming down the stairs. 'Well, why didn't you say so?' She clasped her hands neatly together when she reached the foot of the stairs and smiled at the sergeant. 'Well, now, you seem a nice, understanding sort of chap. Are you married, Sergeant?'

Sergeant Brixham looked wary but was forced to concede that yes, indeed, he did have a good wife back home in Kent.

'Oh, well, I'm sure a fine upstanding *young* man such as yourself can still remember what it was like to be first married?'

At the wrong side of forty it was hard for the sergeant

not to be flattered, particularly since the old lady had such a charming smile. 'Well, as a matter of fact, this is my second wife, and we haven't been wed all that long ourselves.'

Aunt Kizzy looked delighted. 'There you are, then.' The smile on the sergeant's face grew puzzled. 'And where is that, mistress?'

'The young couple are alone, as newly married people usually are, and wish to stay that way. Now is not the moment for strangers to intrude. I am sure that whatever business you might have with Benjamin can very well wait until a more civilised hour.'

'But——'

'No, no. I won't hear another word. Who else would protect their privacy if I did not?' Aunt Kizzy brushed past him to lead the way to the door. She ignored the other half-dozen foot soldiers as if they were not cluttering up her stairhall with their unwelcome presence. Nor did she give any sign of the pitter-pattering of her heart though Dr Livesey would not have been at all surprised. He had always declared her as fit as a flea despite her protests to the contrary. 'Thank you for calling.' She held open the door but, perplexed, the sergeant stayed where he was. If he left without his prisoner, his commanding officer would have his scalp, and if he stayed, this sweet old Southern lady might well do likewise. He didn't care for the way she was smiling at him. It seemed to mean business.

'Good day, Sergeant.' She reminded him of the open door by pushing it well back on its squeaking hinges. 'Perhaps you would like me to call my man, to help you on your way?'

'Are you having problems, Aunt Kizzy?' The unexpectedness of the voice from the open doorway made Aunt Kizzy almost jump out of her skin.

'Oh, my. Oh, Carter. What a relief. Yes, indeed. These gentlemen are being rather a pest at an hour when I'd much rather be in my bed.' She glanced up at him sharply. 'But I might ask the same of you. What is the attraction about my house at five o'clock in the morning?'

Carter had already been thinking fast. When he'd heard how his plans had been foiled by some person or persons unknown rescuing Blake, he'd come straight round, expecting to find him already clapped in irons. Instead the problem grew stickier. Smiling reassuringly at Aunt Kizzy, he led her back indoors, carefully closing the door. 'There, now, wasn't I on my way to the store when I heard all the rumpus going on in the street and thought I'd go take a look-see? When I saw all these soldiers marching up to your place, why, I was worried. Didn't I think they'd come to take away my favourite aunt?'

Aunt Kizzy's frown mollified slightly but she was still puzzled. 'Now, why should you think that? I ain't the only person living here.'

He'd made a mistake and instantly tried to rectify it. 'Why, I thought Hester and her new husband were out of town, on their wedding journey or whatever a newly wedded couple does, so who else was there to care for you, but me, huh?'

Aunt Kizzy was convinced. 'Oh, Carter. You don't know how pleased I am to see you. Would you be so kind as to show these men off my premises? I really can't have them here in the middle of the night. It isn't proper and the excitement of it all is making me quite giddy.'

Then Carter was leading her into the parlour, fetching her a glass of restorative cordial before returning to the sergeant, who had watched the whole proceedings with considerable interest.

Carter jerked his head silently towards the door. 'Thank you, Sergeant, but I will see to Miss Kristina now. And I'd be obliged if you'd confine your visits to more conventional hours.'

'Very good, sir.'

Aunt Kizzy did not hear the brief exchange of words at the door, nor see the sergeant's smile as he left. And when Carter returned she grasped his hand in thanks. 'Dear Carter, what a comfort you are. Whyever did not Hester marry you, I wonder? And now there is some problem with Benjamin and I know not what it can be.'

'I shouldn't worry about it if I were you. It will be of no account.' Carter glanced about him. 'Is he upstairs, do you think?'

Aunt Kizzy gazed at Carter, wide-eyed. 'I don't see how he can be, or else he would have heard the commotion and come down, wouldn't he? Hester too.'

'Would you like me to check?'

'Oh, if you would be so kind.'

It did not take Carter long to confirm that his quarry had indeed flown. Now he would have to think of a new plan. But instinct told him not to sever his links with the family. Aunt Kizzy might be particularly useful there, though he wasn't sure how at the moment. 'Now you get yourself off to bed, and I'll sit for a spell down here until Susy and Jonas start stirring.'

'Oh, will you, Carter? I'd be truly grateful. I do so hate being alone. Where can they have gone, and without telling me? I do declare it is almost alarming.'

Left alone in the parlour, Carter easily found the note addressed to Miss Kristina propped up on the mantelshelf. Quickly scanning the few lines, a smile came to his face. So his quarry had played very nicely into his hands. All was not lost after all. In fact, this could prove to be the very answer. He'd give them a week or two to settle in, then he'd take dear old Aunt Kizzy on a visit.

CHAPTER ELEVEN

BENJAMIN drove the cart in silence for several hours. Hester tried once or twice to open a conversation but was forced to abandon the attempt since Benjamin sat, jaw clamped tight and eyes narrowed to twin slits of steel.

The countryside slid by barely noticed, a blur of pine forest and cypress trees broken from time to time by a creek or swamp. The sky lightened and a pale January sun blinked through the cloud though it did little to abate the coolness of the morning. It was the birth of a new year, 1782. The British had surrendered at Yorktown and America was free. Hester was newly married to a man she loved yet her heart felt as heavy as a cannon-ball lodged in her chest. What had gone wrong? Who had put Benjamin in that stinking hold? And, more importantly, why? And why did he refuse to speak to her? At length she could stand the silence no longer.

'Benjamin, will you please tell me what is going on?'

For answer he turned his head and looked at her, his eyes expressionless pools of blue. 'What would you have me say?'

Hester felt the familiar stirrings of exasperation. 'For goodness' sake, we are man and wife. You said yourself we should not have secrets from each other. *Why* will you not talk to me?'

'Perhaps I am tired of being the subject of speculation and gossip,' he said. 'I came to this country to escape all of that. Perhaps I would like my wife, at least, to trust me.'

'This is nothing to do with trust,' she cried.

164

'On the contrary, it has everything to do with it. You have convinced yourself there is some awful truth or mystery about me, as did your friends Caro and Beattie.'

'Is there not?' she said, stubbornly resolved to have it out with him.

'There is no mystery, only certain areas of my life which I prefer not to discuss.'

'Not even with me, your wife?'

Again that casual, half-dismissive glance as if he could not bear to meet her gaze. 'Perhaps particularly with you, my wife.'

'Can you not see that, as your wife, if you need help I want to be the one to give it? If you need protection I need to be the one to offer it.'

'I need neither help nor protection,' snarled Benjamin.

'Particularly from me?'

'From anyone.'

His rejection of her cut deep but Hester was determined, if only to eradicate the pain in his eyes. 'Who threw you into that hold?'

'Carter Lois.'

'Why?'

'Ask him. How should I know?'

'I believe you know very well.' She was thinking rapidly, wildly almost. Yet somewhere in her mind, in her heart must lie the answer if only she could put her finger on it. 'Wasn't the ship about to sail for England?'

'Probably.' His abrupt, clipped answers were infuriating her, but it seemed impossible to get him to talk. He merely held the reins and stared at the straight road ahead as if it needed all his concentration, which was nonsense.

'Always you tell me half a tale. It has been so right from the start. All that story about your being brought up by an aunt—I didn't believe a word of it. You said that only because I was, and it popped into your head as a convenient way out.'

To her dismay he did not deny the accusation, but a faint smile curled his lips, a smile which somehow chilled her. 'How very perceptive of you. It seemed as good an answer as any other, certainly better than the truth.'

Hester could have screamed at him. 'There you go again. What is the truth? Tell me. I insist on knowing.' And when he continued to sit impassively silent, as ever her temper got the better of her and she lunged for the reins, snatching them from him and yanking poor old Captain to a halt with such fierceness that he snorted with a matching fury. 'I am waiting for an answer.'

'How very angry you sound,' he said icily and then he prised open her fingers without the slightest difficulty and took the ribbons from her. 'Don't ever do that again, Hester. Apart from the discomfort to the horse, I do not like it.' His voice was so hard, so distant, it drenched the heat out of her temper in an instant and she wanted to lean on him, to sob her insecurity against his shoulder and have him reassure her that all was well between them. That he was who he said he was, her own dear Benjamin, and not some bleak-eyed stranger with a mysterious past who had taken his place. Right at this moment she felt as if their entire marriage was a sham. Though she had married him with her eyes open, under no illusions that he loved her, yet she had hoped. Now she felt that hope wither and die inside her. She had promised she would never pry into his past yet those unknown years gripped her to the point of obsession. That word again. She was getting to be as bad as the tragic Sarah and the thought sickened her. But how could she help herself when she loved him so much? He spoke of trust, yet he would not trust her, his own wife?

'I will tell you this much, since it seems to matter to you,' Benjamin said, and, propping his elbows upon his knees, and keeping his gaze fixed upon the toes of his boots, he began to talk.

'I don't know who my parents were, either of them. I was found as a baby in a ship's barrel on the dockside at Liverpool, probably left there by some frightened girl. Old Mother Cooper took me in, as she did countless other strays, whether it be cats or children. We lived, some seventeen of us, in two small rooms in a block of tenement buildings. As soon as we were old enough we got a job on the docks to earn our crust, even if it was only holding a gent's horse for a penny. It was a rough and ready kind of life, but she was kind and our bellies were not left empty any longer than she could help. I'm not sure how Mother Cooper earned her living. To be frank with you, none of us dared ask. But she made sure we knew the difference between right and wrong, and if any of the children made the mistake of trying to line their pockets or stomachs without working for it they felt the sharp end of her anger in no uncertain terms. In the end she died, worn out, I suppose, and we were all left to fend for ourselves, hiding from the authorities mostly at first, since they were anxious to gather us up and clap us in some workhouse or other.'

'Why didn't you tell me all this before?' Hester asked, shocked and humbled by this harrowing tale.

'There is little point in re-telling it. It is not a background to be proud of.'

'Nor ashamed of,' she said briskly, and he looked at her in surprise.

'I suppose not, yet we were. I jumped on a ship at the first opportunity. I think I was about eight at the time. That was all I had ever dreamed of, going to sea.' He gave a wry grin. 'Yet, as so often happens when one achieves a dream, at first I hated it. Not all captains are good to their crew. I decided the only way was to buy my own ship, which, in the fullness of time, I did. Which brought me to America. And so you have it.' He clicked for Captain to walk on, leaving Hester with much to think about. It was only several miles later that she realised she was no nearer unravelling the mystery of his attempted abduction by the British. Risking a sideways glance at him, she decided now was not the moment to pursue it. The tight, preoccupied expression was back upon his face with a vengeance. Crawling into the back of the cart among the assortment of goods and chattels, she pulled a blanket over her and in moments was asleep. Her last thought as her eyelids closed was an almost childlike belief that everything would come right between them once they were at Rhapsody Creek.

Benjamin realised his first mistake as soon as he brought the horse to a halt outside the old house. He had been so anxious to get away, he'd brought no help with them, not that he would have robbed Aunt Kizzy of Jonas as well as her one and only horse, but it was a pity he hadn't given more consideration to the matter. Even as they drove up the long green tunnel of a drive he could see the work that would be needed to be done to turn this place into a feasible proposition.

The fences were broken, the fields overgrown with pine saplings and brambles, and the house itself long past its best. Ivy clung to the once white walls of the wide, porticoed plantation house. The paintwork was peeling and blistered by the sun and the green shutters sagged on their hinges. And all about it hung the drifting skeins of Spanish moss, giving it an ethereal, ghostlike appearance. In the spring, when the azaleas and dogwood were in bloom, it might be passably pretty; right now it looked forbidding and chilled even Benjamin's grim resolve. Yet he must make a success of it. If he could not go back and right old wrongs, then he must find the strength to go forward and hope that eventually those old wrongs would cease to pursue him.

He climbed down from the cart and stretched his lean, hard muscles with relief. The journey had been long and tiring, for he'd wasted little of it in sleep. But a good night's rest would be very welcome now to prepare him to face the future. Surely there must be some folk hereabouts looking for work? At the next town perhaps? Being British, it did not occur to him that they had other ways of doing things here in the deep South. Instead he threw the reins to Hester.

'Ever untacked a horse before?'

'No.' She was startled.

'Now's your chance to learn. See you rub him down well and give him a good long drink and some of the oatbran from that sack there.'

'And what are you going to do?' called Hester, slightly miffed, to his retreating back as he strode rapidly across the forecourt of the house. She didn't object to looking after old Captain at all, but she did object to working while he wandered around viewing the place. Enjoying himself.

'I'll bring back some wood. Presumably you do know how to cook?'

'Why, I. . .' But her words fell on thin air as he disappeared round the corner of the building. Sighing with exasperation, she got down from the cart in a hustle of skirts and temper. If Benjamin Blake thought he could just lord it over her, and boss her around at her own plantation, he could think again. Not unless he came clean about the necessity for their running here, anyway.

Captain patiently suffered her fumbling attempts to relieve him of his bridle and harness and rub him down. He certainly found no quarrel with the generous helpings of oatbran and water she gave him and Hester left him in the stable happily munching. Out in the yard again she looked about her for Benjamin but there was no sign. It was late afternoon and the wind was sighing through the tall cypress trees and live oaks and it brought back a memory of sleepless nights here as a child, when she'd always found the place disturbed her, convinced that it was haunted.

'Hester.' Her name, carried like a sigh on the wind, brought her whirling around, frightened eyes scanning the small outbuildings that lined the four sides of the yard. There was no one there. She was quite alone. An icy shudder licked her spine. In the centre of the yard stood the well, an old wooden bucket upturned on its rim. And beyond that were the slave cabins, empty now that the plantation no longer functioned. No doubt Benjamin would buy more to get the place going again. To her left were a pair of barns which, she remembered, held a perplexing number of rusty old tools and farm implements. To her right was the smoke-house. In here once hung home-cured hams and sides of bacon, taking on that deliciously unique flavour of the oak or hickory wood fire that burned constantly beneath them. The thought made Hester realise that she was hungry.

'Hester.' She jumped as if someone had shot her.

'Benjamin, there you are.' She ran to him in relief. 'Did you call me before?' she asked but he shook his head.

'I've put dry wood in the old stove and it seems to be operating. It's a bit smoky but it will do for tonight. I'll clean the flues tomorrow. Let's get the stuff we need for a meal and a night's sleep from the cart and leave the rest till morning.'

'That has my vote,' agreed Hester and followed happily on his heels. It was the most he had spoken to her since they left Charleston yesterday morning. Even last night, spent huddled beneath a tree with a small fire blazing to warm them, he had kept his distance and neither touched nor spoke to her for the few short sleepless hours he had permitted her to rest. She hoped it would be different now they were home. Home. Hester drew in a sharp breath at the thought. Could she ever think of this place again as home? George had always loved it, though she did not, and had finally persuaded Aunt Kizzy not to pay any more visits.

But at least she had her husband with her this time. She could smell the night air, scented with damp earth and burning pine wood. The stove must be working better than they expected. This would be a new beginning for them, and if it was what Benjamin wanted she must give all she'd got to make it work.

They toasted bread and cheese on the kitchen stove and made a big pot of hot coffee. It was the most delicious meal Hester had ever tasted.

'This place is filthy,' she said, busily rubbing a portion of the table clean enough for them to use.

'That can be your first job in the morning. To clean it.'

Hester paused with the toast halfway to her mouth. 'My *first* job?'

Benjamin met her puzzled expression with a laugh. 'Well, I'll have more important things to do, like giving Captain his first lesson in pulling a plough. Besides, cleaning a house is woman's work.'

For a moment Hester was dumbstruck. 'Do you know how many rooms there are in this place?' she asked, when she could finally find her voice. Benjamin simply looked at her and continued to eat. 'There are nine bedrooms, four main reception-rooms, at least two kitchens and goodness knows how many attics, cellars and servants' quarters. Nobody ever counted them.'

Benjamin shrugged. 'No need to clean them all. We

will only be using the one bedroom after all.' His eyes twinkled dangerously. 'So long as the bed is clean and warm, what more do we need?' He laughed at her expression of outrage. 'And we will need a living-room in addition to this kitchen, which would undoubtedly benefit from a good scrub. Heaven knows what creatures have come to reside in it these long years.'

'You must be mad. I cannot possibly clean all of this house, even half of it, without help.'

'Why not?' He reached for a second slice.

'It is simply too big,' she cried, growing flustered as she thought of the long-echoing corridors and the high-ceilinged empty rooms, which held the ghosts of her parents and her half-forgotten childhood. 'And—and I am unused to such hard labour.' She could have bitten off her tongue, for this gave him the excuse to freeze her with one of his most fearful glares.

'You were happy enough to help out at Aunt Kizzy's, to take in lodgers, and help Susy cook.'

'That was different. There was a war on. It was an emergency.'

'And now the war is over you wish to revert to your ladylike status and be waited on hand and foot?' His lips curled into a mocking sneer.

Hester was so furious for enmeshing herself in this argument that she rounded on him with a fine show of temper. 'No, I do not. I have never played the lady. But for goodness' sake, Benjamin, I don't think you've any conception how much work it takes to run a plantation.' She decided to air her superior knowledge. 'Why, when my parents had this place they had two cooks, more than a dozen house slaves plus a couple of hundred more working in the plantation fields. There's no way we two can manage on our own.'

Benjamin was on his feet. 'I'd no intention of asking you to. Not for very long, anyway. But until I find some hired help we'll just have to cope as best we can.'

'Hired help?' Hester looked at him in surprise. 'You'll be lucky to find any hired help around here. Most folks own their own piece and don't reckon on working for anyone else.' She began to stack the plates with more clatter than was strictly necessary. 'No, we'll have to drive down to Atlanta and buy us some slaves from the slave mart.'

'No.'

Hester stopped in her tracks. 'What did you say?'

She had never seen his face so set, so grim. 'No slaves. No man should have the right to purchase or own another. It may well be your custom here in the deep South, but it will not be the custom on Rhapsody Creek.'

Hester was so astounded, her jaw dropped clean open in a most unbecoming fashion. 'Then pray how do you intend to run this place? Who will plough the fields, mend the fences, plant the cotton? Who will protect us?'

He pushed back his chair noisily and glowered at her. 'I'll manage to find people somehow, people willing to work for a fair wage. Meanwhile, I have you. You've already proved your stalwart strength on the domestic scene,' he mocked. 'Do you think I'd have taken on a milksop for a wife?'

'You married me just to get yourself a *work-horse*?' Hester stood, incensed, in the centre of the kitchen floor, the crockery rattling in hands shaking with temper.

'I wouldn't put it quite so crudely,' teased Benjamin wryly, eyes brimming with laughter, and was forced to swiftly duck as a plate hurled by his head and landed in a dozen pieces on the flagged floor.

In the awful silence that followed he merely turned his head, looked at the disaster and then looked back at Hester. 'I trust it was not valuable. You really will have to work on that temper of yours, Hester.' Very calmly, as if the outburst had not taken place, he continued, 'There will be no slavery here and that is final. You do your job and I'll do mine, and so long as the one doesn't interfere with the other we'll get along fine. Remember, Hester, you are my wife now so you——'

'Must do as you say?' she interrupted, eyes widening in shock.

The lips which had kissed her with a pleasure so sensual that it had curled her toes now mocked her with a dry smile.

'Isn't that what you told me? It won't all be unpleasant, I assure you.' He drew her close into his arms and with an idle finger traced the outline of her lips, causing her body to arch naturally towards him. 'I've lit a fire in the first bedroom at the top of the stairs. I suggest you retire to it at once while I check the locks. You can clear this mess up in the morning.'

Looking up at him through shyly lowered lids, she noticed for the first time how weary he looked. There was a tight white line around the full lower lip, and more fine lines had etched themselves beneath the gentian eyes. It had been a long drive from Charleston, two days and a night of bumping unmade roads on that dreadful cart. Her heart swelled with a rush of love for him. Why was she quarrelling? Secretly she admired his resolution to create his own world in his own way. The Drayton and Mackay families had always been good to their slaves, but that was not the case with all slave owners. Many were ill fed and abused. She too would like to see an end to the practice, were she brave enough to defy convention. She was tired, and this place, as ever, unnerved her. A feeling she must learn to master. Taking a gulping breath, she ventured a smile.

'As you say, Benjamin. I will do as you say. But you'll take care to lock the door securely, won't you?

There've been no Indians sighted out here in the wilds of Georgia for some long time, but there's no call to take chances.' She smoothed a hand along one solid shoulder. 'I'm sorry if I was a little—well, grumpy with you just now. I guess I'm just a mite tired from the long journey. Can't we go up together, to make it more cosy?'

Without a word he put her from him and walked from the room. It was a clear enough reprimand that she had overstepped the mark yet again.

She was glad of the fire in the huge bedroom as she made up the bed with clean sheets. The nights at this time of year were bitingly cold. And as she removed her travel-stained clothes and scrubbed herself all over before the blazing fire with the warm water she had brought her mind could not help but return to the memory of that first night. Whatever she had expected, it had not been that. The experience had thrilled and delighted her. Only thinking of it brought the familiar stirring of excitement to the pit of her stomach and a warm flush to her cheeks.

She slipped on her clean nightgown and slid between the sheets, wide awake now as she listened to the unfamiliar sounds of the night. Why were old houses so unbelievably noisy? Her senses were alert to every creak and groan. Was that a footstep? Did he come? But the waiting was long and at last the warmth of the room and the softness of the bed performed its charm upon her and she began to feel drowsy. Despite all her efforts she found her eyelids drooping heavily. Thirty-six hours or more without proper sleep had finally got the better of her and it became harder and harder to drag them open again. Her last waking thought was that she must not sleep for Benjamin would join her in this delightful bed at any moment. She must stay awake to welcome him.

Benjamin found Hester sleeping soundly. He stood

for some long moments looking down on her. One hand slipped under a softly curved cheek, she lay curled like a kitten in the great bed and his throat constricted at sight of her. He'd forgotten just how young she was, how vulnerable. Little more than a child. Yet she had loved him like a woman, a woman of surprising passion and generosity. He knew that she loved him. She had made no secret of the fact, offering herself to him with a naïve conviction that it would bring love in return. His face grew thoughtful. Was that possible? He had never had any intention of falling in love with Hester Mackay. He had had his fill of love years ago.

When Sarah Rigg had developed that passionate obsession for him, that had been the last straw. He felt somehow threatened, as if she had invaded the inner core of his being without his permission. His one object had been to escape the cloying tentacles of her need. When he had indeed escaped in such a traumatic way, the experience had left him feeling vulnerable and insecure, as if he were not in control of his own life. It was a sensation he did not care for and had no intention of repeating.

Allowing his gaze to travel over the tousled golden-brown curls that fanned the pillow, the innocent white nightgown she still insisted on wearing and on over the delectable curve of her hip, Benjamin knew it would be easy to be lulled into a feeling of false security with this girl. She had such an appetite for life that she met it full tilt, brushing aside all restraints and conventions. She had vigour, and humour, passion and a kind of wholesome beauty that lived in the mind, but what could he offer her? The frozen remains of himself? The empty casing that had once held blood and flesh? If he woke her now, he knew she would open her arms, her whole being to him. But though physical satisfaction was exceedingly pleasant it was insufficient to sustain life. He would not risk hurting her. He could sense already a waning of hope in her. Soon all her love would be snuffed out like a spent candle, and surely then life would be more comfortable for him? Frowning slightly, he turned from the bed and stoked up the fire till the flames danced, added more logs then lay down upon the sofa. He was so weary, he could have slept upon a rail.

Hester realised she must have been asleep when she opened her eyes and found the lamp had been turned off. Save for the faint flickering of firelight on the plasterwork ceiling, the room was in complete darkness and, if the tip of her nose was any judge, had grown colder. She stretched out her hand and found the bed beside her to be cold and empty. She sat up quickly, eyes stretched wide and frightened. Where was Benjamin? Had he left her alone?

And then she saw him. He was stretched out upon an old sofa drawn up to the fire, the blanket he had used to cover himself had slipped to the floor and apart from removing his jacket and boots he lay fully clothed as if ready to leap up at any moment. Disappointment bit deep. Why had he chosen not to sleep with her? Did he care so little for her? In an instant she was out of bed, padding across the sanded boards to kneel by his side. The curl of his dark lashes brushed the high cheekbones, and sleep had smoothed the frown from between the dark brows. Hester put out an exploratory finger to trace the line of his square jaw, so firm, so strong. She found it grasped in an iron grip.

'What the—Hester?' She was sure that if she had not cried out he might very well have broken her finger without a moment's thought. 'Why are you out of bed?'

'Why are you not in it?' she tentatively asked and quailed as she saw the frown return with a vengeance.

'One of us must remain alert,' he said.

'Oh, Benjamin,' she chided. 'What a fib. You were fast asleep, not in the least alert.'

'I caught you quickly enough.'

She took his hand and tugged at him. 'Come to bed, do. You must be half frozen on this sofa, the fire is dying now. And what need have you to stay alert? There is no one for miles around.'

Benjamin swung his feet to the ground but did not otherwise move. His expression was thoughtful. 'Are you certain you left no servants or slaves in charge after your aunt stopped coming here?'

Hester shook her head, looking surprised by the question. 'No. We did at first. But once the war started it became impossible to expect anyone to stay. Why?'

Benjamin shrugged. 'No reason. Only, I thought there were signs. . .' He paused. 'The winding gear on the well looked recently oiled and someone has fitted a new rope.'

'We do take care of our property, you know,' she answered teasingly, not really listening. Her gaze travelled over the rumpled dark curls that fell upon his brow and her fingers itched to smooth them back, to caress the tiredness from his cheeks and light the weariness in his eyes. What was he talking of? She paid little attention.

'And a small fire has been lit in one of the outbuildings. Perhaps it was a passing soldier, separated from his unit.'

'Hm.' Couldn't he tell how she wanted him? Couldn't he feel her need? It was consuming her like the fires of hell itself.

He got up and, kneeling beside the hearth, began to pile more logs upon the glowing embers. 'Go to bed before you get cold,' he said.

'Benjamin.'

He looked back at the sound of the pleading in her voice. 'What is it?'

She knelt beside him, and now she was caressing him. She knew it was wrong but she couldn't help herself. The firelight danced upon his cheeks, made his eyes sparkle and lit glowing patches in his glossy hair. She found her fingers running through those springy curls, smoothing over the nape of his neck and then, as if that were not bad enough, her cheek was moving against his. She drew in the scent of him as if she needed it to give her life, pressing her soft body against the hard muscles of his. Hester knew she was behaving like a wanton, like the dreaded Sarah, no doubt, but she was caught in the mesh of her own desire and could no more keep herself from touching him than she could prevent herself from breathing. Her lips kissed the smoothness of his cheek, which somehow he had managed to shave. The smell of the clean soap and that indefinable scent which was himself sent the need in her escalating to fever pitch. Her kisses moved on to tease the lobe of his ear and she heard at last the soft groan she had longed for. The shudder of his own need transmitted itself through them both and his arms fastened around her as his mouth found hers. She gloried in the excitement that shuddered through him and helped him remove his remaining clothes without fuss or loss of rapture to either of them. He wasted no time in taking her, nor did she want him to, so powerful was her love for him. It was enough to feel him move inside her, to sense his need for her.

And at the climax she cried out his name with love and the joy which exploded from her as she had known it would, and afterwards, as she cradled the beloved weight of his body upon hers, she turned her face to kiss his heated brow with a sigh of deep satisfaction upon her lips. Later, they lay in the big bed together and he made love to her with a compelling sweetness which made her heart ache. He even, at one moment, softly murmured her name. How could such ecstasy not be love?

A movement caught her eye and, glancing into the

shadows, she was sure she saw the great brass knob turn as if someone was quietly closing the door. For an instant cold fear clenched her stomach and she cried out with fear.

'What is it?' Benjamin was instantly alert, but even as she told him she laughed at her own foolishness. She was no longer a child, imagining ghosts. Hadn't she just proved she was a woman, full-grown?

'Indeed you have, Hester,' he agreed, lying down beside her again, but as he watched her curl up into a kitten ball once more, her head tucked in the crook of his arm, he lay staring into the darkness, the creases of his frown deeper than ever.

CHAPTER TWELVE

'WAKE up, Hester, the day has begun.' Hester was tugged sharply from the warmth of her dreams by a cold hand upon her bare shoulder.

'What is it?' she mumbled, languorously drawing the sheets higher. But they were pulled from her and the icy morning air nipped harshly at her bare flesh. Shame flooded through her as memory returned. She hardly dared meet Benjamin's eye as he placed a cup of hot coffee on the table beside the bed, the delicious aroma tantalising her taste-buds. Reaching for her nightgown, she quickly pulled it over her head, feeling her cheeks start to burn, and heard his deep chuckle, aware that he was watching her.

'I'll tear that thing to shreds one of these days,' he threatened.

'Indeed you won't,' she hotly retorted, and, seeing how his eyes sparkled with a keen wickedness, blushed all the more.

'Drink your coffee quickly, there is work to be done.' And as Benjamin strode from the room her heart sagged in her breast. Had she truly behaved like a wanton last night? It would seem, if her recollection was correct, that she had. Hester squirmed inwardly at the thought. What in heaven's name had possessed her?

Yet still she felt that he had kept back a part of himself. Why should that be? And how could she reach him? Tears brimmed suddenly and trickled over to run in scalding channels down her cheeks. Was it the deprivation of his childhood or the death of the poor, spurned Sarah which had caused him to build this powerful shell of protection about himself? Or perhaps a combination of both, robbing him of faith in those close to him, and making him over-protect himself. Hester could well understand how that might have come about and, though it did help to explain the way he held himself distant from her, learning to live with the man hidden behind that shell was quite another matter.

But her own behaviour must carry some of the blame. She had flung herself at him when he had made it clear from the start that he had no taste for yet another female fancying herself in love with him.

Hester realised, with a sickening of her heart, that she must put aside this naïve dream that she could make him fall as hopelessly in love with her as she was with him. She was not such a fool as to imagine that the performance last night on the hearthrug or that repeated later in this very bed had any connection with love. Caro, who was Hester's mentor in all things pertaining to the opposite sex, had most carefully explained to her that such was not necessarily the case. That if Hester was to win Benjamin's heart she must gird her temper and exuberance and learn to practise compliance. In this Hester could see that her friend was quite right. But it was a hard lesson to learn when all her instincts cried out to show him the strength of her feelings.

'Are you coming, Hester?' The deep tone of his voice echoed up the stairs and for a moment she closed her eyes. Work. That was the only thing he needed her for. If that was the case then so be it. She had entered this marriage with her eyes open; now she must simply close her mind to her need of him. Biting back a tiny sob of misery, Hester slipped out of the high bed and reached for her clothes.

She worked harder that day than she had ever worked in her life, but to her complete surprise found herself actually enjoying it. After Benjamin had finished cleaning the flues she polished the stove until she could see her face in its glossy black surface. Dressed in her oldest gown and with her hair tied up in a kerchief, she scrubbed the kitchen from floor to ceiling and took her sweeping broom into every corner of stair and hall, vigorously banishing dust and cobwebs. Their bedroom was given an equally thorough treatment, the grate swept out and relaid, and tenderly Hester smoothed and remade her marriage bed, scented it with rosemary, and, wistfully recalling their love-making, wondered if Benjamin would ever see it as anything more than a mere essential of life.

They sat together at luncheon in the small parlour, eating the cold meats and bread they had brought with them, and Hester gave serious thought to the question of food.

'I know we brought plenty of basic supplies with us, Benjamin, but we must have fresh food. Do you know anything of trapping?' she asked, but he ruefully shook his head.

'Can't say I've found much call for it at sea. But I can fish and will go and catch us some from the creek this afternoon. Then I intend to clean up the old plough and give Captain his first lesson. How do you think he'll take to that?'

Hester wrinkled up her nose and shook her head, making Benjamin laugh out loud.

'Well, until we get a proper work-horse he'll have to swallow his pride and knuckle to, like the rest of us. It's too soon to plant corn or vegetables but we can at least break up the soil. When we have recovered from the journey, I intend to visit Atlanta, buy more stores and hopefully find some help.'

'You won't leave me here alone, will you?' Hester's voice was sharp with panic and Benjamin cast her a questioning look.

'What is this? I thought you said there was no one around for miles? Don't tell me the valiant Hester Mackay is afraid of the dark?'

'Not at all,' she retorted. 'But I confess to disliking being left alone for long in this place, with not a neighbour in sight. What if I should fall in a swamp, or break a leg or some such?'

'Or the alligators come to get you?' he joked. 'I'm sure you wouldn't do anything so careless and the alligators wouldn't dare to touch a Mackay.'

'Don't tease me,' she fired back at him. 'It isn't funny.'

To be fair, he was at once contrite when he saw how rigid her mouth had become, how stiff her back. 'You really don't like it here very much, do you?'

Avoiding his probing gaze, she shook her head. 'No.'

'Why is that?'

Hester shrugged her shoulders and cut herself more bread. The energetic cleaning had made her hungry and it was their last loaf. Oh, well, she would just have to get up even earlier tomorrow and bake fresh. 'I don't know. Strange things always seemed to be happening here when I was a child. I've always thought it rather spooky.'

He leaned over and kissed her cheek, only a light peck but it warmed her a little. 'Then we must make Rhapsody Creek into the finest house the South has ever seen. That should banish your spooks. You shall naturally come to Atlanta with me and while I hire field hands you shall choose yourself a maid, and a cook, buy fine dresses, drapes for your windows and new furnishings for your rooms. And someone to clean them of course. I couldn't have my beautiful wife soiling her expensive new gowns with housework. And when that is all done to your great satisfaction you must deliver your card to all the neighbours and have them call.'

Hester stared at him in disbelief. 'Do you think they would come? And I thought you said I was to do the work myself. Are you funning me? If so, I think it in uncommon bad taste.' And to her complete astonishment he burst out laughing, a rich peal of laughter which made her chuckle along with him.

'No, I am not funning you. Would I tease you on such a serious matter? And of course you cannot do all the work yourself. Didn't I say that was only a temporary arrangement?'

Hester was not at all sure that he had, but did not intend to argue the point. Plans and ideas flooded her head. 'New drapes, you say? And dresses? Carpets too? These are quite moth-eaten.'

His eyes kindled merrily, enjoying the brightening of her face. 'As many as you like.'

'But can you afford so much luxury?'

Benjamin got lazily to his feet, the length of him uncoiling with the grace and strength of a mountain lion. 'You can safely leave such concerns to me, Hester. Concentrate on drawing up a list of whatever you require and we will order it in Atlanta. I'll tell you when to stop spending, but I assure you it won't be for a long, long while. I would not have my sweet young wife restrain her pleasures one bit. Only the best is good enough for Rhapsody Creek and Benjamin and Mistress Blake.' His blue eyes shone with a mischief that held also a touch of sadness, and she wondered why. Perhaps because he had never had a real home before.

But Benjamin, anxious to fill the dawning emptiness of a life far from her relatives and friends, yearned to offer his young bride more. He loved to see her eyes light up, those sweet lips smile. Yet what else could he give? And why did it matter? Why did it hurt him so, to meet the anguished appeal in those soft brown eyes? Wasn't he supposed to be immune to feeling, inured against the soft and languid glances of the fawning female? Last night she had taken him by surprise, revealing a part of her nature he had never dreamed existed. Hidden in that childlike body beat the heart of a sensual, exciting woman and, if he could not love her as she deserved, then he could at least try to make her happy in other ways.

'We shall make this house the envy of the entire county, shall we not?' he said, pulling her to her feet and holding her within the circle of his arms. 'And everyone will vie for an invitation to one of Mistress Blake's fabulous balls.' Overcome with emotion, Hester clapped her hands in delight and laughed up at him.

'I should enjoy that, if only in memory of my dear mama and papa, who loved this place so much. And perhaps, if I do restore it, I can learn to love it too. Do you think that is possible?' she asked and her eyes begged for reassurance. Willingly, Benjamin gave it.

'Anything is possible.' And for one breathless moment she thought he was going to say more, that he might admit it was possible for him to fall in love with her. But then he was putting her from him and the moment was past.

'There is much to be done if you are going to have it ready for the summer season, so jump to it, wife. No time for dallying.' He took her chin and smoothed it between his finger and thumb. 'The damp, like your ghosts, must likewise be banished, so light lots of fires. But do not work too hard. See that you rest this afternoon. I would not have my pretty woman exhausted.' And, with a telling smile, he left her to her blushes and the knot of confusion tightening in her breast.

The expedition was planned for a week towards the end of the month and if all her plans were to be complete by then Hester knew she would have her work cut out. But somehow it all became a pleasure. She almost forgot her dislike of the place and enjoyed exploring and investigating the damage that long neglect had done to the house at Rhapsody Creek. She chased the lingering damp from the remaining rooms, as Benjamin had instructed, by the constant lighting of warming fires. He told her that she used up so much wood, they would need to buy another fifty acres to feed the bedroom fires alone. And employ a boy to chop the kindling for her.

She made notes in a small black book of all the work needed to be done to make the place habitable and a second list of tasks she would dearly like done if funds permitted. From time to time she would show her lists, with trepidation, to Benjamin and with scarcely a glance he would nod and smile and agree.

'Don't trouble me with every detail,' he said, not unkindly. 'It shall be done.'

But the best part of her day was the time she spent with Benjamin out in the fields. She insisted on helping him, for Captain was proving an unwilling pupil and there was much work to be done. The weather was clear and dry, even bringing out patches of freckles upon her glowing skin. She had never felt more alive, more whole, more in tune with life, and with her husband.

And at night he came to her in the great bed where she lay, sweetly scented, heart beating fast with anticipation and hope, and they would make love. He taught her the joys of anticipation, and the skills of fulfilment, and she was a willing pupil, offering all of herself and more with an open and adventurous heart. She could tell that he loved to stroke her hair and the silky softness of her skin, though he never said as much, for she could sense the tremor in his long, tapering fingers as they traced their path of ecstasy.

But if Hester dreamed of eventual proclamations of undying love she was to be disappointed. He did not always stay for the entire night, and sometimes he would not come until she had almost given up hope and had very nearly lost the battle of fighting off the weight of sleep on her eyelids. Then the bedroom door would creak open and Benjamin would slip quietly between the sheets and lie in silence for a long while, not touching her, scarcely breathing, it seemed. And in the darkness she was certain he must hear the pounding of her own heart. But then his hands would slide over her and, with an indistinguishable sound deep in his throat, he would pull her towards him and his lips would seek hers, teasing her into startled awareness till sleep was the last thing she wanted, and make love to her as if he could not get his fill of her.

She wondered sometimes if perhaps he tried not to come at all, but failed in his determination time and time again, often looking as if he had tried to sleep elsewhere but had finally come to her just as dawn was breaking. A most accurate assessment, had she but known it. Yet always she responded eagerly to his caresses, and once she playfully tried to entice a few loving words from him.

'What would Aunt Kizzy say if she saw my skin now, almost weather-beaten? I dare say she'd have me working with one hand plucking up the weeds and another holding my parasol.'

But Benjamin only chuckled, kissed a freckle and declared they would soon go. 'This weather cannot last. Take care not to stray too far from the house.'

'Whyever not?'

'The weather may suddenly change and a storm blow up. It is but January.' Benjamin had other reasons for keeping her close, but, since he was still unsure of his ground, preferred not to elaborate at this juncture.

But worse than his coming late to her bed were the

times he left it the moment the lovemaking was over. Almost as if he were ashamed of having loved her, and did not want to be reminded. Then the bed would grow cold along with her hope as she lay unmoving, holding back the tears, going over and over in her head what it was she had done wrong. Well aware of her lack of experience in these matters, still her feminine intuition, her very love for him told her there should be more to lovemaking than this simple coupling, beautiful though it was. There should be a coming together of souls, of hearts. There should be sweet words, smiles and kisses, and lovers' talk. But with Benjamin there were none of these things. His silence was almost grimly maintained, and she too must keep her own counsel. They loved with their bodies, and with their minds, and in Hester's case, at least, with her heart, but always there was a slight restraint, an aftertaste that there could have been more.

Often she felt him looking at her in the pale light from the moon that shafted through the tall window and she would hold her breath, thinking he might speak to her, or at least say her name. But then he would turn away, almost leap from the bed and hasten from the room as if the matter were done with, most pleasurably maybe, but that was that and he could not rid himself of her presence quickly enough.

Yet there were compensations. Benjamin Blake was a delightful, considerate companion and Hester loved his sense of humour, his wickedly cheerful smiles, and his continuing thoughtfulness for her welfare.

'Do not overtire yourself. Let me carry that bucket, Hester. Haven't I told you not to work too hard? The sooner we go to Atlanta the better.'

And equally satisfying. 'How do you manage to produce such delicious meals from so little? I swear I shall never leave you, Hester Mackay Blake, if only for your cooking.'

Yet still she wanted more. If the naïve Hester Mackay she had once been had guessed for one moment the pain involved in loving with no hope of return, and without being allowed to fully show that love, she might very well have thought twice before committing herself to such a marriage. Yet how could she live without him? However much heartache the situation might bring would be multiplied a thousand-fold if she were to never see Benjamin again.

She determined to be content with her lot and tried hard to keep her mind fully occupied. But often as she worked she would pause in her chores to glance over her shoulder, half expecting to see someone standing there. And for no reason a shiver would run up her spine as she returned with reluctance to the task in hand.

These feelings reminded her of her childhood when she remembered experiencing the very same sensitivity to the atmosphere of the place. Even as a small child, no more than two or three years old, she could recall waking screaming in her cot-bed as if the devil himself were after her. It was a foolishness she had hoped would have dissipated with the passage of time, but it seemed that was not the case. She began to acquire the chilling certainty that she was being watched.

And as if that were not enough, as in her childhood, strange things began to happen. At first Hester found there was nothing positive she could put her finger on, only a feeling that some things were not quite as she had left them. A jug or a plate in a different place. A water-bucket empty that she had believed filled. But then came the incident of her shawl.

She had been working in the log store, splitting kindling for the many fires and she had removed her shawl and hung it, she was almost sure of it, on the peg behind the door. But when she went to collect it later it had gone. She searched everywhere but could find no trace. When she asked Benjamin at lunchtime he declared he had never set eyes on it and that she probably had taken it into the house herself and left it in one of those nine bedrooms or four reception-rooms.

'But I didn't. I know I left it in the wood-shed.'

'Hester, this is a big place, and you are busy. You are bound to forget things. Anyway, it is only an old shawl. Surely you have another?'

She began to tell him that that was not the point, that she had any number of shawls, but once as a child the same thing had happened with her favourite doll. It had disappeared from its cot only to be found days later, soaking wet and half buried beneath an azalea bush in the garden. No one ever believed that she hadn't left the doll there herself. Was there truly a malevolence in the house, or was it simply that it affected her in some strange way and made her behave oddly?

She found the shawl two days later when she was sweeping out the smoke-house. It was in the salting trough, ripped to shreds, and someone had tried to set fire to it. She showed the charred remnants to Benjamin.

'Now why would I do such a thing?' she cried, heart pounding with fear. 'Besides which, I have not been in the smoke-house these last few days. And only went in today to sweep it out.'

He stared at the shreds in her hand as if he did not see them, then turned unfocused eyes upwards as if to scan the far horizon, yet Hester knew his thoughts did not follow them. 'You have been overworking, Hester. Perhaps that is a different shawl,' he said at length, and she almost choked with exasperation.

'Why will you not believe me? Why should I lie? What is happening?'

Benjamin regarded her thoughtfully for so long that

she thought he had not heard her, but then, without another word, he turned on his heel and left the room.

In a flurry of frustration she flung the scraps of charred wool to the ground and stamped upon them with her foot. 'Drat the man. He has no feelings,' she cried out to the empty room, and nothing but the ticking of the kitchen clock replied. Eyes brimming with a sudden gush of tears, she looked about her in despair. Was she really going mad? With not a living creature to talk to all day when Benjamin was not with her, was it any wonder if she was going out of her mind?

She made herself take a calming cup of coffee and gave herself a strict talking to. Perhaps this was a different shawl, or perhaps she had indeed torn it and set fire to it herself when she was too tired to think what she was doing. Sometimes she felt in such agonies over her problems with Benjamin, she might be demented enough to do anything. Often she found herself pacing from room to room as if she were seeking something but could not find it.

The silence was oppressive. Hadn't she always found it so? And winter was not yet over. If they did not go to Atlanta soon, they could well be trapped in alone here by an ice storm or gales. Though memories of childhood days spent at Rhapsody Creek were hazy, so effectively had she blotted them out, she recalled storms so severe that they brought even branches from the great trees crashing. And, much as she loved Benjamin, it was a scenario she did not welcome. Yet wallowing in self-pity would not help one iota. With a valiant strength of purpose she wrapped a fresh shawl about her head and went to join Benjamin in the fields.

'I'm sorry,' she told him, with a sheepish smile. 'This place has always done odd things to me. But no more. I am determined to beat it.' And, picking up the hoe, she set to with renewed vigour.

Benjamin watched her as he went about his work, and had Hester been able to read his mind she would have been sorely troubled by it. For not only did he fully believe that she was not responsible for the burning of her own shawl but he rather thought he knew who was. From that first day when he'd studied the well-oiled winding gear on the well he'd been puzzled, and since then there'd been other signs. A banging door, a tool missing, and once the still warm remains of a fire. He'd spent long nights watching and waiting for a sign of the intruder, which he had welcomed in an odd way since it kept him from Hester's bed. His mind was a riot of confusion when he was not with her, and worse when he was. Yet his weakness had always taken him to her in the end. He even asked himself if he was coming to care for her more than he would admit. And so he had been glad of an opportunity to cool his growing ardour in the chill of the night. And his patience had been rewarded, for he had spotted their silent companion, and the young wiry body with its familiar face and crop of brown hair had been unmistakable.

He glanced across at Hester where she bravely toiled. He could not bring himself to tell her his fears. Yet he could not have given a satisfactory reason why not. It was certain that he must do something. Her rosy cheeks were quite gone.

'On Monday we go to Atlanta,' he called across to her. 'So have those lists ready.'

With a squeal of delight Hester dropped the hoe and flew the short distance between them to wrap her arms about his neck. 'Oh, how kind you are to me.' She wondered then how she could ever have thought him cold for wasn't she the luckiest girl in the whole world? And when Monday came they set out before dawn, well wrapped up in coats and rugs against the chill of the morning, with hot bricks at their feet. And as

194

Hester watched the sky turn to pink and gold over the distant Blue Ridge mountains she vowed, most fervently, to be content with her lot, and never again to indulge in a fit of the glums.

George Mackay pulled the speared rabbit carcass off the shaved willow wand and stuck it in a pot on the hot stove. He had learned to be careful these last weeks where and when he'd lit his cooking fires, but he was cold and hungry and meant to take advantage of having the place to himself at last.

He smiled as he stoked the flames in the stove. He'd had some fun making Hester jittery, though. He'd forgotten just how much fun it could be but she was every bit as soft as she had been when they were children. It had been so easy then to dupe her with tales of phantoms and spooks when he played his tricks on her. It was almost laughable to find it equally easy now she was a woman grown.

He limped across the kitchen and got himself a cup from the dresser. Hester surely wouldn't miss a drop of this delicious coffee she'd made, and he was mighty thirsty. His darned leg was aching more than ever in this cold weather. Still, he was lucky he'd only broken it during that first dreadful winter when he'd fallen through the rotten boards on the bridge, and not had it bitten off by the gators in the river below. Sheer grit had kept him going through the dark, pain-filled days that had followed. But then nothing had been easy these last two years. Against all the odds he was still here, and he sure as hell wasn't going to risk losing the freedom he'd so painfully achieved to salve Hester's prickly conscience. And he knew that if she ever found out he was alive, and a deserter, she'd have him back in that army billet quicker than a squirrel could climb a tree.

But he wasn't going. No, sir. They'd string him up

for sure if he did, or shoot him, as they had poor Jethro. Best friend a man ever had, was Jethro, and now he was dead all because he couldn't stomach killing. George had no such inhibitions, being a country boy at heart who loved nothing better than pitting himself against man or nature. But filth, squalor, men screaming from gangrene and fever, and semi-starvation, he could not tolerate. All he wanted was to be left alone, in peace, in his own home. And not even Hester's over-developed sense of duty could make him do what he didn't want to. So often when they were children she'd forced him to own up to his pranks and naughtiness, but she'd bossed him for the last time. He didn't care a button for patriotism, only for George Mackay. What else mattered when in the long run it was every man for himself? Just so long as Hester thought him dead, and continued to hate this place, he could work on her enough to make her leave, and that surly husband would go with her.

But George was worried. They'd gone off to Atlanta today in fine fettle, laughing and joking together as they always seemed to be these days. He'd heard them talk of hiring hands and buying pretties for the house. A bitterness clenched his heart. This was his plantation, and he wouldn't have it stolen from him by some damn Englishman. Since he hadn't succeeded yet in sending the pair of them packing, perhaps he should use more direct methods? Maybe he should turn his attention to lover-boy himself.

As George tore into the succulent pink flesh of boiled rabbit, he stopped to smile or frown from time to time as plans were hatched, examined, or rejected in his agile brain. He'd think of something, nothing was surer.

CHAPTER THIRTEEN

WHILE in Atlanta, Hester was having the best time she'd ever known. She called in just about every shop on and around Peach Tree Street. And Benjamin seemed to take a real interest in choosing fabrics, patterns, carpets, lamps and bric-a-brac to brighten Rhapsody Creek. Hester guessed it was probably the first home he'd ever had the pleasure of furnishing and he entered into the spirit of things with relish. It was the most enthusiastic she had ever seen him, and she loved him for it.

Hester never stopped talking the whole day for there was so much to remark upon. She loved Atlanta on sight with its straight, wide streets that criss-crossed the town, fine, elegant houses and smart new shops. She loved to watch the carriages ride by and peak inside to see what the young ladies were wearing. It was all most exciting.

'A town in its infancy,' Benjamin told her. 'But going places. Like me.' And he grinned at her with that totally disarming grin which squeezed the breath from her lungs and left her curiously light-headed.

Benjamin surprised her even more by taking a decided interest in the question of her wardrobe. He took her to a charming little salon where they were attended personally by the proprietress herself, a Madame Levoir, late of Paris. Young and ambitious, determined to bring style to this new land and riches to her own pocket, she sat them upon gilded chairs while she quietly measured Hester with her eyes, and the size of her husband's pocket with her head.

Pattern books were brought out and pored over,

196

together with a bewildering choice of fabric swatches. And just as Hester was trying to decide between a sensible blue merino or a more daring lavender satin, with the entertaining she would be doing in mind, Benjamin took her breath away by buying both and proceeding to order more gowns than she could ever know what to do with. True, a number were merely serviceable for everyday wear, for she had insisted on those being included.

'While we are living on a plantation with all the work that that entails, even with servants, I must have the proper clothes to wear for my chores,' Hester said repeatedly until Benjamin laughed.

'Very well, but you must also have the correct clothes to entertain, as my beautiful young wife. Something entirely frivolous.' He held up a length of soft velvet in a deep rich red. 'This, for example. With a low-cut neckline and sweeping skirt, and perhaps a fall of cream lace at the elbows? It would look superb on you, Hester.'

Hester enquired of the price and turned pale. 'I think this blue cord will do just as well,' she protested.

'We'll take the red,' said Benjamin, handing it over to the young matron, 'and see that it is made up by noon tomorrow, as I said. We'll take this one home with us and you can send the rest on.'

'Yes, indeed, sir. I have here a hat which I think would match perfectly; perhaps Madame would care to try it?'

That too was selected and Benjamin also chose a fur-lined cloak with a wide hood, and Hester was sure that had she seen the price on the ticket, which Madame Levoir ensured that she did not, she would have fainted clean away, for it was the most perfectly beautiful cloak she had ever seen.

Next came shoes, and fans and gloves and all manner of gewgaws. And so it continued for a long, long time, until Hester's head was spinning and she could scarce tell the difference between green or gold, satin or silk. At last Benjamin left, claiming that he had to attend to his own affairs, leaving Hester with Madame Levoir to deal with the more personal items of clothing that she needed and enjoy a most welcome cup of coffee.

'And now we must make the first basic pattern in a simple white cotton fabric,' said Madame Levoir in her businesslike fashion. 'That way we can use it as a guide for all the clothes we make up for Madame. We can then deliver the items without asking you to call for constant fittings, which is not always possible,' she explained.

Thinking of the long distances involved, Hester wearily agreed, and gave herself up to a long and tiring afternoon enduring endless pinning, tacking and tucking when she would much rather be with Benjamin choosing horses and a carriage. And would he find enough men to help him on the plantation? She very much doubted it. He still had very little idea of the amount of work involved. If only he would listen to her more. But then that was half his charm; he was so decisive, so strong. He knew exactly what he wanted and went right out to get it. She admired that in a man. And surely all this extravagance on her behalf must prove that he liked her at least a little. Or else that he felt pity and shame for her in her dowdy, outmoded gowns. Hester's fragile optimism crumbled and her mouth turned down in almost childlike despair.

Madame Levoir noted the loss of confidence at once. 'If Madame is newly married, then she would perhaps like a new nightgown, in fine French lace, yes?' asked the clever little seamstress. 'It would please Monsieur, no?'

'Oh, yes,' cried Hester, brightening. 'It would be the very thing.'

And as she stood brushing her hair in their hotel

room with the eyes of her new husband riveted upon her she guessed that Monsieur was indeed pleased.

He came to rest his hands upon her shoulders and look into her eyes through the cheval glass. 'Do I detect the influence of Madame Levoir?'

A tell-tale flush crept up Hester's cheeks but she tossed her chin and outfaced him. 'I dare say a woman may buy herself a new nightgown if she has a mind to.'

Benjamin threw back his head and almost shouted with laughter. Then, before she guessed his intent, he swept her up into his arms and carried her to the bed. 'I think you are simply protecting that awful tent which I promised to shred.'

'Would you shred this one?' Hester asked, daringly provocative as she lay looking up at him, and slowly he shook his head.

'But it is so beautiful, we must take care not to crease it.' And, smiling at her with a compelling warmth that none the less sent shivers of delight along her spine, he helped her to remove it. 'Though I confess I'd grown quite fond of the other. It issued a kind of challenge.'

'Benjamin Blake, you are wicked.'

And, with a gleam in his eye, he agreed. That night in Atlanta proved to be the most beautiful, the most fulfilling of their marriage thus far. Their lovemaking was somehow different, more relaxed, more giving. Far from the plantation, Hester put aside her restraints and worries and at last loved her husband with open candour. And Benjamin responded with an achingly sweet tenderness which she would hold in her memory for all time. He smoothed back her slender arms and cupped and caressed her breasts and each sensitive part of her until she was wild with desire for him. And when fulfilment came she felt at last that it was much more than a physical union for he cried out her name, breaking his long silence, and gazed down into her eyes, something he had never done before.

'Dammit, Hester, but I——' The sentence was bitten off as he rolled from her. But, warm and relaxed by his side, Hester sank that night into sleep with a small smile upon her lips, for hope had been born again, and with it a small bud of confidence which one day might flower.

The drive home was accomplished with greater speed in a spanking new carriage. The cart followed behind, pulled by a pair of huge chestnuts. Benjamin knew more about boats than horses, but these two seemed strong and broad enough of shoulder to pull the heaviest of weights. He rather thought they would be called upon to use that strength in rooting out the many old tree-stumps he'd found about the place, and, since Captain had proved uninterested in ploughing, they could do that too. The old horse would need to be returned to Aunt Kizzy somehow, for farm work did not suit him, he always managing to give the impression that even pulling the old cart was beneath his dignity. He was clearly much more interested in the new carriage, for he trotted along happily enough now with ears pricked and head held high. In any case the cart would have proved too heavy a load for him on this occasion, for in addition to fresh supplies it carried a cook, two maids, and three field hands.

'Three?' Hester had repeated, when Benjamin told her, but he simply tightened his lips and said three was plenty for now and he could easily get more as spring came nearer. He had not backed down on the slavery issue.

And tied to the back of the cart were also a couple of riding horses, which would prove useful for getting about the plantation. One of them, a small grey mare, was for Hester and she had been delighted with the gift.

'I shall call her Charlie,' she declared, rubbing her cheek against the soft face of the horse and Benjamin had laughed at her.

'Isn't that a boy's name?'

'I don't care. It's in memory of Charleston, my home. Oh, I know I must make this my home now, with you, but Charleston will always be special.'

Benjamin regarded her with an expression so sad that it chilled her. 'You can go home to Charleston if you wish. We have horses enough for the journey now. I certainly have no desire to keep you here against your will.'

Hester could have kicked herself for her foolishness. The last thing she wanted was to leave him, particularly now they were growing so close. 'Oh, no, I have no wish to go without you. It is only—only——'

'Only what, Hester?' And now the expression softened as he took in her confusion. Did she miss her friends so much? Somehow the thought disappointed him and, wrapping an arm around her shoulders, he pulled her gently to him in the carriage. 'It will be better when the house is done. You can invite the Marshall family from Ashlea, and I hear the Calverts have a daughter your age. You will not be so lonely then.'

She met the kindness of his smile with brimming eyes. He was not so cold and unemotional after all for there was genuine sympathy in his expression. 'Thank you, Benjamin.'

'For what?' He was looking at her with a quiet thoughtfulness, the memory of their last night together in the forefront of his mind. He hadn't seen her quite so vulnerable before and it disturbed him; the warmth of her trusting body leaning against his gave him pleasure and offered a strange kind of comfort.

'Oh, I don't know, for being there, I suppose.'
Hester looked contrite. 'I'm just an old silly, I know. I
shouldn't let the quiet get to me the way I do. And you
are probably right. Once Rhapsody Creek is fixed up
good, I'll get over my jitters.'

Benjamin gave her a reassuring squeeze. 'You shall
have the biggest party Georgia ever saw, and we'll
invite everyone we can think of. Fill the place with
light and colour and noise.'

Hester looked quickly up at him, her eyes shining.
'A party? Do you really mean it?'

Benjamin chuckled at the excitement in her voice. 'I
really mean it.'

'Oh, you are the best of husbands.' And Hester flung
her arms about his neck and gave him a bear-hug
followed by a kiss. She had meant it to be sweet and
loving but only short, and very by the way. But for
some reason one kiss gave her the appetite for another
and she waited breathlessly, hopefully, her eyes fixed
upon the sensual droop of his lower lip so close to her
own, wanting desperately for him to feel the same and
repeat it, to show his love for her outside of the
bedchamber. In the long, hushed moment she could
feel his eyes moving over her face but dared not meet
his gaze for fear of what he might read in it. She was
almost sure she could feel his heart pounding against
her own. Then he simply looked over her head and
spoke in a practical matter-of-fact voice.

'Get some sleep, Hester. It's going to be a long drive
home.' And without demur she obeyed.

Several hours later, when the little party turned into
the long drive of Rhapsody Creek, Hester leapt forward in the carriage to gaze over Captain's head,
incredulous joy in her face.

'There's someone here. Look, there's a carriage at
the door.' And, indeed, waiting for her on the wide
white steps was none other than the tiny figure of Aunt

Kizzy herself, a pile of boxes about her feet and a wide smile on her dear face.

'Why, I've missed you, girl,' she cried, giving Hester a hug that near robbed her of breath. 'The place has been that quiet, I've taken to talking to myself. So when Carter offered to drive me over on a visit, I couldn't pack quickly enough, I can tell you.'

Turning, Hester smiled up into Carter's bland face. 'Hello, Carter. I appreciate your bringing Aunt Kizzy to visit. It was kind of you.'

Carter rubbed thick fingers through the sprouting tufts of pale blond hair. 'I would have come anyway, Hester.'

She was surprised. 'Would you?'

'Sure would.' He looked at her for a moment, grey eyes boring into her as if he was trying to read her thoughts, and then he glanced across at Benjamin's retreating back as he led the horses away. 'I had to be sure you were being well cared for. 'Cause if you ain't, I'd have to take steps to do something about it now, wouldn't I?'

Hester gave a little laugh that came out sounding foolish and nervous, feeling that all too familiar tide of hot embarrassment mingled with irritation which Carter brought out in her. 'Really, Carter, how you do fuss. Why shouldn't I be fine?' The thought of the ineffectual Carter Lois tackling the mighty and power-ful Benjamin Blake if it had been otherwise almost made her want to laugh out loud.

But Carter was looking unusually grim. 'You don't look too well. You lost weight?'

'Only a little. I've been working hard. But I have help now, see.' She indicated the little procession carrying boxes and packages into the house. 'So no need to look so disapproving, and do stop this foolish interrogation about my health, and come inside, do.

You must be worn out from the journey and I'm just longing to hear all your news.'

'Nothing untoward happened to you at all?' persisted Carter, as he followed Hester through the stairhall to the small parlour and watched as she set a match to the ready-laid fire in the grate.

Hester paused for the slightest fraction of a second before snapping, 'No, nothing at all. What should have happened? Benjamin and I have been kept fully occupied with our daily chores, I can tell you.' She had no wish for either Carter or Aunt Kizzy to suspect any hint of nervousness on her part at living out here. She got to her feet and turned quickly to face them, hoping her smile of welcome effectively masked the uneasiness that seemed to be an inherent part of her nature the moment she set foot in the place. Somewhere in the depths of the house a door banged in the wind, and despite the swift leap of flames around the dry logs behind her Hester shivered. 'Now, if you will excuse me for one moment, I would like to give my new staff their instructions. We shall certainly all require hot water and food, and bedrooms for you both, of course.' She kissed Aunt Kizzy effusively on her wrinkled cheek. 'I can't tell you how happy I am to see you.'

'There are matters I would like to discuss with you, Hester. In private, if I may,' announced Carter portentously as she strode to the door.

'Oh?' Despite herself she stopped and half turned to him, curiosity in her voice. 'What matters?'

'I came because I reckoned there are things which should be made plain to you, Hester, without any more delay. I've talked to Miss Kizzy about it, and though we don't entirely see eye to eye she has agreed that I may put certain new facts before you which have come to light over this new husband of yours. Facts which might just alter your opinion of him and make you think twice about staying out here all on your lonesome selves. If you see what I mean?'

Hester stared at him, confounded, the irritation growing to a hot ball of tight anger in her chest. 'No,' she said very quietly. 'I'm afraid I don't see. If by "this new husband of yours" you mean Benjamin, then I would ask you to have the manners to use his given name. And I can't think of any facts, new or otherwise, which can't be spoken of openly before both of us. Perhaps at dinner? In the meantime, pray make yourselves comfortable by the fire while I organise refreshments.'

As she swept from the room, through the stairhall and out the back to the house kitchens, she was unaware of a figure standing by the front door who watched her in silent admiration. Hester Mackay had come a long way from the hot-tempered miss who had wanted to box Carter Lois's ears and boxed his own instead. Now she possessed self-reliance and burgeoning sophistication and Benjamin, despite his frowning expression, decided he liked that in a woman. He liked it rather a lot. It was almost a pity they'd been interrupted in this new discovery of each other.

Despite her brave words, Hester could scarcely concentrate. Throughout the rest of that endless day she dreaded what Carter might have to tell her, yet perversely could hardly wait to hear what it might be. Hadn't she always guessed there was some secret concerning Benjamin which he had kept from her? It seemed she was now about to hear what it was. But how was she ever to find the opportunity to be alone with Carter?

There was no opportunity that evening, which began pleasantly enough with convivial glasses of peach wine and a re-telling of their shopping trip in Atlanta. For once Hester was free to enjoy the delicious meal of celery soup and bird's-eye peppers with tabasca sauce prepared by Mango, their new cook. The negro had been astonished to learn that he was to receive his freedom, and wages for his work, and had at first been suspicious, not quite believing that this family was genuine, but Benjamin had been at pains to prove his worth by offering a hiring fee in advance and, thus encouraged, the surprised and delighted man had been more than willing to help purchase stores and equipment for his new kitchen. And though he declared it 'shore would take some gettin' used to,' he seemed to be managing well enough and Hester proudly explained their new policy to her guests, wondering what their reaction might be.

'Doesn't surprise me in the least,' stated Carter, mystifyingly.

'Are you going to join the anti-slavery lobby?' asked Hester, surprised, frowning slightly as she sensed Benjamin tense beside her.

'I meant that I can quite see that someone of Benjamin Blake's persuasion would be against hiring slaves.' Carter's tone was caustic as his pale eyes slid over Hester to rest challengingly upon Benjamin.

'You mean because he is English?'

Carter almost smirked. 'No, I don't. I mean because he has spent time as a captive himself so no doubt appreciates freedom more'n most folks. But then I dare say he has told you all about his spell in prison by now?'

The air became charged with an unidentifiable atmosphere as he waited for Hester's reply, and she looked from one man to the other, her thoughts whirling. Here again was the hint that Benjamin had spent time in prison. Could it have been more serious than Caro and Beattie had supposed? She dared not think that it was. For some reason she had no desire for Carter to think she was in ignorance of it.

'I am well aware of Benjamin's murky past,' she said, and with a brave attempt at a girlish giggle continued, 'I'm sure we must all have some skeleton in our cupboard we'd much rather not remember. Maybe even you have secrets, Carter. Do tell us?' Her joking sounded stiff and unreal but she felt an unquenchable desire to keep up some kind of pretence. Casting a quick glance sideways at the tautness of Benjamin's high cheekbones and the now familiar way he sucked in his lower lip when angry, she wished very fervently that he would speak, deny the accusation and have done with it.

Instead he got to his feet and, taking her elbow with a hand that felt more like a grip of steel, he twisted his lips into a parody of a smile. 'Shall we retire to the withdrawing-room and enjoy our coffee there?' And, turning to Aunt Kizzy, blithely continued, 'You can perhaps give us your opinion, Miss Kizzy, on how best to re-cover the two sofas. They are in a sorry state but Hester is a little overwhelmed by all the work to be done, I'm afraid.'

'Yes, of course, by all means. I should be delighted to help in any way.' Aunt Kizzy was on her feet, giving no indication that she had noted the atmosphere or the weakness of the excuse to change a conversation that had grown difficult. And for the next hour the two ladies discussed the relative merits of stitched braiding and panel pins, round or square cushions, pale blue or turquoise, and whether the drawing-room walls should be completely redone or merely cleaned. Meanwhile the two gentlemen took part in a polite if desultory conversation somewhere in the background, punctuated by long, pained silences. Hester was so intent on trying to overhear the stilted words exchanged between the two, she had great difficulty sometimes in keeping up with Aunt Kizzy's busy chatter. The old lady, with notebook and pencil in hand, had already made a list at least as extensive as the one they had so recently fulfilled in Atlanta.

But Hester could take no interest in the proposals. She felt the whole episode was becoming increasingly embarrassing and she could not help but wonder why. If Benjamin had nothing at all to hide, as he had made such a point of assuring her, why was he behaving in quite such an odd fashion with Carter Lois? Surely he could at least make the effort to be open and friendly? Why did he not put paid to the rumours once and for all?

'Dear me, no, Aunt Kizzy. Not rose-pink; I could not live with it. I simply am not a pink person.'

'Tush! It is the very latest fashion.'

And then Carter's voice rose as if he wished it to be heard over the female chatter.

'This must seem a dull spot to someone such as yourself, Benjamin, used to the more fashionable cities of Europe.'

'I can't say I care much for fashion,' growled Benjamin in a voice barely above civil.

Carter's pale eyes seemed to take on new colour as he fastened them on his adversary. 'But it is true that you have travelled extensively, particularly in the Netherlands and France?'

'Indeed I have never denied it. I have several ships, after all.' Sarcasm was strong in his tone.

'And, if not a dandy, a lady's man, eh? Or so I've heard tell. What is it they say about sailors? A lady in every port. Is that the way it goes?'

'I know not.' Benjamin clinked the decanter against his brandy glass as he refilled it. He did not offer Carter any.

'Not now, Carter,' interposed Aunt Kizzy, for no apparent reason so far as Hester could see. A slow smile stretched across Carter's flat face as he flapped a dismissive hand at the old lady.

'He'll have told you two ladies all about it, in any case, I dare say. About his uncommon bad luck with the fair sex. Never was a man so jinxed, eh? Ain't that right, Benjy?'

'Don't call me that.' The words came through slitted teeth.

Triumph spilled over into a chortling gurgle of laughter from Carter, who was quite unlike his normal restrained self, and Hester felt her spine tingle with unexpected fear. 'No, indeed, sorry. That was your first wife, wasn't it, who called you that?' Carter adopted a considering look of glazed puzzlement. 'Or was it the second?'

The silence was appalling. It ran through Hester's veins like forest fire, eating up every emotion in its path. It left her stunned, empty with shock.

It was Aunt Kizzy who was the first to rally and her voice was as crisp, her words as direct as ever. 'Carter Lois, didn't I tell you to keep your mouth shut? I was going to break it to Hester gently, what it is that everyone was saying, so's she had some warning before she came on a visit. Now you've gone charging in like a pig in a parlour, upsetting everybody and everything and achieving nothing. Why can't you learn to hold your fool tongue?'

'My sentiments entirely.' Every head turned towards the sharp, clipped tone.

'I'm sorry I let him fetch me now,' mourned Aunt Kizzy, looking up at Benjamin beseechingly. 'If I'd known, I wouldn't have agreed. You know I wouldn't.'

Benjamin smiled reassuringly at the small, distressed woman and patted her shoulder kindly with one large, tanned hand. 'I know that, Miss Kizzy.' Then, turning to where Hester stood as stiff as a pillar of solid rock, he continued, 'However, now is not the time to discuss it, and certainly not in company. I'll speak with you tomorrow, Lois. It has been a long day for us all and I can see my wife is dropping on her feet. I'll give you goodnight.'

And, scooping Hester into the curve of his arm, he swept her out of the room and up the wide staircase before she had time to think or protest.

Once in their bedroom, however, Benjamin closed the door with a sharp click and turned Hester to face him. After a long empty silence, in which he seemed to be struggling with his control, the words began to come.

'And now I expect you are ready to rant and rail at me for supposedly keeping further secrets from you? I well know that temper of yours, Hester, and I'm sure it is just bursting to let fly. Well, go ahead. You are free to do so. We are quite alone. Here is a pottery vase to hurl at me to start you off.'

She accepted the ornament from him as if in a daze. Hester had never felt less inclined to temper in all her life. She felt stunned, drained, and, worst of all, betrayed. Why had he not told her that Sarah had been his wife? All that talk of the woman meaning nothing to him was just so much nonsense. And with rare clarity of insight into her own character she realised that she only ever resorted to temper when she wanted her own way in something, and was in danger of not getting it. But such an outburst would never win her Benjamin Blake. And, if nothing he had said to her so far was the truth, did she even want to win him?

Hester stared across the bedroom at the bed where he had come to her these last weeks almost as if he couldn't help himself. They had fused their bodies one with the other as if they truly were lovers, and in the deep dark of the night Hester had pretended that his lovemaking meant that Benjamin returned her love in very truth. And in their last night in Atlanta she had begun to hope the days of pretence were almost over. Now, looking at him where he stood by the marble fireplace, at his most inscrutable and unfeeling, a terrible fear invaded her stomach that it had all been a lie, a fantasy of her own making. Benjamin did not, nor ever would love her. He had rejected her love from the start, not because of his lack of family background, nor because he had been disturbed by Sarah's so-called obsession with him, but because he was still in love with Sarah, his *wife*.

Hester thought again about Carter's words. Benjamin's *second* wife? Then there had been a first? How could a man forget to mention *two* wives? To her dismay she found her body was actually shaking and, setting the vase very carefully down, she turned away and walked to the window. It would never do for him to guess that she was out of control. Yet she was. Her agony was almost choking her. She had become every bit as possessed by him as poor sad Sarah, despite all her well-meant efforts to the contrary. Every waking moment Hester thought of him. Every night she longed for him with every fibre of her being.

She spoke now with commendable composure, successfully controlling the threatening tears.

'I dare say you had your reasons for not telling me these things, though for the life of me I cannot at this moment imagine what they might have been. But I do assure you that I am not in the least concerned or even interested. We agreed from the start that the past would be a closed book to us both. Our marriage is nothing more than a financial arrangement, therefore I am not in a position to ask for any explanations nor throw a tantrum if you do not offer one. I suggest we continue as we are without recriminations or criticism. We owe each other nothing.'

His eyes narrowed alarmingly as he stared at her in a manner which made her feel excessively uncomfortable, as if she had said something offensive, yet she had spoken no more than the truth.

'You consider our marriage nothing but a sham?'

'I didn't say that.'

'You are not in the least little bit curious about whether Carter Lois spoke the truth?'

She shifted uncomfortably and turned her attention back to the window. A wind was getting up outside, ruffling the tall cypress trees so that they creaked and moaned as if to echo her distress. 'For all his faults I have never known Carter to lie.' She heard a guttural sound of unexploded anger in Benjamin's throat and she flinched. Yet again, it seemed, she had said the wrong thing. Swirling about to face him squarely, she flinched again as she found him close behind her. 'You did not deny it.' There was the faintest quaver in her voice and though she tried to tear her eyes from his face she could not.

'Was it necessary for me to do so?' Benjamin asked, deceptively soft, and Hester felt herself quaking before his barely suppressed anger, as if it were she who were the guilty one, she thought resentfully. His hands came down upon her shoulders, pinioning her firmly against him so that there was no question of escape, and his face came down to within inches of her own. 'Do I look like a murderer? Did you imagine you shared your bed with one?'

CHAPTER FOURTEEN

ALL vestige of colour fled from Hester's cheeks as shock bounced through her. 'Murderer?' It was little more than an ashen whisper spoken through stiffened lips, and she could frame no more words, for the expression in Benjamin's glittering blue eyes was awesome.

'Carter's facts were a little inaccurate, but without doubt he has stumbled upon the nub of my story, so you'd best hear it all.'

'I don't want to hear.' She was turning her face away, desperately trying to shut her ears to the droning harshness of his voice.

'No, sweet Hester, you must listen, since if I don't oblige Lois most certainly will.' He forced her frozen limbs into a stiff-backed chair and, stepping back, regarded her with an expression of taunting cruelty. She believed, in her distress, that it was directed entirely at her. Had she fully understood the inner bitterness Benjamin felt, she would have known otherwise.

He did not walk away when he started to speak, and she found herself riveted by him, her eyes fastened to his in a kind of macabre horror, not wishing to hear yet unable to resist drinking in every word. The facts fell starkly upon her ears without preamble, without explanation or excuses.

'Sarah was not my wife; in that Carter was wrong. But it is true that I have been married before. My first wife was called Jane. She was a child of sixteen when we married, and I was twenty-two. I suppose you might call us childhood sweethearts. I went away to sea and when I returned found that she had died in childbirth.

213

I swore never to marry again and devoted my energies to making a fortune, for which I appeared to have an aptitude. But then Sarah reappeared in my life. She too had been taken in by Old Mother Cooper and had been wont to follow me about like a doting puppy throughout my boyhood. But what was faintly amusing to a nine-year-old became an embarrassment to a man of near thirty. I have told you of her obsession so I will not repeat it.' He paused and dropped his chin to stare moodily at the ground, legs apart, fists clenched as if it cost him all his effort to continue.

'She begged me to marry her but I would not. When she realised that I meant it, that I was going away back to sea, to America. . .she hanged herself. She left no note, for of course she could not write. But she had warned me of her intention and I had not believed her, putting it down to a disappointment which would soon pass once she accepted I was gone for good. They charged me with her murder, naturally, and I could convince no one of my innocence. I spent two years in gaol while my case waited to be heard.'

Hester was staring at him with a shocked appeal in her wide eyes. 'And were—were you found innocent?' she managed at last.

Benjamin gave her a long, considering look before his wide lips twisted into a smile, but the eyes remained flint-hard. 'Now that is the crux of the issue, is it not? Carter says that I was guilty. And Carter never lies. Half the population of Liverpool said that I was guilty. I have crossed the world to be rid of the cruelty of such taunts, yet still they follow me. You know me as well as anyone. What do you think, Hester? Tell me. Am I a murderer, or no?'

If Hester slept at all that night she was not aware of it. A strange ethereal light, filled with pain, seemed to pierce her eyes and split her head in two. Of course he was innocent. How could he be otherwise? *Then why did he not say so?* It would surely be the simplest thing in the world to set her mind at rest?

She almost staggered from her bed the next morning, and long before the pink of dawn came to melt away the dark of night she was in the kitchen brewing coffee on the old stove. They left it burning day and night and Benjamin's first task each morning was to replenish the depleted wood-pile stacked by the kitchen door. Possibly because of their trip to Atlanta and the huge amount of cooking, and extra fires they had lit last night on their return, the pile was all used up.

Hester riddled the embers with the poker, chewing thoughtfully upon her lower lip. Benjamin had spent the night in the small dressing-room and, since she had heard no sound from there thus far this morning, he must still be asleep. She considered waking him, but it was only coffee she wanted; it was too early yet for anyone to be asking for breakfast. It couldn't be much beyond five and she had no wish to face Benjamin's ire in her present fragile state. Making her decision, Hester picked up the log basket and, pulling a shawl over her head, left the cosy warmth of the kitchen. She could surely manage a few logs by herself?

Crossing the back yard without benefit of moonlight was an uncomfortable experience but she could not carry a lantern as well as the log basket. She could feel the small hairs prickling on the back of her neck. An owl hooted and somewhere in the far distance was the cry of a less friendly night creature. She quickened her pace. Almost there. The wood-stack was just beside the second of the old barns. Here was the well with its cold stone rim. Her fingers found the bucket balanced on the lip and settled it more safely. The winding gear had proved surprisingly easy to use and had not rusted up as much as she would have expected over these long years. Feeling her way with care, she moved on. Hester almost cried out as she heard a door creak on old hinges, then laughed softly at her own foolishness. It was only the wind. Ahead of her were the slave cabins, unused and broken down now they housed no slaves at Rhapsody Creek. Benjamin's new field hands occupied the former overseer's house in much greater comfort. Soon she should reach a picket fence and if she followed that to her left she would come to the wood-stack. Fingers outstretched in the darkness, breath held tight in her chest, she located the smoothness of freshly painted wood and, breathing more easily, traced a swift path to the barn.

Hester found the wood-stack without any difficulty. It towered before her, leaning rather drunkenly against the side of the barn and she began to hastily fill her basket. She was anxious to be done with the job and return to the comparative comfort of the kitchen. Once the fire was stoked up and the coffee humming, Hester planned to sit for a while with her own thoughts and try to sort out her confusion. But she mustn't try to carry too many logs, she thought, taking one last one from the pile. Perhaps her haste made her careless but as she picked up her basket and turned to go she heard an odd grumbling sound. Spinning round quickly to check where it came from, her eyes flew upwards to the top of the log pile. And as logs began to fall upon her and she heard her own scream in her head she was almost certain she saw the outline of a man, stark against the lightening sky, and even heard him laugh.

Benjamin lay unmoving on the narrow bed, his thoughts in turmoil. She had not believed in him. She had stared at him with horror printed on her innocent face, as if he were the devil incarnate. And for the first time in his life Benjamin had wanted to kneel before a woman and beg her to understand. He gave a grunt of self-derision in the darkness. Why should she understand? And why should it matter? Why had he ever imagined that Hester Mackay was in love with him? She had made it plain enough just now that that was not the case. Oddly enough the thought did not bring the expected flood of relief. He felt suddenly bereft, as if he had lost something of inestimable value. What in heaven's name was wrong with him? Hadn't he made a pact with himself all those years ago after Jane had died, and again when Sarah had hung so obsessively to his coat-tails, that he would dally with women where he willed but never—*never* become involved with one ever again?

He flung himself from the hard bed and, dressed only in shirt and breeches, threw up the window to breathe in the chill morning air. He would go for a swim in the small lake behind the house. Perhaps the pain of the cold water would banish this perplexing depression. Tugging on boots and a long overcoat, he let himself quietly out on to the landing. Outside Hester's closed door he hesitated, one hand upon the brass knob. Should he go in? His hand began to turn the knob, then it stopped. For what purpose? What was left to be said? He had told her the full facts and she had turned from him as if it were all of no account. Tightening his lips, he let his hand fall from the knob, turned away from the door and went down the stairs.

He heard Mango whistling happily as he passed the breakfast-room but he did not go in. He did not slow his stride until he had reached the lake. He stared out over its glittering surface, not a ripple marring its smoothness, as dark and passionless as he himself had behaved these last months, years even. He had begun to wonder if he had any feelings left. If he was a man still or merely a parody of one who ate and slept and went through the motions of normal life but never quite succeeded in joining it. Yet during these last weeks with Hester, and in particular that night in

Atlanta, he'd begun to feel like a human being again. The credit for that must surely go to her.

Shrugging off the long coat, Benjamin dropped it on the turf, then looked quickly about as a sound caught his ear. Did someone call out? He half turned. Should he go back to the house? Why should he? It was probably only Mango bursting into one of his lively shanties. Peeling off the shirt, Benjamin dropped it beside the overcoat. The water would be ice-cold at this time of year and his muscles contracted in readiness at the thought. Then he heard it again and this time it was unmistakable. It was indeed Mango, but he was shouting, screaming almost in a high-pitched, petrified voice.

'Massah! Massah!'

Benjamin was running across the grass, thrusting aside the clinging brambles and dogwood, racing for the house.

''Tis Mistress Blake, massah.'

'Where is she?'

'By the wood-pile. It collapsed, massah. But what she doin' there, I shore don't know.'

Now was not the time to waste words. 'Fetch Miss Kizzy. Run, man.'

Fleet of foot, the negro sped into the house and, while pausing only to snatch up the lantern, Benjamin made for the old barn, his heart pounding with the fear of what he might find. To discover he did possess feelings after all and then to lose the source of them would be more than he could bear.

George, on the other hand, had long since given up such luxuries. His eyes followed the gleaming bronze of the half-clothed figure as it bent over the supine form of his sister. He saw her being lifted in strong arms and carried towards the house, the broad back glistening with the ripple of powerful muscle. He had not missed the tenderness which emanated from that awesome figure, nor failed to observe the ashen quality of the cheeks or the grim set of the square jaw. The man looked as if he was having difficulty quelling his anger and George conceded to himself that he would not care to be at the butt of it.

Ironic in a way that it had been Hester. He hadn't been able to curb his laughter when he saw her, and still chuckled at the thought. Always so independent and precise. Always telling him what to do, for all she was younger than him. She'd spent so much time as a busybody child nagging him to take more care when he'd wielded woodaxe or wittling-knife more recklessly than she, yet it was goody-goody Hester who lay injured and not himself. He was a survivor. Hadn't he proved it a score of times?

But in all his planning George told himself he had never meant to seriously hurt Hester, only to scare her off. And how could he have known that his latest plan would backfire? It should have been Blake's perfect body which lay among the pine logs, not poor Hester's. What if she was dead? He shook his head as if chasing away unpleasant thoughts. In any case, how could he be held responsible if she insisted on poking about where she shouldn't? Doing men's work when she should be confining her attentions to filling empty bellies. It'd taken no more than the slightest push to have the log-pile, so artfully unbalanced by his own hand the night they were away, tumbling down upon her. But it would have been better if it'd been the Englishman. It could have been George's final grand gesture for his country, to kill one of the enemy. And, once widowed, Hester would have left at once, he knew that. She would never stay out here alone.

George chewed thoughtfully on his thumb, brow creased in a deep frown. He could only hope this 'accident' would now make her change her mind and leave anyway.

He curled himself up into a tight ball, high in the oak tree. From here he had an excellent view of the whole yard and house area. He could hear Aunt Kizzy issuing orders in her usual forthright manner and he half smiled to himself. What a shock she would get if he simply walked into the kitchen and told her that he was here. The old lady might very well die of fright. But the smile faded as the thought travelled on. She must never know, none of them must. The sooner they all took the road back to Charleston, the sooner he could find peace again and have his home to himself.

Hester opened her eyes on to dazzling light. Even her dreams had taught her to expect Benjamin to be beside her when she woke and she looked hopefully up into the face hovering closely above hers. It was Carter's face. Round and flat with its thatch of unruly corn-coloured hair sprouting out the top of it. If she hadn't hurt so much all over, she would have laughed out loud at sight of it. But the emotion which bit deep inside her was one of disappointment.

'Carter?' She said his name with trembling lips and felt him grasp her cold fingers and rub them with his own. But his hand was even colder than her own and gently she pulled herself free of it. 'Where is—where is Benjamin?'

The grey eyes hardened. 'Stacking logs,' he said crisply.

Hester stared at him in disbelief. His own wife had just suffered a terrible accident and all he could think of doing was stacking logs.

'One is tempted to wonder why,' sneered Carter. 'Covering up evidence, perhaps?'

'Evidence?' The nightmare was deepening.

'That it was not an accident at all,' hissed Carter close against her ear and a ripple of loathing, quite shocking by its intensity, slithered through her. Then he was grasping her hands again and the pain caused by his hold made her wince. 'You have to get out of here, Hester, before you are really hurt. Didn't I tell you, honey, that the man was mad? He's had two wives already. . .'

'One.'

'Begging your pardon?'

'He's had only one wife,' said Hester in a hoarse whisper, 'and Sarah.'

'One wife. Two wives. Don't matter none. What matters is your safety and you sure as hell ain't going to find it here. You must leave, Hester, right away. You can come with me and Aunt Kizzy back to Charleston. Put an end to this shambles of a marriage and start afresh as we always meant to do. We can have it annulled or some such. I'll have the house finished on Meeting Street in no time and you'll want for nothing, I promise you.'

Hester stared at him, transfixed. What was he saying? Her whole body felt as if it had been pummelled, as it probably had by the falling logs. Pain shot up and down her legs and her chest felt as if it still carried the weight of one huge log upon it. But Carter was implying that these injuries had been deliberately inflicted. Suddenly she recalled the sight of a man outlined against the sky, high up on the log-pile. Her heart set up a low thud. Benjamin? Who else could it have been? Could she truly trust him? The memory of that gunpowder of which he'd claimed himself innocent came back to her with powerful force.

'Oh, my, there now, Hester is awake. Didn't I just tell you to call me, Carter, the moment she opened her eyes?' Aunt Kizzy flustered up to the bed and began plumping up pillows and smoothing sheets. 'How you feeling, honey? Got a mighty headache, I'll warrant?'

Hester offered her relative a weak smile. 'You

always did warn me for taking too much upon myself. Seems I did it proper this time.'

'Tch. Always were stubborn as a mule. How do you feel about a sip of lemon tea?'

Hester began to shake her head then thought better of it. 'I'd prefer coffee,' she said, then smiled. 'That's why I went out there, and I never did get a cup.'

'Carter, go and fetch Hester a cup, and some of those fresh-baked biscuits,' ordered Aunt Kizzy, in a voice not to be denied. When he had gone she sat on the edge of the bed and gathered her niece's hands between her own, warming them where Carter's dry touch had cooled.

'Your poor husband has been quite demented. Sat for hours beside you, he did, desperate you might not wake at all.'

Hester gazed wordlessly up at her aunt's homely face as questions formed and reformed in her mind.

'Oh, I know he ain't here now,' she continued. 'But that's because I made him go and lie down a spell. He was plumb exhausted, I can tell you.'

'He's in bed?' Hester asked, expelling a small breath. 'Oh. Carter said he was stacking logs.'

'And so I was. Someone had to do it, since they were all over the yard and like to cause another accident.' Right on cue her husband was standing at the foot of her bed, smiling down upon her, and Hester's mind flew into a turmoil. How could he be guilty of trying to injure her when he looked so—so——? She could think of no word other than beloved, standing there with his glowing eyes, smiling at her with what looked very like tenderness. 'Do you realise how lucky you were, young woman, not to have been killed?' He was frowning at her now and the room grew silent on a held breath. 'As it is, so far as we can tell, you seem to have got off with minor bruising. Can you move everything?' Gently drawing back the sheet, he made her flex every limb, ignoring her embarrassment and her crimson cheeks.

'I am perfectly all right,' she insisted, then gasped as his fingers pressed upon her ankle. 'Almost.'

'In future you'd best confine yourself to the house,' he said bluntly. 'No more doing chores too heavy for you. Besides, there is no need now that we have servants. See she keeps to that, Miss Kizzy.'

'Oh, but I like to be busy——' Hester began.

'No buts,' he bit back. 'For once, Hester, do as you are told.'

And for the next few days rest was what she wanted more than anything. She felt decidedly shaken by the occurrence. But by the end of the week she was beginning to fret at the restrictions and wanting to be out and about again but Benjamin would not hear of it. Every time she set foot on the front step he seemed to be beside her, ordering her back inside. The furthest he would let her visit was the small knot garden at the front of the house, and then only on a bright sunny day.

'But what am I to do with myself all day?' she protested one morning when he would not even allow her out of bed.

'Whatever women do do,' he casually replied. 'You were always fond of mending, do some of that.'

'But now I no longer have your crew to take care of, there is little to be done.'

'Then embroider something. Start on the new cushion covers for the drawing-room. You should come to no harm there. But stay within doors.' And, having settled her day to his satisfaction, he strode to the door only to find Hester had run to reach it before him. And, leaning with her back against it, she faced him squarely.

'We have to talk.'

'About what?'

Hot fury flooded through her at his tone. 'Don't turn so cold and haughty with me, Benjamin Blake, not after all. . .' She faltered slightly as his eyebrows lowered, but then resolutely continued, 'You know well enough what about. We must clear this matter between us.'

'Do you mean the one Carter raised?' asked Benjamin in blithe innocence.

'You know full well I do.'

He brushed her aside with a careless hand and tugged open the door. 'I was under the impression it was all cleared up. Carter, after all, never lies, and if he says I am guilty I can see it is impossible for you to deny it.'

Hester let out an explosion of fury. 'Why will you not tell me with your own lips?'

Benjamin paused at the top of the stairs and considered her thoughtfully for a long moment. 'It should not be necessary. Think what you must, Hester. Live your own life, and stop expecting me to solve your doubts and fears. I have enough problems of my own. All I ask is that you keep yourself close to the house for a while and out of the way. Now do as I say and stop arguing.' And, taking the stairs two at a time, he ran down them as if he could not put enough distance between them.

Hester ran to the top of the staircase, tears blurring her vision. 'Fine,' she called after him. 'If separate lives is what you want, that's what you can have, Benjamin Blake.' She waited for him to turn, to run back to her, to take her in his arms and tell her that was not what he wanted at all. But he did no such thing. At the front door he did pause to look back up at her, standing at the top of the wide stairs in the diaphanous lace nightgown, the one he had once enjoyed removing, and a sudden dryness caught at his throat at what they had lost.

'Do as you will, Hester, but stay close to the house.

Otherwise you may well live to regret it.' And then he added more menacingly, 'Or, worse still, you may not.'

She watched him go with an overwhelming sense of emptiness and shock in her heart. It was over. All that had begun to grow and blossom between them had now quite gone. Perhaps it had never existed at all except in her imagination. And then the kernel of soothing anger exploded within her and the restraining walls of the house were too much for her. Whirling upon her heels, she stormed back into her room, calling for her terrified maid as she began to fling open closet doors.

Moments later, dressed in her new warm cloak, she strode out along the magnolia walk which led to the lake. And as she walked she went over and over in her mind everything that had taken place between them. The happy days working together on the plantation, the nights of lovemaking where they had begun to discover each other as people, that glorious night in Atlanta when for the first time she had felt sure he was giving himself to her alone. And she knew, without a shadow of a doubt, that it had all started to go wrong the moment Carter Lois had arrived. In some indefinable way Benjamin had changed. And what did the past matter in any case? Why would he not tell her?

'It should not be necessary.' Benjamin's own words came to her with a startling intensity.

The night's raindrops dripped from the dark, shiny leaves on to her head. Brambles encroached across the path, catching at her pumps and cloak as she walked, and her temper soaked away, leaving despair and misery in its wake. He was implying she did not trust him. Yet if he would not tell her the whole story then it showed that he did not trust her either. And where there was no trust, how could love flourish? And what was left for her here with no prospect of love? She saw their relationship now as a fantasy of her own mind, insubstantial, unreal, and now the pretences were over. Benjamin did not and never would love her and he had made it quite impossible for her to settle for anything less.

Carter still constantly repeated his offer. It was not a prospect which filled Hester with any pleasure, but it might be a way out of her dilemma. Certainly she needed transport to take her from Rhapsody Creek, and she would prefer not to make the journey alone. She kicked a stone across the path and it rolled with a plop into the lake.

She recalled childhood picnics by this lake, camp fires, a punt, childish laughter. Rare moments of pleasure. She smiled wryly to herself. How foolish of her to imagine she could ever attain happiness at Rhapsody Creek. Hadn't the place always defeated her? Stopping to gaze out over the dark water, so menacingly still, Hester was unheeding of the tears flowing freely over the soft curve of her cheeks. It was foolish to stay on. It was all over. She would speak with Carter at once and begin the arrangements. Tomorrow they would leave.

A bird flew up from the undergrowth behind her, squawking loudly, and, startled, she spun on her heel, a cry upon her lips. The next instant she was falling backwards, her heel slipping and sliding in the wet mud, perilously close to the edge of the banking. Twisting her head, she saw the loom of dark water below. Her fingers clutched at something then closed on thin air. The breath slapped from her body as she hit the water. It was over her head, the folds of her heavy cloak dragging her down, down. Water weeds curled themselves about her face and wrists, binding and plucking her down to the muddy depths of the lake. She tugged at them, fighting for breath, pushing up to the sparkling light. Again and again she fought, an iridescent blur of water filling her eyes, her nose, her mouth, desperate to find a hold, with the sure and certain knowledge that it was not accidental that she had fallen in the lake. She had distinctly felt a push from firm, determined hands. Benjamin's?

CHAPTER FIFTEEN

AT LAST Hester's frozen fingers found the solid form of a branch and she held on to it. She wasn't sure how long she hung there, the overhanging weeds and branches brushing against her head and scratching her face, but tenaciously she gritted her teeth and concentrated on keeping her head above water, fighting the overwhelming desire to let go and sink into oblivion. If only she could rid herself of the dragging cloak but she dared not let go to struggle with the wet neck-cord, nor did she have the strength to pull herself from the water up through the prickly undergrowth that lined the steep bank. Then, when her hands were raw with their scrabbling for a hold, and she was certain she could hold on no longer, miraculously someone was grasping her by the wrists and lifting her with apparent ease from the water.

'Damn you, Hester,' said the all too familiar voice, 'why will you not do as you are told?'

And, meeting the fury of that blue-eyed gaze, Hester pushed at him desperately with her sore hands and, with a heartbroken sob, gathered up her sodden cloak and ran down the slithery path.

She refused to see him. She refused to speak with anyone, even Aunt Kizzy. Hester merely handed over the soaking clothes to her new maid and instructed her to inform Carter and Aunt Kizzy that she wished to leave for Charleston first thing in the morning.

'And if they ask why,' she told the startled maid, 'tell them I feel unwell and believe the sea air will benefit me. For today, I shall spend it in my room. Pray have my meals sent up and start packing.' She said nothing of how she came to be so wet, of how her husband had pushed her into the lake.

When the maid had gone Hester sat in her dressing-gown staring out of the window. There were no tears now, nor any doubts about the rightness of her decision. Only a deep, pained sadness. For whatever he was, whatever he had tried to do to her, he was still her husband and she loved him.

No one came to her. Even Aunt Kizzy respected her wishes for privacy for once, but strangely this neglect had an unsettling effect upon Hester, for though she longed to unburden her fears she dared not. Not for the world would she risk endangering Aunt Kizzy's life. If Benjamin was indeed the madman he seemed, the less she saw of him until she could make her escape, the better. But the long, lonely day gave her too much time to think and she was glad when night came and she could climb into the great bed and close her eyes. But here she found less peace. And as the sleepless night wore on she was spared no agony of memory.

She could remember their first night in this very bed, his tenderness and generosity towards her, the joy she had felt at being close to him. Yet something about Benjamin Blake had always seemed withdrawn. Right from that first meeting he had refused to be drawn about himself. He had always kept the private inner core of his being from her. And now she knew why.

Hester could almost coolly consider her rashness in marrying him. Was that what he did with his life? Persuade innocent young women to fall in love with him and then prey upon their fears and set out to demolish them, culminating in their murder? What manner of man was he that could do such a thing? A monster, no less. She found she was trembling and whimpering in her sleep.

'Hester.'

She was sitting up wide-eyed in bed, heart pounding. 'Don't touch me,' she cried, wildly slapping Benjamin's hands away.

'No hysterics, please. I shall not hurt you but you must listen to me.' Something in the quiet certainty of his voice prevented her from screaming though every instinct cried out so to do.

She pulled the sheets up to her chin. 'If you touch me I'll——'

'I won't touch you,' he said softly. 'Hester, you must believe me, it was not I who pushed you into the lake.'

She gasped. 'How then do you know I was pushed?'

'I can guess.'

'Who else could it have been? Surely you are not accusing Carter, who is still asking me to marry him? And it cannot be Mango or any of the other new hands because strange things were happening even before they came. Oh, nothing quite so dramatic, I know, but none the less odd. You remember the shawl, for instance?'

'I remember. That is why I wanted to speak to you.' His eyes were compelling and much as she longed to turn from him she could not. 'There is one other person who could have done these things to you.'

'Who? I can think of none. You are simply making excuses because you hate me for loving you.' A sob caught in her throat. 'If I did I must have been mad. But not as mad as you. I'm leaving tomorrow and nothing you can say will stop me.'

He grasped her by the shoulders and almost shook her and, as she cried out in terror at his touch, abruptly released her. He sank his head, his chin almost on his chest, his shoulders slumped, and she had to fight the overwhelming urge of pity and love which rose inside her. Then he lifted his head and stared steadily into her eyes. 'You have to know, Hester. There is no way I can protect you any longer unless you know the truth.

I believe it was George who did these things. George who created these accidents. I assume because he wanted you, both of us, out of his home. That is why I have urged you to stay indoors.'

'*George?*'

Benjamin slowly nodded and there was sympathy in his gaze now. 'I suspect he has been holed up here for some time. I've been trying desperately to find him for weeks, but he knows the place so much better than I, and is obviously very clever at hiding.'

'George is *dead.*'

Benjamin shook his head. 'No, Hester. I believe your brother is very much alive.'

'Don't lie to me any more, Benjamin. I can't bear it.' She was out of bed in an instant, her vow to stay calm forgotten. Never in her entire life had she felt so completely angry. 'How can you do it?' she screamed. 'How dare you blame my poor dead brother for your own madness? Get out! *Get out!*'

'Hester, listen to me. . .'

Wildly she looked about her, then picked up the pottery vase he had offered her not so long ago and flourished it at him. 'Get out of my bedroom, out of my life.'

For a long moment Benjamin hesitated then moved to the door. 'As you wish. Perhaps we can discuss this when you feel more rational.' The vase hit the closing door and smashed in pieces all over the new carpet, and, bursting into tears, Hester fell upon the bed.

She woke Aunt Kizzy and Carter early and insisted they leave before dawn. Carter was only too willing to comply, so readily assisted Hester in talking the old lady out of waking Benjamin, 'to bid the poor dear boy goodbye.'

'He knows we are going,' Hester told her with barely restrained patience. 'I said goodbye last night.'

'But he is your husband, girl.'

Not without difficulty Hester finally persuaded Aunt Kizzy to leave by assuring her the separation was merely temporary, and as soon as Hester felt quite herself again she would return.

'I will be back come spring,' she assured her aunt and felt dreadful about making up this lie, but persuaded herself it was permissible in the unusual circumstances.

And so, with their boxes strapped on the top and Captain and Charlie, the new mare, tied to the back of Carter's carriage, they set out eastward towards the rising sun. But instead of the expected joy and relief in her heart Hester felt heavy and unutterably depressed. Behind her lay life and warmth and love. Before her was loneliness, misery and an empty mockery of a life without Benjamin. How could she ever tolerate it?

To make it worse, the sun did not choose to rise at all that morning. Instead the sky remained overcast though with a strange effervescent light. It was bitterly cold and the hot bricks beneath their feet soon cooled to the point of uselessness. Hester tucked her fur-lined cloak, the special gift from Benjamin, around both her own and Aunt Kizzy's knees but still they shivered. Carter, up front driving the horses, would have to see to himself.

An icy wind sprang up, cutting effortlessly through all their layers of clothing and frosting every branch in seconds.

'Looks like we're heading for an ice storm,' called Carter over his shoulder. 'Stick close together or it'll freeze your blood.'

And as the carriage bowled along at as brisk a pace as the frozen rutted track would permit they heard the ominous creak and groan of ice-laden branches swinging overhead. Hester knew that it was common for whole trees to be snapped in two by the icy winds that sometimes scoured the deep South in winter, and if only a branch were to fall upon their carriage they could all be killed. Guilt was now added to her depression that she had put her friends into danger, and she shrank closer to Aunt Kizzy in total dejection.

Carter stopped briefly to put extra blankets over the horses but he was soon back beneath his tarpaulin, shaking with cold.

'Don't look like we picked too good a day for it, Hester, honey. This wind is picking up something terrible.'

'Perhaps we should find shelter.'

'No. Reckon we'll keep going while we can.' The horses bent their heads into the wind and struggled on. After they had been travelling for about three hours they came to a rocky outcrop which could offer a modicum of shelter. And since it was impossible to make effective progress against the cruel wind by this time and a white-out of frost swirled about them they were all more than ready to give the horses a rest while Carter lit a fire and brewed a pot of welcome hot coffee.

'It must be well below freezing,' groaned Aunt Kizzy, wrapping her hands, already clothed in a double pair of mittens, stiffly about her mug. 'I'm sure I cannot see why we had to leave in such a hurry. Another week or two wouldn't have made much difference, and by then the weather would be kinder.'

'I'm so sorry, Aunt, but I really felt I couldn't stay another day in that house. You know I have never liked it.'

'But you were with your husband this time, Hester, and a grown woman. You should have long since given up those spooky fancies you used to have.'

'What spooky fancies?' Carter spoke through a mouthful of chicken. Food, he'd decided, was the only answer to provide warmth, and he pressed it upon the two ladies. 'Eat up, girls, it's a long haul home.'

Hester reached for a chicken leg though she was sure her stomach was too tied up to eat a morsel. 'Only childish imaginings,' she confessed and briefly outlined one or two incidents that had happened to her as a child. 'And always the sensation that I was being watched. The place simply makes me nervous,' she admitted. 'Though I know it is foolish, I imagined it was sending me quite mad.'

'Don't you fret none, honey,' mumbled Carter with his mouth full of bread. 'You ain't going mad. Wasn't it only that brother of yours playing games on you? That's what I heard tell. Why, didn't he laugh like crazy about it when he told me once?'

Hester's eyes flew wide and she stared at Carter in stunned disbelief. 'George? You mean it was George playing tricks on me all the time?'

Carter looked so astonished at her ignorance that he even stopped chewing. 'Surely he told you that when you both growed up.'

'No.'

Carter began to look uncomfortable. 'Well, I ain't one to split on folks but I know he had a reputation for being a pesky rascal when he was a nipper.'

'He certainly did.' This from Aunt Kizzy. 'Wasn't I always having to scold him for this or that? Not like dear Hester, who was such a dream of a child to bring up. George never did seem content, did he now, Hester?'

But Hester wasn't listening. Her mind was whirling as frantically as the frozen leaves in the icy wind. It made sense. George had always been ready to plague her with his odd sense of humour, even at Charleston when he was quite a young man. Why had she not thought of it herself? Why had she not realised that he was the obvious answer? But then why should the nervous child she had once been think to accuse her own brother for her nightmares? And now the cold that settled in her stomach, banishing the coffee's warmth, had nothing to do with the weather.

If George had been the cause of the odd goings-on at Rhapsody Creek when she was a child, then who was responsible for them now?

She was on her feet, stiff with shock. 'Dear heaven, Aunty, Benjamin was right. George did not die of the fever, he is alive. Alive and living at Rhapsody Creek, where he has done his worst to scare me away these last weeks.' Her eyes were dark pools in her ashen face. 'Benjamin. Benjamin is *alone*. We've left him all alone with poor, tormented George. Oh, we must get back at once.'

She was flinging back the fur cloak, climbing down from the carriage, heedless of the quick cry of protest from Aunt Kizzy and Carter.

'I must get to him, don't you see?' She was busily untying the mare from the rear of the carriage. 'Who knows what George might do? If he has been living all alone there these last two years he will be even less responsible for his actions than he was when a boy, and heaven knows he had little enough control in those days.'

'You can't deal with him on your own, child,' cried Miss Kizzy. 'Even supposing you are right, then George won't be at all rational and he could hurt you as well as Benjamin. We must drive on somewhere and get help.'

And Carter, alarmed by his bungling, added his own vehement protest.

But Hester was already preparing to mount. 'There isn't time. You and Carter follow more slowly if you wish. It's too cold anyway to cross the Smokies. We were no doubt mad to try. But I'm getting back there just as fast as I can.'

And, without waiting for any further argument, she kicked her heels into the mare's flanks and put her to a canter which quickly, and rather recklessly in view of the state of the roads, turned into a gallop.

In spite of the icy wind, the treacherous roads and several detours around fallen trees Hester made better progress alone than they had done in the carriage, so did little to curb the madcap pace of the little horse.

When, some hours later, the mare finally skittered to a halt on the icy cobbles of the yard it was late afternoon and the light was failing in the short winter day. The wind had dropped and nothing stirred, not even the Spanish moss which hung pale and ethereal, frozen stalactites of ice hanging from ghostly trees. In the fading light the place looked even more desolate than normal and the usual misgivings and apprehensions flooded in upon her. A tug of self-doubt now made her wonder at her own supposition. How could it be George? George was dead. Why would he not present himself as soon as he saw them if he were truly alive? It was the place itself which gave her the creeps, not poor George. It was her husband who was the murderer, not her brother.

She got down from the horse and took her to the warm stable, where she fed her on hay and water. And as she rubbed Charlie down she began to tremble with fatigue. She would have to go into the house and confess all to Benjamin. But, turning to the door, she just as quickly recoiled from doing so. It had been Benjamin himself who first told her that George was responsible, and she had disbelieved him. Could she now admit that she had been wrong, that she had learned of George's secret childhood pranks on her, and so accepted all Benjamin said? That George was alive? She shook her head in a dazed fashion. Which was the truth? Childhood pranks of moving dolls about was one thing, attempting to kill her was quite another matter. George would never do such a thing. Her mind in a turmoil of confusion, Hester stepped out into the yard.

She could hear nothing, see nothing untoward. The place was deserted. Staring across at the big house, she could not even see a light in the place. But wait, there was a light. But not from the main house. From the smoke-house.

She started across the yard. 'Benjamin?'

Pushing open the door, she peered inside. It was warm in here. Someone had lit a small fire. Oh, how cold she was. She stepped inside. 'Benjamin?'

The door slammed shut behind her, and in the same instant the stone walls echoed with the sound of maniacal laughter. Whirling about, she came face to face with reality.

'Oh, dear God in heaven.' She uttered the words softly, in disbelief. 'We thought you dead.'

'As you can see, sister dear, I am very much alive.' The smile was as beatific as she remembered, but she was more critical now, after what she had so recently learned and experienced, and she did not warm to it as she had been wont to do in the past.

'Why did you not tell us?' Hester whispered. 'Oh, how we worried about you. And were you here all the time? Even when we held the funeral? How could you do it to Aunt Kizzy?'

The smile died. 'Don't start hectoring me, Hester, I won't stand for it. Not any more. You have to under-stand I did what I had to do. Nothing else for it. Not going back. Can't go back.' The fingers began to pluck at his lower lip in agitation.

She stepped closer, a smile of sympathy on her lips. 'I can understand that,' she said. 'But you needn't worry about those old gambling debts any more; Benjamin has paid them.' An uneasiness was spreading within her as her brother stood fidgeting from one foot to the other, like a nervous horse about to bolt. George was clearly in deep distress but where was Benjamin? 'I'd be interested to hear your story,' she said kindly. 'Were you badly injured? I see you favour one foot?'

'That isn't anything.'

'Well, nothing matters now, does it, except that you are alive. Oh, George, I cannot tell you how pleased I am to see you. Let us go into the house and you can tell me everything.' She made half a move towards the door but George moved too, to block her exit.

'No,' he said, and his abruptness alarmed her. 'Stay here.' He spread out his arms as if to ward her off and she hesitated, uncertain what to do.

'But we cannot stay here,' she said, with a shaky attempt at a smile, desperately fighting the fear which was growing inside her.

'Why not? Warm in here. Have lit a nice fire.' His eyes gleamed.

Hester glanced around at the small fire smouldering in the corner. 'Yes, I can see that you have, but it is very smoky in here for it has no windows, and you know smoke is not good for your chest. Let me make you a warming posset on the kitchen stove, or fresh hot coffee if you prefer.' Again she tried to move but he slapped at the door with the flats of both hands and pressed his back against it.

'No, no. There you go again, lecturing and scolding, lecturing and scolding. Knew you would. Didn't tell you because of that.'

Hester frowned. 'You didn't tell me you were alive because you thought I might scold you? Oh, George, how can you think such a thing? Whyever should I do that?'

'You'll make me go back. Deserter. You don't like deserters. But I'm not going back. Not ever, ever, ever.' The voice rose at the end and she recognised in it the growing note of hysteria and hastily tried to reassure him.

'I wouldn't dream of making you go back. Besides, the war is over now, George.' The smoke was getting to her, making her eyes water, sticking in her dry throat, and though she tried not to show it panic was rising within her. She must attempt to keep him calm, offer him a way out. 'And, though there may still be trouble for you, I would speak up for you, George, and see you had the proper treatment and help.'

It was the wrong thing to say. He leapt towards her in one agile movement and though all her instincts cried out to flinch from him she did not. Too late did she see the twine in his hands.

'George?' Now the panic revealed itself in all its painful vulnerability and he stopped for a second and smiled.

'George is a clever boy.'

'Y-yes, of course you are.'

'They thought I had the fever like the rest, but I hadn't.'

'I'm glad, George.'

'That's why no one ever liked me, because I was too clever for them.' He was taking hold of her hands and stroking them very gently with his own.

'But everyone liked you, George.'

He shook his head. 'Not as they liked you, the perfect little Hester. You wouldn't have run away, would you?' He stared at her and she tried to think of a fair but non-provocative reply, but saw by the expression in his eyes that he would recognise a lie. For it was true. She would never have deserted. She'd have died sooner.

'We can tell them you were ill,' she crooned, much as she had done when they were children. 'Your commander will understand, I'm sure.'

Again he was shaking his head and now he drew one

finger across his throat and let out a horrific gurgling sound. 'That's what they'd do to old George. Or string him up. That's what they did to Jethro. Just shot him. Never gave him a chance to explain how sick he was.' He looked down at her hands. 'Pretty hands. You always had pretty hands, Hester. Always sewing, sewing, sewing.' He smiled at her, a boyish smile and she returned it until his next words penetrated her consciousness and the smile died. 'Give them a rest. Done enough work. No more pretty sewing.'

He was winding the binder twine around her wrists, weaving it in and out with great concentration. Hester stood watching him in helpless fascination. Nothing seemed quite real to her. She was sure that at any moment she would wake and find it all a nightmare. But she could not stir herself from her stupor.

'What are you doing, George? You are hurting me.'

'No, no,' he shook his head. 'Never meant to hurt Hester. You should have stayed away. I meant you to go away. To go home. But you would never do as I wanted, would you?' He lifted up her arms and began to tie the twine to one of the cross beams. Along these beams were once hung a line of hams, bacon and pork. Now they carried nothing but cobwebs and dust.

'George, what are you doing? Let me go, this is the silliest game.' But she could see he wasn't listening to her, and he wasn't playing games, not any more.

He was stoking up the fire, pushing clumps of damp hay on top, which made it smoke all the more. Terror clawed its way through her patient civility and as he moved, chuckling, towards the door she began to beg.

'Don't leave me here alone, George. You know how I hate to be alone. Put out the fire, please. I can't breathe. There is no air in here.'

He looked at her as he opened the door, and smiled as he closed it, very softly and very firmly.

And now she was alone and terror was a living

monster that was eating her stomach and gnawing at her brain. Her hands were tied so tightly, it was impossible for her to move. Tears from the smoke streamed down her face, and her throat was rasping with pain. With no windows in the smoke-house how long could she hope to endure it? She drew in a lungful of the evil stuff and screamed, putting all her failing energy into it for there was nothing else she could do. She was trapped, here in the smoke-house, and, like the hams of yesteryear, she would stay here until she was pickled and ripe and very, very dead.

The trees were dripping with moisture. Just as quickly as it had come, the ice wind had gone and in its wake came a kinder, softer night breeze, melting the ice fronds above Benjamin's head as he rode wearily down the long drive. He had searched all day but could find no sign of her. Drat that Carter, dropping his poison into her ear, pleading with Hester constantly to leave. If only the man hadn't interfered, everything would have come right.

But Benjamin knew in his heart of hearts that that was not so. The blame lay not with Carter Lois but with himself. He had held himself a prisoner of his own problems, shutting Hester out. Benjamin had acquired independence and self-reliance in a hard school and it was a hard lesson to unlearn. He could see that now, oh, so clearly. He could see many things more clearly.

How pretty she had looked in her bright new red dress with its froth of lace on that first night when they'd returned from Atlanta. So young, so sweet, the bloom upon her cheeks as soft and fragrant as the southern peaches themselves, she had graciously entertained Aunt Kizzy and Carter Lois with consummate skill and beguiling sensitivity. And how had he behaved? Like a peevish schoolboy who saw no reason to be polite to someone he despised. And instead of showing a degree of sensitivity in the telling of his tale he had bludgeoned her with it as if it were a blunt instrument and then wondered why she reeled in shock.

And now she was gone.

Benjamin leaned back his head and stared up at the night sky, which was as black and cold as his heart had been. But not any longer. When exactly had the pain of memory left him and this incredible longing for life been born? He knew not. What he did know was that he had lost her, and he hung his head as if he could not bear the weight of the pain. But he couldn't leave it like this between them. He would rest his horse, and himself if necessary, then pack sufficient food for the long journey and leave at first light for Charleston. He could think of nothing more dreadful than spending the rest of his life without Hester at his side, and he'd been all kinds of a blind fool not to have seen it before.

'Have you been looking for me?' The voice rang out in the darkness and Benjamin pulled the horse up and pressed him to be still. He had never heard the voice before but knew at once whose it was.

Very slowly he dismounted. 'Aye. I've kept my eye open for you these last weeks,' Benjamin said mildly, and began to walk the horse towards the stable.

'Stay where you are. I have a gun.'

Benjamin hesitated. In the gathering gloom of dusk he could make out a man's figure, half crouched by the well, but whether he held a weapon or not it was too dark to tell. 'I wouldn't hurt you, George, any more than you would me. You and I have much in common.' Very gently, so as not to startle him, he confined his attention to pulling up the girth straps. 'Never was in the army myself but I've spent time in prison so I know all about confinement, the stink of sickness and dying men about me. Doesn't surprise me that you avoided going back to it. I wouldn't welcome returning to prison either. But the war is over now, George, and America is free. So are you, to do with your life as you wish. You can go anywhere you want.'

'This is my home. I stay here.'

'I can understand that. Then you must have it back. I suspected you were still alive, teasing us all.' Benjamin gave a little laugh. 'So I waited one night, and watched you. But I lost you and never could spot you again. You like jokes, eh, George?'

'I'm good at them.'

'Indeed you are. And this is the best one yet.'

'No. Not the best one.'

Benjamin frowned, wondering just what that might mean. The poor boy's mind had clearly been turned, first by the horrors of war, and secondly by two long, lonely years spent in total isolation here at Rhapsody Creek. The effects upon a sensitive, introspective personality had proved disastrous. But Benjamin knew instinctively that he mustn't let the boy see how worried he was. 'So all this time it was you playing jokes on Hester, eh? And she never guessed.'

'I'm cleverer than Hester. Always was.'

'I dare say.' Benjamin moved a fraction nearer with the horse but the voice rang out again.

'I have a gun. I swear it. Look.' Benjamin was near enough to see the shape of it in his hand and began some rapid thinking. If he jumped him, they might both get killed. He could stampede the horse but he had no desire for a dead horse either. Yet if he turned his back on George and walked away there might well be a bullet placed in it. Who else was here? The field hands were way out of earshot in the overseer's house. Mango was no doubt peacefully sleeping in his attic bedroom. The two little maids were of no use at all. Thank goodness Miss Kizzy and Hester were far away. But for the first time he would have welcomed the presence of another man, even Carter Lois. And then a thought struck him.

244

'Does Carter know you are here?'

'Course he does. We had a pact. I scare Hester back to Charleston. Finish you off.' A gleam of white teeth in the darkness. 'Get Rhapsody Creek to myself again. And he can marry the grief-stricken widow. In the fullness of time. Arranged it all, we did. Clever.'

'I see.'

'Only she will never do as I want.'

Not understanding, Benjamin smiled with genuine affection. 'Yes, Hester is nothing if not stubborn. Your sister sure has plenty of spirit,' he laughed, in an attempt at an American accent.

'She won't ever do as I tell her. Till now. Has to now.'

Benjamin's smile faded and a chill of foreboding crept through him. 'Why? What have you done, George?' No answer. 'Where is she, George? Where is Hester?'

And now it seemed the boy's concentration was slipping, for George suddenly started muttering to himself. 'Always bossing me, she was. Always knew best. Didn't I say she'd make me go back if she found out? Had to stop her. Can't go back. Jethro went back.'

'You wouldn't shoot Hester, would you, George?'

The boy looked at him, startled, and then he started to cry, heart-rending sobs that racked his whole body, shattering the quiet of the night. It was as if all the agonies he had ever endured were at last finding voice. Benjamin saw the boy drop the gun and sink to the ground, curling himself into a tightly compressed ball of misery, his thin arms wrapped around his head as the keening sound went on and on.

Very quietly, taking care not to startle him, Benjamin secured the horse to a tree and, walking over on soft feet, picked up the weapon. It was nothing more than the broken branch of a tree. He tossed it to one side and stood staring down in pity on the broken figure beneath him. What victories war wrought from mankind.

He lifted his face into the breeze, eyes narrowing keenly as he listened. He'd thought for one moment that he'd heard his own name called. Benjamin shook his head. How could that be? There was no one here. And then, 'Hester?'

He was running. His long strides crossed the yard easily and he started to fling open doors, calling all the while. 'Hester? Hester!'

George, demented though he was, had said something about Hester having to do as she was told now. Why? Could she possibly have come back? Was she even now tied up in a barn somewhere? Frantically Benjamin flung back door after door and then he heard her, as if she spoke directly to his heart, for not a sound rifled the air. Turning on his heel, he strode to the smoke-house and, after wrestling with the lock, broke open the old door. Inside, slumped in the smoke-filled chamber with her hands fastened above her head, he found the woman he loved.

'I knew you would come,' she murmured in a hoarse, rasping voice before passing out in his arms.

CHAPTER SIXTEEN

HESTER was sitting in her favourite spot on the piazza at the house in Charleston with Benjamin seated beside her on the rocking-board. In the week that had passed since they left Rhapsody Creek she was only just now returning to a feeling of normality.

Following the events of that fateful night, George had taken himself off into the swamplands to the east, where Benjamin and Mango had found him after several days of searching. This time the funeral had taken place at Rhapsody Creek, where George's torments had finally been laid to rest on the land which had so obsessed him.

Carter had been only too ready to abandon his forlorn hope of winning Hester when Benjamin pointed out the advantages the West had to offer to a man of opportunity such as himself, in comparison to serving time in gaol for harbouring or assisting a deserter. Arrangements were to be put in hand for Benjamin to sell Carter's store and invest the money for him in one of the new, more sound, banking houses.

Aunt Kizzy, no less than Hester, was happy to be back in her own home and was no doubt crocheting contentedly in her bedchamber at this precise moment. All, in fact, appeared to be settled, save for Benjamin.

Hester crossed neat ankles, placed her hands demurely in her lap and drew in a deep breath. The matter had to be dealt with and there would never be a better time than now, when they were at last alone.

'Benjamin.'

'Hester.'

They had spoken at the same moment, almost,

Hester thought, as if his thoughts had been following the same direction as her own. Nervously, struck with a sudden attack of shyness, Hester giggled. 'You first.'

Silence once more descended and as Benjamin fidgeted on the rocking-board it jounced him an inch or two nearer to Hester. For a long time they both sat without speaking but then, compelled by a force too strong for her to resist, Hester raised her eyes to meet his. And in that second she saw his face fill with love for her. It left her astounded, humbled by the intensity of raw emotion revealed in that telling moment.

'I love you, Hester.'

She caught at the sob that rose in her throat. How could this man, whom she loved more than life itself, who told her with apparently genuine sincerity that he loved her, be a convicted murderer? She went weak at the knees just to think of it. It could not be true.

'I should have believed in you,' she said, with disarming simplicity, and Benjamin smiled, the tightness easing in his chest. It was going to be all right. He could sense it. Quickly he gathered her hands in his.

'I should have been more open and honest with you but for so long I have shielded my privacy, I found it impossible to let it go. I never actually lied to you, Hester, but I certainly withheld the truth. But then no one had ever believed in me before, so I was not even prepared to give you the chance.' He was caressing her cheek, one arm slipping around her shoulders, drawing her close, and the coherence of her thoughts were blurring into the study of his bewitching smile and the glitter of his beloved eyes. 'There is so much I need to tell you,' he said.

She shook her head. 'It doesn't matter. Nothing matters, except that you love me.'

But very firmly he put her from him. 'No, my precious darling, you must hear me out. The jury acquitted me of Sarah's murder but somehow I never felt free of the guilt. It was as if I believed it was my fault she had developed the obsession in the first place.'

'I can understand that, for didn't I feel the same way about Carter? Yet I'd never encouraged him. He just seemed to take everything for granted without even asking.'

Benjamin seemed to relax as for the first time he opened his heart and rooted out the long-held pain and guilt. 'Stefan, my bosun, admitted to me that he had been deeply in love with Sarah and refused to accept the verdict as the true one. He'd vowed to take revenge for her death, for which he held me entirely responsible. I dare say in a way I was.'

'Oh, no, that cannot be so, any more than I am responsible for Carter, or for George's behaviour. We are our own people.'

'Yes, I believed so once, but after Sarah's death it was hard to rid myself of guilt, particularly since I had already lost one wife. And now, however unwittingly, had caused the death of an innocent woman. I didn't care what happened to me, whether I lived or died. I deliberately courted danger, as if seeking a higher hand of justice. And Stefan, my old friend, encouraged me in that belief.'

'Was he always one of your crew?'

'We were friends ever since we met as boys in Holland, so he was the obvious choice as my second-in-command when I bought my own ship.'

'Yet he wanted you dead?' Hester was appalled but Benjamin only gave a wry smile.

'A man in love does not think too clearly. He has had his opportunities to finish me off but could never quite bring himself to it. I think our friendship would have won through in the end but when Carter was seeking dirt about me Stefan would be ready enough to supply it. But he went too far or else Carter jumped to the wrong conclusions, and believed that I was still sought in order to answer charges. That is definitely not the case. I did not escape. I was released, acquitted. If Carter had succeeded in shipping me back to England I would have been quite safe, if a mite furious. Stefan must have hoped for a different end for me. The last thing he wanted was to have me shipped back to England, a constant reminder of his misery. He confessed all to me in that brief and telling exchange of words, as I told you at the time. What I could not bring myself to tell you properly was why. I could not bear to have you see me as a murderer.

'It was true that I carried guns willingly for England, despising the danger as much as I despised myself, but the store of gunpowder found on my ship, destined for American hands, was not of my making. Stefan was clearly happy to see me hanged as a traitor, or delivered to the Indians by Carter Lois, but in the end, my sweet, your good nature, and perhaps our long friendship defeated him. Whatever it was you said to him, I know not, and though our friendship will remain scarred he now feels able to resume his life and leave me in peace to enjoy mine. As I fully intend to do.' Benjamin traced a kiss along her earlobe. 'For you have done much for me also, little one. You have taught me to care about life once more, to feel, to love, to trust. I'm so glad I decided to come to America, to try for a fresh start, that last cry for freedom if you like, to find somewhere far from the whisperings and the pointed fingers. Then I stumbled upon you.'

Hester giggled. 'Literally.'

Benjamin smiled. 'Indeed, yes. Yet I foolishly believed that you threatened that freedom, for you unsettled me so. But the more I tried to push you away, the firmer you seemed to lodge in my heart. It took me a long time to admit the reason why this was so, that by refusing you entry into my soul I was robbing myself of the very thing which would cure me.

Your love. But I promise you, Hester, my darling, I shall devote the rest of my life to making you happy, if you will allow me.'

The kiss which followed this entirely satisfactory statement was everything a kiss should be and Hester curled up her toes in delight.

'Wait one moment,' she said, bouncing away a little, not without some difficulty on the rocking-board, whose sole purpose was to jounce people back together again very quickly. 'You said that you had never truly lied to me, only withheld the whole story. Yet you told Caro a most enormous fib.'

'And what was that?' His eyes were merry. 'I told Caro a good deal of nonsense; she has that effect upon a man.'

'Oh. Oh, yes, I do so agree,' said Hester, filled with a rush of sympathy for anyone attempting to contend with Caro's interrogations. 'But she is still my dearest friend. You told her that you were half Dutch and half Irish. Now how can you know such a thing if you were found in a ship's barrel on the docks?'

And now Benjamin was laughing out loud. 'The barrel was from a Dutch ship and when a child has no background at all he tends to invent one. I decided that my father was a Dutch sea captain, and, since Old Mother Cooper declared that I had the luck of the Irish, an Irish mother. Why not? It might well have been the case for there are plenty of Irish in Liverpool. It seemed as good a story as any and better than nothing.'

'Oh, I can see that it would be,' breathed Hester, her heart swelling with new love for him.

'Heaven forbid that a child of mine should have such a start in life,' he said, with a touch of his old bitterness.

'I think there is no danger of any child of ours being found in an old sea bucket. And wouldn't he have all the background a person needs, with the best of both worlds, the old and the new? A fine English seaman for a father, and an American for a mother, even if the hot blood of the Scots does still flow in her veins!'

Benjamin's eyes shone with delight, and a new warming pride. 'Long may it do so. No milk-and-water miss for me, nor for my daughter. An event I anticipate with pleasure.'

'Son.'

'Why must you always disagree with me?'

'Because it is such fun,' Hester said, teasingly nibbling at his ear.

'Then let us say both,' he said with a low groan, 'for I have better things to do with our time together than fight you.' And, claiming her lips very decidedly with his own, he set about proving his point.